THE FIRES OF HELL

THE FIRES OF HELL

PAIN AND AGONY™ BOOK FOUR

MICHAEL ANDERLE

DISRUPTIVE IMAGINATION

Copyright © 2022 LMBPN Publishing
Cover Art by Bandrei at 99designs
https://99designs.com/profiles/bandrei
Cover copyright © LMBPN Publishing
A Michael Anderle Production

LMBPN Publishing
PMB 196, 2540 South Maryland Pkwy
Las Vegas, NV 89109

Version 1.00, February 2022
ebook ISBN: 978-1-68500-599-3
Print ISBN: 978-1-68500-600-6

THE FIRES OF HELL TEAM

Thanks to the JIT Readers

Deb Mader
Dave Hicks
Wendy L Bonell
Peter Manis
Rachel Beckford
John Ashmore
Zacc Pelter
Kelly O'Donnell
Larry Omans
Angel LaVey

If I've missed anyone, please let me know!

Editor
The Skyhunter Editing Team

DEDICATION

*To Family, Friends and
Those Who Love
to Read.
May We All Enjoy Grace
to Live the Life We Are
Called.*

— Michael

CHAPTER ONE

Another day, another stakeout, and another suspected abduction —merely another day at the office for the P & A Investigations team. They had parked and were seated in Bertha on a city street across from a block of row-houses that were neither completely dilapidated nor gentrified.

Pain, first initial M, turned to his partner. "So says you."

"Sorry, bucko." Alicia Goni—known to all who loved, loathed, or downright hated her as Agony—replied. "Maybe knit one, pearl two is more your speed?"

"No." He was firm. "We're only thirty moves into this and you're a novice. There's no way you'll have me in checkmate in five more moves."

Stakeouts could be so boring that even the fires of hell would come as a welcome relief. He had tried to learn how to knit and failed magnificently. So far, all he had been able to produce was a two-foot-long scarf that any puppy with an ounce of self-respect would be embarrassed to wear in public.

It was also damn hard to knit while trying to keep a camera focused at the same time.

She had studied her ass off and Googled chess moves every

chance she had. As they sat in their faithful retrofitted minivan Bertha on their latest operation, she knew she had him. His mind was far more nimble than his fingers, and he had given too much attention to whatever he was currently trying to knit than he had to the chess game she was about to bring to a tragic end through his white king.

Agony sighed. "You missed a stitch two rows ago and you also run a very sloppy Slave defense. Either stop mumbling under your breath and go French or go home."

Damn! He could deal with her being right now and then but not twice in the span of one minute.

Pain stopped his mumbling about chess moves, put his knitting needles down, and picked up the camera. Something had to break soon across the street, and that something should probably be what he focused on.

She interrupted her partner's attention to his camera. "My side. Coming from the front and walking with intent."

"He looks too well-dressed to be hitting us up for spare change."

His partner agreed, took her S&W from the compartment between the front seats, and rolled her window down. They didn't have time for this and she wanted to send the man on his way as quickly as possible.

In his early thirties and the possessor of a gentle smile, he raised his hands and in a soft southern drawl, spoke as the window lowered. He tried to keep his focus on the eyes of the occupants of the minivan more than on the gun the woman seemed ready and willing to pull the trigger of—and probably not bother to ask questions later.

"I am so sorry. I did not mean to startle either of you two. But I was led to believe that I might find Pain, first initial M, in a minivan matching this description."

Agony kept her S & W in plain sight of the stranger but out of view of any other pedestrians who happened to be walking by. "You were led to believe wrong."

"Ah, yes. I can see that perhaps I was."

The man neither stepped forward nor retreated but did keep his hands in clear view, which the partners appreciated but didn't quite trust.

"I merely tried to pay a courtesy call to a Mister Pain to let him know that someone has passed away. But I might have been provided the wrong information regarding the vehicle he often travels in. My apologies."

He started to back away but Pain had been hooked. "Who died?"

"Mister Pain?"

"There are many men named Pain so I cannot confirm that I am the one you are looking for. The New England Payne's spell it P-a-y-n-e. My bloodline comes from other climes and we go with the more traditional P-a-i-n but yes, I carry that name. Who died?"

The man didn't step any closer. Agony's gun—combined with the look in her eyes that told anyone who paid attention that she wasn't concerned about firing a well-deserved round or two— confirmed the stranger's suspicion that keeping a safe distance was his wisest choice of action.

"That would be a Ms. Esther," the gentleman with the southern drawl continued. "A Ms. Esther Chongrak. Her *SISTER* shall dearly miss her."

Pain didn't believe a single word. Chongrak was too contrary to die. If the grim reaper tried to pay her a call, one of them would end up being sorry they'd ever met and it wouldn't be Esther. "Well, at least someone will. But don't count me in if you are looking for someone who will contribute money to the flower arrangements at her funeral."

"I was forewarned that Mr. Pain's response would be something similar to that. I'm sorry to have bothered you. It is simply that Agent Chongrak's demise was brought about by circumstances that some have deemed to be suspicious."

"What kind of circumstances? Did she finally visit a doctor who confirmed that she had been born without a heart and it was a medical conundrum as to how she had managed to live so long? And out of shock, she collapsed and expired? That kind of suspicious circumstance?"

The news-bringer shook his head gently. "No, sir. I fear it is a little more complicated than that. As I stated near the beginning of our conversation, I have been requested to pay Mr. Pain a courtesy call to inform him that a former colleague has cast off her mortal coil."

"Lucky coil." Both men heard Agony's under-her-breath utterance, but Pain was the only one who had to fight to stifle a chortle.

He dismissed the informant. "Thank you. Message received and understood."

Instead of giving them a polite nod and walking away, the stranger remained in place.

The partners needed to return to their surveillance, but the man stood silently and gave every appearance of having no intention to walk away yet.

Pain sighed. "Is there something more to this courtesy call that you need to add?"

"Only that the heads of the agency are convinced that you are in no way responsible or connected in any way to Agent Chongrak's untimely demise."

"So the heads finally pulled their heads out their asses and realized that all on their own? I am relieved."

The stranger nodded his affirmation. "The heads believe so, yes. The only issue—which is the second of the two reasons why I have been sent to pay you a call—is that Agent Chongrak had a partner she shared duties with as one of the two heads in charge of the Special Expunging Unit, and that agent isn't quite as sure as everyone else is that you were not involved."

The detective sighed again. "Of course. Nothing with SISTER is ever non-complicated."

"And I have been sent to inform you that the partner has gone dark and might be coming after you. That is the last of my messages. I shall be on my way now."

Pain, at the risk of the stranger setting up shop on the sidewalk and chatting for another hour, chanced one more question. "Before you go, does the late and not quite lamented Esther Chongrak's partner have a name?"

"Yes, sir. Her name would be Oksana Baran. Do you need me to spell that for you?"

"No! I do *not* need you to spell it for me."

For the first time since the conversation started, Agony turned her head and looked at her partner instead of the bearer of the sad-glad tidings. She saw no signs that he was in any danger of breaking out in a smile in the near to distant future.

The gentleman with the soft drawl and friendly smile added one more comment. "I don't wish to overstay my welcome, but there is one more thing I forgot to mention earlier."

She turned her focus to the stranger and gritted her teeth. "Exactly how many one more things do you have?"

"Only this and then I shall be on my way. SISTER wishes, out of courtesy, to inform or warn Mr. Pain that they are planning no direct intervention to try to protect him or derail Agent Baran from pursuing whatever her goals may be."

Agony had never held Pain's former governmental employer —the black ops agency known as SISTER—in very high regard, but she had now become seriously pissed.

"You are telling us that you have a rogue agent—a supervisor no less—who has gone dark and seems determined to spill Pain's blood for something everyone except her thinks he was not involved in? Is that what I'm hearing? Because if so, I have a few suggestions for you to take to whoever the hell you answer to. Tell them—"

"Don't!" Pain interjected and took his partner by surprise. "Agony, trust me on this. If Oksana Baran doesn't want to be reined in, the only thing that could stop her would be a nuclear strike where she was target ground zero—and even then, there would be no guarantees."

"I am afraid he is right, ma'am."

She didn't know where to start. On one hand, she could grill her partner about how dangerously bad a bitch this Baran chick must be to cause even him to hold her in such high regard. Or she could lash out at the stranger for using "ma'am" with her.

Before she had time to make up her mind, however, all thoughts changed direction when bullets erupted from the direction of the row-house that had been their stakeout objective when the day had started at what now seemed like seventy-two hours earlier.

The partners were seriously outnumbered and indisputably outgunned. This wouldn't be the first time, but they had been there to take a few photos and maybe sneak away with the captive. They were not prepared for eight trigger-happy bangers to burst out of the row-house with AKs. Agony had her collapsible baton and her S&W. Pain had half a bag of stale bagels.

Fortunately, the attackers came from the other side of the street, so Bertha and her bulletproof windows took most of the assault. The mild-talking messenger, though, was still outside Agony's window and was wounded in the shoulder. No one argued the fact that partners had to escape quickly. There was no disgrace in living to fight another day.

"I'll open the tailgate," Pain shouted and the messenger managed to scramble to the back and climb in before the automated door closed and Agony accelerated away. Four of those who had rushed out of the house jumped into an SUV while each of the other four hopped into four muscle cars that had suddenly appeared, souped-up and ready for action.

"We hadn't even taken any photos yet!" She raced through a light and got lucky.

"They don't know that! If we have any proof, they will want it before we have a chance to deliver it."

Their pursuers, their engines revving and mufflers roaring, had stopped at the light, possibly on the assumption that it should not be too hard for them to catch up to a mommy-mobile. That pause gave the partners a twenty-second head start. She used the first five of those seconds to screech to a halt and leap out.

"You fly! I'll buy!"

Pain slid across and behind the wheel as she scrambled around the front and into his seat where she could fire a shot or two—or ten, or a hundred. She had three spare magazines in the container between the seats and wouldn't be shy about using them all.

Bertha was a beautiful beast of a minivan but she was not built for speed, and the SUV and four muscle cars would catch up quickly. Pain looked in the rearview mirror and waited for the light to change. They were in a residential area of the city and on a two-lane street where there was no parking. His intention was to let the pursuers run and gun and rush after them as if all their firing had damaged the soccer-mom-mobile and immobilized it.

The light changed. The SUV hung back as it brought up the rear and the four muscle cars surged forward. The detective spun the wheel and thrust the accelerator down hard to head back toward them on their side of the street.

Like Monopoly, Candy Land, Clue, some classic games never went out of style and didn't need any real expertise to play. Such was the game he knew as Chicken, although it wasn't played on a fold-up board. It was played in the streets. I race at you. You race at me. Pain loved Bertha but no love was meant to last forever and he was willing to risk her life to save his and Agony's—oh, and the wounded agent's in the back.

"What the hell are you doing?" his partner shouted.

"They have at least eighty G's invested in each car—ten grand on the mufflers alone. Buckle up in case I'm wrong!"

She strapped in but fortunately, he wasn't wrong. The first car swerved to his left, ran onto the curb, and barreled into a fire hydrant. At least the water spewing into the undercarriage would help to dampen any fire coming from the engine that now had a bright red addition to it courtesy of the city's fire department.

The next car swerved to Pain's right, then farther to his right to avoid the oncoming pick-up truck that outweighed it by two thousand pounds. The second hasty swerve caused the car to catch the curb at a bad angle and it flipped onto its side in the front yard of Henry and Georgetta Harris. They had been enjoying the weather on their front porch and shared a pitcher of orange juice with a touch of vodka in it.

Henry took another sip of the concoction. "Now that, Georgie Girl, is worth missing a soap or two."

She sighed. "I'll go fetch the shotgun in case they aren't the friendly types."

The third and fourth cars each swerved to the right and managed to get back into their lane without any accidents happening. He didn't count the fact that one rear-ended the other before they spun and continued the pursuit.

Pain braked at the light that was still green and turned hard left, leaving Agony a clean line of sight to the front of the SUV that had hung back. She emptied an entire magazine in the five seconds it took before he screeched into motion again. Two fender-bendered muscle cars and an SUV with a windshield full of spider web cracks and a shot or two into the radiator brought up the rear, again in hot pursuit.

"Do you have any suggestions?" He was never too proud to ask for advice.

"Could you tell if the abductee was brought out to the SUV?"

"Not from my angle but I wouldn't doubt it. They wouldn't want to chance leaving her alone. She has a reputation as an escape artist."

"Shit! Muscle cars first. Save the SUV for last."

They were going fifty in a thirty-five zone and Pain braked and spun the wheel. The pursuers were left facing Agony, who glared at them from her side and fired. They could take their chances and ram the minivan or swerve to the side. The decision was made for them when Agony shredded four front tires in rapid succession and the muscle cars were forced to run on their rims before they shrieked to a sparks-flying halt.

The driver of the SUV made an executive decision, spun the wheel, and accelerated as fast as he could in a different direction.

Agony shouted, "You can't let them get to the freeway!"

"Do you think I don't know that? If they do, Miss Missy may never be seen again! How many are in the SUV?"

"Four, I think, not counting Missy."

"They gotta go left to reach the freeway. Hold on."

As predicted, the SUV went left at the light. Pain had gone left into a strip mall parking lot and cut diagonally across it to emerge side by side with the SUV. His partner emptied two more magazines before the SUV finally swerved to the right and rolled over one and a half times until it came to rest, wheels-up, on the outer edge of a church parking lot.

They knew now that they wouldn't block traffic but also that they didn't have any time to waste before the nine-one-one-calls calls rolled in from the cell phones of the witnesses. With this in mind, they rushed out of Bertha and toward the overturned SUV.

Agony lay prone, ready to empty another magazine if anyone inside decided to return fire while strapped upside down. The gangers dropped their weapons and held their hands up—or down as the case may be.

9

Pain hurried to the back of the vehicle and opened the tailgate door. "Got her!"

He leaned into the back and cussed as he came out with what was left of the plastic pet-carrier crate.

"Is she alive?" She rushed forward and looked at the carrier that had several bullet holes in it.

"Only because you're a terrible shot."

"Hey. If I wanted the dog dead, the damn dog would be dead."

The dog in question was Miss Missy, a prized Pomeranian whose custody battle had been the main sticking point in the divorce proceedings. The animal had been caught between Freaky-Freddy, the gang leader with one blue eye and one green eye, both of them pale and crazed-looking, and his soon-to-be ex-wife.

The soon-to-be ex was the partner's client and she wanted full-time custody with no visitation rights. Freaky-Freddy— Freak Fred to his friends—didn't want to leave the decision up to a judge and had taken matters into his own hands.

Pain took the carrier to Bertha, popped the back door, and was startled when he found an agent waiting for them with a bleeding arm but otherwise unharmed.

He apologized. "I'm sorry. We forgot you were back here."

"Apology accepted." The man scooted farther toward the front to give him room to put the carrier down and inspect its whimpering contents.

"I had everything under control but you had to keep shooting and shooting, didn't you?" the detective protested.

Agony looked a touch guilty as she holstered her S&W. "They started it."

"Seriously? That's what you're going with?"

"Is she still—intact?"

Pain opened the carrier door, pulled Miss Missy out, and made soft cooing noises as he held her up to inspect her for wounds. Finding none, he held the small dog close against his chest and whispered, "Does Miss Missy miss mommy?"

The dog whimpered and deposited a couple of puppy kisses on his chin, which he gladly received.

"Maybe a little traumatized but other than that, she's fine."

"Well, that's good to know." His partner moved toward the driver's door. "Hopefully, Missy's mommy can find her a good doggy shrink. But right now, we have to get a move on."

"I'm sorry, Missy. We're still working on her bedside manner." Pain handed the dog to the agent with the wounded arm. "She needs cuddling and comfort now more than she needs a cage. We'll try to drive calmly."

CHAPTER TWO

Missy and the wounded agent bonded immediately. They both needed a little cuddling after their recent ordeal and found comfort in each other.

Agony moved Bertha away from the scene as quickly and innocently as possible. Pain pressed the button that allowed them to communicate with their passengers in Bertha's retrofitted back cage.

"Your arm needs attending to. We don't have time to stop for me to do triage, so the closest hospital or would you prefer a different location?"

"It hurts but I am in no danger of dying," the man replied calmly and recited an address that the detective put into Bertha's GPS. "If you would be so kind as to drop me off there, I shall be able to receive any further care that is required."

Twenty minutes later, they found the parking lot and pulled up at the front of a store that took both partners by surprise. Pain headed to the back and assisted the soft-spoken agent out of Bertha.

"Are you sure you gave us the right address?"

The man managed to extract himself and handed Missy to him.

"Very sure. Thank you, sir. You might want to now direct your focus to Missy here and not give me a second thought as you head out with all due haste."

He nodded as he closed the hatch, carried Missy to the front with him, and took his seat.

Agony studied the building. "It seems like a strange location."

"From your brief experiences, has anything involving SISTER ever seemed not strange?" he asked.

"Good point. Buckle the dog up. We're moving again."

Pain held Missy on his lap as he strapped them both in. "Honestly, little girl, she does love you. That is why she is so worried about your welfare."

"Has anyone ever told you how sappy you sound when you have a puppy on your lap?"

"I've never had a puppy on my lap before. I'll have to study up on it."

"Study hard," was his partner's only advice as she headed to the nearest pet store to buy a new carrier for Miss Missy. No one disputed the reality that the old one could no longer be presented as even halfway suitable, what with all the bullet holes.

When they located the store, he left Missy on his seat as he hurried inside to find an appropriate carrier. The dog stared out the window after her rescuer and whimpered.

"Hey. What about me? I helped. Don't I get any thanks?"

Agony immediately regretted having spoken as Missy scrambled over the console between the seats and landed in her lap.

"Don't pull the puppy eyes and whimpering routine on me, you little manipulator. You are nothing but a rich, spoiled— bitch." She enjoyed the fact that she could use the term bitch in the most appropriate of contexts.

Missy took the hint and leapt back to the friendly guy's seat. The Pomeranian didn't know the difference between the words bitch and asparagus but if she did, she wouldn't have used the vegetable to describe the mean lady she had wanted to make friends with.

Pain returned not a moment too soon with a carrier that did the prize-winning Pomeranian proud. He scooped her up, set her in her new temporary home, and loaded her in the back of Bertha for the short drive ahead of them before they could return her to her mommy.

The client—as opposed to her soon-to-be ex—currently still had possession of the house. She also still had a private security protective detail, which was not a bad idea given who her ex was.

Agony pulled into the circular driveway, parked, and rolled her window down.

"We have a dog delivery! Please don't shoot."

Her partner slid out of his seat with his arms raised and moved to the back of Bertha. He extracted Miss Missy's new carrier and held it up for all to see.

The guards immediately recognized the spoiled pooch's yapping. They had a betting pool going as to whether or not they would ever have to deal with the little bitch again. The odds were fifty-fifty. Everyone had bet the under and were all saddened to have lost. It wasn't the money so much as a matter of having to deal with the spoiled dog again on a day-to-day basis.

"Missy, Missy, Missy!"

They all winced at the grating voice when Missy's mommy rushed from the house.

Agony snatched the carrier out of Pain's hands. "Payment first. Puppy second."

"Jesse. Pay these good people."

Jesse, the head of the security detail, pulled out the ready-cash fund he kept in his pocket for such emergencies and turned to the woman in possession of the puppy. "How much?"

"Pain?" There was no way she would let go of the carrier. "Tell the man how much."

Between the happy squealing of both Missy and her mommy, only Jesse heard the price the big man quoted. It was very high but only the detective heard the security agent's response. "Damn, man, we would have paid you twice that to have failed."

Only Jesse heard the big man's apology. "Sorry bro. A job's a job."

"Don't I know it."

Having seen the cash exchanged, Agony set the carrier down and worked out how to open the door so Missy and Mommy could have their joyous reunion. If either she or Pain expected a word of thanks, they would have been seriously disappointed as mommy ignored them and carried Missy back inside. The guard detail and the rescuers were now no more than an afterthought.

Pain shrugged his apologies. "We'll be on our way now."

The guards watched as the woman slid behind the wheel of a minivan that all the guards could see had taken some damage. The big man slid in on the shotgun side and the minivan pulled out slowly, reached the end of the circular drive, and disappeared down the road.

"Damn, Jesse," someone mumbled. "I thought we had it rough."

"We all got it rough," Jesse replied, "except those that don't."

The partners wanted to return to their apartments above Kwan's but also wanted to visit their office since the repairs had been finished the week before. Pasha and Masha's delis were still in business on the street level and the only remaining issue was the fact that the temp agency had failed to find a new administrative assistant to send them. The rumors of gunfire while trying to answer the phone and doing a small amount of filing had gotten around, so the temp agency was running out of willing applicants.

But still, it was their office. Agony parked and led the way up the stairs.

"Well, wasn't that all more giggles than a girl can handle."

"If memory serves," Pain replied, "I don't remember anyone getting any giggles out of anything."

"Maybe you've taken one too many blows to the head because I was laughing a mile a minute."

Having reached the second floor, they paused to admire the etched-glass window in the top half of their recently repaired office door.

P & A Investigations, the window read. The repair company had done a fine job and even changed the font a little to give it a special touch of class.

She paused before she punched the numbers into the keypad to let them in.

"At least we've had no uninvited visitors while we were out." She led the way in and took a couple of micro-brews from their mini-fridge. They entered the reception area and she sat in the chair behind the desk and put the beers down where notes and messages would normally be laid out if they had a proper receptionist-office assistant.

Although she wasn't sure that her partner deserved a cold beer, she was about to grill him. This left her with only two choices. It was either ask him his preference for a last meal— which meant she would have to trudge down the stairs to Pasha's —or let him enjoy one last cold one.

Pain took the offering and settled into a visitor's chair, where he took one long, very satisfying draught. He leaned back and rested his head against the wall under the print of where one of MC Escher's numerous mind-twisting staircases hung and closed his eyes.

"You were saying?" he prompted,

Agony twisted the cap off her micro-brew, took a sip, and

answered in a voice that dripped innocence. "I wasn't saying anything."

He took another sip and kept his eyes closed. "True enough. But the current elephant in the room is one Oksana Baran."

"Oksana Baran...Oksana Baran..." she mused dryly. "Why does that name sound so familiar? Oh, right. I remember now. It's because I never heard the name before today and now wonder why the hell not."

Pain's eyes might have been closed but his ears picked up every note of agitation in his partner's voice. He couldn't honestly blame her for any anger she wanted to spew at him. Not that there was anything resembling simple about his SISTER days, but the truth was that he had hoped to never hear the name again.

He kept his eyes closed as he replied with a sigh. "If wishes were horses, then beggars would ride."

"Where the fuck do beggars and horses figure into the current equation?" She often had trouble following her partner's flights of fancy and sometimes wondered if he needed to have his meds checked daily. But as far as she had observed, caffeine in a finely-brewed pot of light beans was his only choice of daily drugs.

"There was a time—" he started before she interrupted him.

"At least you didn't start with once upon a time. That would have been seriously annoying."

Pain understood her attitude. He straightened, opened his eyes, and faced her as he tried to explain the layers of the history behind him and the agent in question.

"My relationship with SISTER hasn't always been as antagonistic as it is now. I will not say where it was. It could have been Central or South America. It could have been in an African or Asian or Middle Eastern or even one of the former Soviet Union's satellite countries, so please don't ask."

"Got it. You weren't sightseeing in Minnesota." There were some details he could not reveal, but she needed to hear as much of the story as he was allowed to tell or at least the part about the woman she had already come to think of as Oksana the bitch Baran.

"There was an agent who went rogue—" he started and was again interrupted before he could get rolling.

"Huh. A SISTER agent who went rogue? I've never heard of that ever happening before."

"May I finish the story or at least be allowed to finish a sentence?"

"My bad. Please, continue." Agony made a serious effort to remain quiet. She decided that as well as taking a sip or two from the bottle of brew, she would also try to semi-distract herself by attempting to peel the label off of the bottle. At least that gave her something to do with her hands that didn't involve her wrapping them around his throat and choking him to death.

"Not only did the agent go rogue, but he took half his team with him. Since Kip and I were the agents in the closest vicinity, we were pulled off our assignment and Chongrak and Baran were sent to help coordinate the effort to quickly put an end to the developing situation."

She had been able to focus on peeling the label off long enough to have allowed him to at least finish a sentence, but she still needed to keep track of the players involved.

"So, it was you and your partner, Kip, the bitch twins, and how many others?"

"No others. Only the four of us. Chongrak did most of the coordinating, Kip, Baran, and I did most of the heavy lifting. I'm telling you, Alicia Goni, that I have never met a woman who can handle shit like Oksana Baran."

That statement truly caught her attention. Pain had used her full name and had implied that she—Alicia Goni—might come in second if it ever came down to a fight between her and Agent Baran. He had seen them both in action and since she respected his ability to evaluate talent, she decided to not take it personally and instead, tried to rib him on his sexism. She had the top-quarter of the label peeled and looked at him and smiled.

"So there big strong Kip and you were, and there was a woman who had the audacity to be able to keep up with you? How dare she?"

He acknowledged the dig with a nod and a slight smile for having been called out but had to make sure that he was being clear enough while remaining adamant about his assessment.

"Everyone has different skill sets, preferences, and abilities. But when it comes to strapping on gear that damn near matches your weight and trudging across rough terrain for extended periods of time... Well, the simple truth is that the male physiology provides too many advantages to tabulate. Can we at least agree on that?"

Agony had half the label peeled by now and grudgingly acknowledged his point.

"But Oksana Baran made up for her physiological disadvantages, and with nothing more than an incredible awareness of her surroundings combined with an extreme efficiency of movement, she often ended up being the one running point. I think part of that was merely her sheer determination to be the first one on the scene because she didn't want to miss out on any of the action."

She was halfway through her brew and three-quarters of her way through the label.

"So did the little girl manage to beat the big strong boys to their goal?"

Pain took a sip and seemed to suddenly be caught up comparing his pristine label with that on his partner's bottle.

"I asked you a question, sir."

"The answer is yes. We didn't stand a chance against her determination and sheer willpower. We eventually reached the compound of the tin-pot dictator-wannabe and the rogue agents. After the firefight was over, only four people were left standing, which is why the whole episode never made it onto the nightly news. Mission accomplished. Chongrak—who, by the way, had held her own—called in a chopper to get us back to civilization."

Agony had the last quarter of her label almost off and without looking up, asked, "Can you define civilization?"

"It was a city with hotels large enough to have heliports on their rooftops. We landed and were guided from the rooftop to our rooms for the night before we headed out again the next morning."

"It sounds like a happy ending all around to me."

"And it would have been if Oksana and I had spent the night in our own rooms."

She tried not to chuckle. "Oh, were you a bad boy?"

"Let's say that two of the four SISTER agents decided to take a week's vacation time and never left the hotel."

"Lust or love?"

"On my part, love. Maybe on Oksana's part too, but you would have to ask her about that. I've never been good when it comes to understanding women."

Well, there's an understatement. She kept the thought to herself before she could finally celebrate having peeled the label off in one piece.

"I am only guessing here, but was there perhaps some fallout about the two agents bopping their brains out?"

"Maybe a little."

"How little?"

Pain sighed and did not meet his partner's gaze. "Esther Chongrak might have had some mixed emotions about it."

"No. Charming Esther being pissed off? Now that is hard for me to believe."

"Sarcasm noted. Please, also note that it's not nice to speak ill of the dead."

"I will believe she is dead when I can stand over her certifiably dead body. Finish the story, please."

He drained his bottle in one long draught and put it on the desk as he leaned back and completed his trip down memory lane.

"Everything went south after that. Whether Esther wanted her for herself—which would never happen because Oksana wasn't a switch-hitter—or maybe she was jealous because there had been an inter-agent assignation that did not involve her—or hell, maybe she thought two agents fucking for a week after the month we had all spent together somehow seemed exclusionary and unprofessional. I don't know. All I know is that ever since then, Chongrak developed a hard-on to make my life miserable and by extension, Kip's, and she never let up, which led to the death of my partner."

Agony thought she had enough to go on now. "Your work partner, Kip, died but your bed partner Baran managed to avoid Chongrak's rage?"

"Only because Chongrak was a master manipulator, which explains why she kept Baran close and left me to swing in the wind."

"And Baran, your soul mate? How do you think she felt about that?"

"What are you—my shrink now?"

"I was merely asking."

Pain wanted to end this discussion and move on to whatever they had to do next but took a moment to finish it.

"I haven't seen Oksana since we left the hotel room and I enjoyed every minute of our time there. But if Chongrak has turned her against me, we could be in some deep and dangerous shit. Chongrak may have been a manipulative bitch who knew how to work the system, but Oksana was the button-woman, the one of the two most likely to pull the trigger and dispose of the evidence."

"You two sound like the perfect couple. It's a damn shame that things didn't work out. You would have been the most fun-loving parents on the block. Is she seriously that dangerous?"

"Much more dangerous than me," he admitted with a sigh.

"Oh my, have I offended your delicate male ego?"

"No, dear ever-concerned-about-my-welfare partner of mine, but you did remind me of our current reality."

"Which is?"

"That for the moment, we should avoid all windows. That woman could shoot the wings off a fly and still leave the poor wingless bastard alive to live out the rest of its meager lifespan kicking its legs in self-defense as it rolled on its back and tried to fend off whatever kind of predators eat flies."

"That is a very specific and elaborate way of explaining that someone is a good shot."

"Sorry." Pain wasn't. "I merely thought it was a nicer way to say that with a gun in her hands, she does spray and pray as efficiently as you do."

Agony snorted huffily. "I do not spray and pray."

"Right. You spray and everyone else prays. Shall we go ask Miss Missy her opinion?"

"That damn dog needs to learn how to tough some things out. Not every occasion calls for whimpering."

"Regardless. Look…all I'm trying to say is that we've been safe in the inner office but we need to start avoiding all windows."

"Along with what else? Should we do gymnastic contortions down a sidewalk to avoid being easy targets? Neither of us is as young as we used to be."

"Look, partner. If I am the one she has her sights set on, I will understand if you want to take a personal week or two of vacation time while this plays out."

She stood to collect the two bottles and deposit them in the trash but paused, sorely tempted to thunk one of them against his skull.

"So…you're saying I should take two weeks off and come

home to find out that I need to find a new partner because one of the eight friends he has managed to accumulate decided to send him on to his next existence?"

"Something like that. Yeah."

"Then think again, pal, because I finally have you almost fully trained and I have no intention to start over again with someone new. Someone needs to go down, but it ain't gonna be one of us. End of discussion."

CHAPTER THREE

The partners managed to travel from their office to their apartments above Kwan's without either of them or Bertha having sustained any death-inducing wounds. They stopped when they reached the top of the stairs.

"You," Agony informed him, "will be the one to go out and pick up the donuts first thing tomorrow. You are also the one who will have the coffee ready when I arrive. If neither of them is presented, I will chalk it all up to a love gone wrong and endeavor to persevere while I try to find another partner."

"White," was Pain's one-word reply.

"White, what?"

"White flowers, white dresses, and white anything. I've lived too much of my life in the dark. I don't want anything dark to appear at my funeral."

That statement left her almost speechless but she managed to respond, "*Mañana?*"

"*Mañana.* Hopefully with donuts and coffee waiting for you."

She scowled as her partner turned the key and headed into his apartment without a backward glance that might include a sly wink to let her know everything was under control.

Agony again wondered if he had anyone in any kind of position of power that he could truly trust. She also knew that being just this side of anathema to the boys in blue network—except for a former sergeant who would offer what he could if able, and the chief of police, Chauncey Morris who they now had by the short-hairs—she was helpless to ensure her survival. He had swum in deeper waters than she ever had.

Pain's door closed and she stood outside hers across the hallway. She wasn't sure if she simply thought it or spoke the words softly out loud.

"If anyone wants the first crack at killing you, bucko, the line forms behind me. The rest will simply have to wait their turn."

She slipped the key into the lock, turned it, and opened her apartment door, slightly taken aback by the fact that nothing blew up as she stepped inside. Her nightly routine came next. She brushed her teeth, ran her hands through her short hair, and changed into her favorite set of sleepwear that consisted of a nightshirt and ready-to-go shorts. Finally, she placed her S&W on the nightstand and slipped her collapsible baton beside her head on the pillow as if it were her favorite stuffed animal.

With an eye on the digital clock on her nightstand, she watched as each minute passed. Everyone had their own way of trying to get through a night when sleep was hard to come by. She knew it was probably not the most traditional alternative to counting sheep, but she would occupy herself by waiting for specific sets of numbers to appear. Duplicates and consecutives were her favorites. 12:34, 1:23, 2:34, 3:45, 3:33, 4:44, 5:55, and if she got to bed early enough, the granddaddy of duplicates —11:11.

The last one she remembered before she finally dozed off was the reverse consecutive of 3:21.

Her first regret the next morning was having sent her partner on the donut run. While she preferred the traditional hole-in-the-middle, he was more of a cream or jelly-filled fan. She gave her ritual coded knock on his door and he called his ritual response.

"It's open."

Pain had helped himself to a cup of coffee. He had been on a Sumatra kick lately but had held off on eating anything until she had arrived because he felt polite. She filled her cup, sat at the table, and immediately snatched the Boston Cream up. She didn't care much for the Boston Cream but knew it was his favorite. In all honesty, she simply wasn't up to his politeness standards after what they had been through the day before, most of it thanks to her partner's past transgressions.

He settled for a powder-covered raspberry jelly. "After careful consideration and extensive research, I have come to the conclusion that Oksana Baran will allow me to live long enough for her to be able to confirm her suspicions about me being the one responsible for Chongrak's death."

"And what did this extensive research consist of?"

"I walked twice around the block before I stopped at the bakery and presented a clear target for her to have a crack at."

Agony bit the end off her Boston Cream and squeezed the cream out into her coffee. The result was an edible donut and a rich blend of Sumatra with a cream cloud that she swirled in her cup until the whole concoction was a very light-brown color. She took a sip and congratulated herself on her inventiveness before she responded.

"So you set yourself up?"

"It's better to find out sooner rather than later. I don't like living with the suspense of not knowing if my next breath will be my last. Now we can focus on what we need to do to get back into everyone's good graces—oh, and that is a terrible abuse of a perfectly fine Boston Cream."

"So says you." She took a sip of the coffee and smiled gloatingly. Maybe that would teach him to buy more than one next time. "Do you have any ideas on our next move?"

"All I can come up with is to go to SISTER and request whatever information we can about Chongrak's suspicious death. If we can discover what happened, we can clear our names with SISTER and not spend the rest of our lives with the feeling that we are in the cross-hairs of whatever scope Baran is peering through."

"But half of your intra-agency fling has gone dark. How will she know?"

"Don't believe everything you hear. SISTER always has ways to keep in touch."

"Then why the hell isn't someone at your agency at least trying to rein her in?"

"Because no one knows for sure exactly who took Chongrak out. They are assuming that either you and I will be able to sort the whole mess out or failing that, Baran will remove me from the equation. In that case, SISTER will have one less target to worry about while they are now short-staffed and have to find a replacement for a very senior agent."

Agony licked the powdered sugar off the top of the Boston and took a good solid bite, knowing it would annoy Pain to see her further desecrate the delectable prize. "All right, so what do we have to go on?"

"I wasn't able to catch the plate number of the car our southern gentleman used. There was too much gunfire to stop and write it down but it probably doesn't matter. I doubt it was a personal vehicle but we do know where we dropped him off. That seems as good a place to begin as any to try to start peeling back the onion layers."

"It did seem like an odd location for a safe house."

With the donuts finished and cups and plates washed, dried, and packed away, the partners arrived at the safe house half an hour later. It was a one-row, one-level strip mall with ten storefronts, four of them empty. At Pain's request, Agony guided Bertha on a tour to inspect the back of the building.

The little excursion made him feel much better about their choice of where to start. "There is some serious security surveillance equipment behind Unit E."

The cameras were discreet but she agreed with his assessment. "I also noticed that Units D and F were vacant in the front but the cameras also seem to cover their back doors."

"Which leaves one functional storefront with maybe three back rooms, one of which has a roll-up door wide enough to drive a car through."

She moved on, not wanting to spend too much time in the vicinity of the cameras. "Something here does not quite add up."

"Which means this has SISTER's fingerprints all over it."

Agony pulled around the front and parked in front of Unit E that the awning above the windows identified as Little Angel's Consignment Shop.

They exited Bertha and couldn't help but notice that the storefront's windows hadn't seen a squeegee in quite some time. With the parking lot being only a quarter full, the whole place gave the impression of a strip mall where every business was barely hanging on.

As they approached, she couldn't help but comment, "It looks more like a thrift store setting than a consignment shop."

"Judging books by their covers now, are we?"

Pain opened the door to the tinkling of a bell and, being the gentleman he was, stood aside to allow Agony to enter first.

"Welcome, welcome." A friendly clerk in her mid-twenties greeted them from behind the counter that was positioned a dozen steps ahead of them. "Please feel free to browse. My name is Nickie. And if you have any questions, myself and Matthew will be happy to assist you." She raised her voice and called, "Matthew, we have shoppers!"

A thin six-footer only slightly older than his co-worker stood from behind a chest of drawers toward the back that he may have been either repairing or polishing and waved. The partners returned the gesture, thanked Nickie for her welcome, and ambled around to inspect the items with one eye and the security cameras with the other.

Pain looked at a full-length mirror mounted on horizontal hinges so it could be tipped either up or down and opened to reveal a convenient set of drawers that could hold small pieces of jewelry inside. "They have serious security inside as well as out."

"And serious prices, too." Agony looked at a tag on a not quite pristine dining room table and chairs and wandered away.

He headed to the counter, not sure which persona to try. He settled for steadily employed but not with money to burn as he approached.

"Nickie? We've seen several things that we like but are these prices at all negotiable?"

The assistant put her sad face on. "No sir, I'm afraid not. All the items are on consignment and the owners set the prices. We always try to convince them to keep the tags reasonable, but you know how stubborn some people can be when it comes to letting go of some of their favorite possessions."

Their conversation was interrupted when his partner yelled, "I won't leave without this one!"

They both turned to see Agony seated in a cushioned, swiveling rocking chair.

"I guess I'd better go see what has struck her fancy."

Pain wound through the aisles and found his partner rocking and twirling as if she were on one of her favorite childhood carnival rides. He slowed her motion enough to be able to get a glimpse of the price tag and gasped.

"Is there any possibility of you getting out of that over-priced piece of Naugahyde so you can try to stay on task here?"

"You have to try it." She stood and pushed him into it. "Lift your feet!" It was more of a command than a request.

He did his best to gather his legs up as she gave the chair a spin. While he had to admit it was a fun little chair, he planted his feet firmly after two spins and stood. The chair was still way over-priced and they hadn't made any actual progress yet in the real purpose of their visit. He told her so in a voice that only she could hear.

Her response was to call, "We'll take it!"

Pain's response was to call even louder, "No we won't!"

"Yes, we will!"

"No, we won't!"

They continued to bicker loudly enough that both Nickie and Matthew had no choice but to converge on the arguing customers in an effort to stop the fighting. They seemed determined to either make a sale or get the two of them out of the store as quickly and quietly as possible.

A third worker exited from the back room and hurried to where all the commotion was coming from.

"Excuse me. Excuse me!" the newcomer announced. "I am the manager here and was on my break. Is there a dispute that you two need to take outside and discuss there? I would prefer that you don't traumatize my staff any further."

Pain turned on the man, who was in his early-forties and slightly out of shape but dressed in what must be the very latest style of khaki meets plaid.

"Maybe you can help us settle our dispute right now because if we take our disagreement outside, the only decision we'll have to make is whether we want to use red or yellow as the color of the spray paint we return with to use as we tag the whole storefront with, *SISTER safehouse*."

"I thought we would go with either black or blue." Agony pouted.

"I think red or yellow would be more noticeable," her partner retorted.

"But I think black and blue would be more appropriate because there will undoubtedly be some hurting inside here after we're done."

The manager stepped between them. "Is it possible that we all may be operating under a slight misunderstanding here? What is a sister safe house? I can assure you both that we are not some kind of a battered women's shelter in disguise, although I believe it would be a very noble cause if we were."

The partners stopped their sparring long enough for Agony to turn to the manager, read his name tag, and respond, "No, Tony, there is no misunderstanding. We delivered an agent here yesterday afternoon and have now returned to ask him a few questions for clarification purposes."

The look the three employees exchanged signaled to each other that their cover had been blown, at least as far as the two new arrivals were concerned. The manager was the one who had to do the conceding.

"The agent's wound is healing nicely. Follow me and we'll all go to the back so you can see for yourself."

Tony turned and led the way in single file with Pain immediately behind him and Agony following. Nickie and Matthew brought up the rear. They were almost at the door to the back room when the man turned with a gun in his hand.

He might have planned to give some type of lecture about how he ran a very secure establishment but all he managed was a startled yelp as his gun ended up in Pain's hand. The sound of two sharp thwacks let the detective know that his partner's baton had taken care of whatever weapons the other two agents had drawn.

The three agents suddenly positioned themselves in a group. None of them were bleeding or in need of a visit to an emergency room because both detectives had pulled their punches. The agents, however, with only ten combined years in SISTER's service between them, were still willing to make another attempt to stand their ground and challenge the interlopers.

Pain and Agony looked at the brave but out-matched threesome and then at each other.

He shook his head. "I'm not into child abuse."

"Nor should anyone be," a man said in a familiar southern accent from the direction of the door leading into the back room. "Thank you, Agents. These two are friends of mine, and I apologize for not being available to welcome them myself. Please excuse us now. I believe we have some things to discuss."

The soft-spoken man turned and walked through the door by which he had entered.

Pain chose to follow him. Agony chose to do the same thing but not before she turned and gave the SISTER group a warning. "No one leaves this store with that twirling rocking chair except me. Got it?"

All three held their bruised hands, wrists, and egos and nodded. She smirked as she stepped through the door behind which negotiations above their pay grades were about to be held.

Once in the back room, the wounded agent led the partners to where four chairs were arranged around a table. Although it wasn't as large as they expected, the area could pass as either a break room or a small improvised conference room without any walls.

The partners' earlier drive-around assessment had been right. The Little Angel's rear space took up all of Units D and E and F, but that was not their concern at the moment. Fortunately, the wounded agent chose to avoid the impending grilling before either of the visitors could decide on which of the hundreds of questions they wanted to ask.

"My name is Christopher Hollund. That is Hollund spelt with a U, not an A. The Netherlands is a lovely country and I hope to pay it another visit one day, but my family name does not derive from there."

Pain took it upon himself to put the man at ease. "I know the history of the name. Those who carry it should carry it proudly. So please, Agent Hollund, can you help us here?"

The agent smiled and continued in his soft southern accent

that she was falling in love with and he continued to be envious of. "Miss Missy?"

Pain answered first. "Miss Missy is back in the arms of her Mommy Dearest."

Agent Hollund breathed a sigh of relief. "So she will be fine. I am glad to hear that."

A little surprised, the partners exchanged a glance that confirmed that neither of them thought this was the proper time to discuss Missy's current or future well-being. Pain brought the conversation back to the reason for their visit.

"Agents Chongrak and Baran. We know you don't know anything about Agent Baran's current location or agenda but could you please give us whatever information you have about Agent Chongrak's death or her body's current whereabouts? Out of respect to her, we would like to pursue the details surrounding her demise a little more closely than what has currently been done."

"You do realize, Pain, first initial M, that she was…how shall I phrase this? Not your biggest fan."

The detective's voice turned cold. "I don't have any fans, either big or small. So either tell us what you know or we will simply leave and not waste any more of your time or ours."

Christopher Hollund had looked up to the agent who had taken his inexperienced self under her wing ten years earlier and had guided him as if he was her younger brother or a potential protégé. Out of respect to her, he decided to pass along more information than what SISTER had originally sent him to provide to one Pain, first initial M.

"You need to know that I knew Esther as a dedicated agent and a very patient teacher. I worked under her for almost a decade and hold her and her memory in the greatest regard."

Pain wondered if maybe there had been two Esther Chongraks who worked for SISTER because Agent Hollund did not describe the one he knew. "I'm sure you'll do wonderfully at the funeral when you give her eulogy. Now please, tell us what you know so we can try to get to the bottom of why your mentor is no longer able to help to guide you along and we can get ourselves out of Baran's sightlines."

"As you are probably aware, Agent Chongrak often played things close to the vest so she only let a few details slip. As far as anyone has been able to piece together, she was delving into a new player on the professional provocateur scene."

Agony knew what the words meant but not in a SISTER context. "Professional provocateur?"

"Assassinations, espionage, weapons acquisitions and re-distribution—little things like that," her partner elucidated.

"Ah, so no one worth worrying about?"

"What has most people concerned now is that the new player is claiming the name Havoc."

The partners shared a quick look of confusion but Pain was firm when he spoke. "Havoc is dead. Whoever it is ought to choose a more original name."

Agent Hollund did not argue the point. "All our sources have confirmed that, but there is something to be said for name recognition. The static we hear is that the new mantle-carrier seems to be reviving old networks and alliances but operates in a far more direct mercenary fashion."

He was almost afraid to ask. "How much more direct?"

"The old Havoc was more of a shopkeeper with a warehouse who kept a lot of inventory on hand and would sell whatever he had to the highest paying bidder. The new Havoc takes special orders and manages to procure whatever is requested, as long as the fee is right. Esther—sorry, Agent Chongrak—tried to determine what the new Havoc's connection was to the old and how much of a threat he posed."

"And then she died."

"Then she died." Hollund didn't exactly choke up but it was clear to both partners that the agent had looked up to his late boss. "No one knows exactly how far she had gotten and it will take some time for the rest of us to piece everything together."

"Then why the hell is Oksana Baran coming after me? Shouldn't the new Havoc be the one she is gunning for?"

"It might have something to do with this." The agent pulled out a copy of a photo and handed it to him. "That and the fact that you threatened her the last time you encountered each other."

"We always threatened each other whenever our paths crossed. If we had sounded all syrupy toward each other, that would have alerted the red-flag brigade."

Agony repositioned herself so she could look over Pain's shoulder. The photo did neither Pain nor Esther justice. Her partner looked too angry and the bitch looked too innocent. The agent handed him another print, this one of a text message that the partners read at the same time.

P will come after both of us once he finds out about Havoc.

"That text was sent by Chongrak to Baran shortly before Chongrak got into her vehicle in which a car bomb was detonated moments later."

"So everyone thinks I am the P she referred to?"

"Agent Baran certainly seems to lean that way. There are also numerous earlier texts going back over a significant period of time where she referred to you simply as P when not using more colorful terms." Agent Hollund showed a trace of a smile and no doubt recalled exactly how inventive his mentor could be with terms of not-quite-endearment.

"Do you have anything that might show that the new Havoc had been setting me up as the fall guy for Chongrak's murder? Or any other concrete evidence that I was involved in any way with whatever investigation she was running?"

"I am afraid that I do not, nor does anyone else I have been working with. I truly wish I did."

Agony was curious. "And why is that?"

Hollund turned toward her. "Because your partner is either guilty—in which case it may never be proven and will be left to Oksana Baran to exact her own form of justice—or he is innocent. If so, I believe he is the best hope left for trying to solve the who and the why of it."

Pain had heard enough to compel him to action, placed his hands on his knees, and stood.

"I do want to find out. Esther could be a grade-A bitch—no one knows that better than me—but she deserved to go down in a firefight, not an ambush. I want to inspect what is left of the car and her body. Will anyone at SISTER be opposed to that?"

The agent also stood, pulled a couple of sheets out of a drawer, and handed them to him. "I will grease whatever wheels I can to give you full access to the car and the body. These are the locations where you can find each. As for Agent Baran?"

"Yeah, yeah, I know. She has gone dark."

He shoved the sheets in a pocket so he could examine them alone with Agony.

They thanked the man for his time, wished him well in his recovery from the recent wounds, and headed out through the showroom. The three official staff members of the Little Angel, having had enough action for one day, were huddled out front near the register. Agony broke away from Pain and approached them.

"I'm sorry about the arm taps. I am glad no bones were broken, but I will come back for the chair and if it is not waiting for me, I can't guarantee that bruises will be the only things you will come away with. Understood?"

They all nodded their understanding. Satisfied that an agreement had been reached, she took one last, longing look at her soon-to-be new used chair before she turned and followed her partner out the door.

CHAPTER FOUR

Bertha had looked better, but there was no damage from the gunfire the previous day that couldn't be patched, painted, buffed, or polished out. By the time Agony slid behind the wheel, Pain was already in the shotgun seat and studied what soft-spoken and earnest-sounding agent Christopher Hollund had given him.

"Find a place to hover." Pain remembered his manners barely in time and added, "Please."

She understood the reasoning and guided Bertha to a place off to the side where they could keep an eye on both the front and back of the small strip mall in case any cars acquired occupants who wanted to make a quick run to their mother—or in this case, their SISTER.

Once she'd parked and turned the engine off, she gave him enough time to look at the printouts—in other words, about thirty seconds—before she became impatient. "What do we have?"

He passed the first sheet to her. "If I read Hollund's shorthand properly, the first location is another SISTER site. Its cover is as a family-owned vehicle repair shop, although I assume that other than a flat tire, there is probably not much the mechanics would be able to diagnose or fix. That is where the car is being stored."

Agony scanned the printout and agreed. "And the second location? The one where Chongrak's body is being hidden—I mean, looked after?"

Pain handed her the second sheet. "Read it and weep."

All she needed to do was see the address. By now, they knew it by heart.

She was tempted to crumple the sheet and toss it out the window. "You have to be kidding me!"

"My guess is that SISTER needed a place to store the body long enough for them to come up with an appropriate cover story."

"But still, even Agent bitch-on-wheels Chongrak deserves a better final landing place than Miles and Ignatius."

"They aren't necessarily her final resting place. Think of them as a holding station."

"Let's hope they know the difference between holding and cremating."

"Either way, let's hit the garage first. I want to have a look at what may be left of the car and the bomb before any more evidence gets lost or mishandled."

They had been parked for twenty minutes and no one had come out from either the front or back of Little Angels. She punched the address of the garage into Bertha's GPS and headed out.

As was their custom when they had the time, she drove past and circled back to park. In this instance, they found the destination on their right as they drove down a four-lane divided highway with regularly-spaced U-turn lanes in the median.

Agent Hollund had said he would try to grease the wheels, but neither partner knew what kind of wheels would be waiting for them inside Buckman's Auto Plaza whose sign stated *Family-owned and operated-0017.*

Once parked in the front lot and in plain sight, Agony frowned at the sign. "What kind of number is zero-zero-seventeen?"

"Maybe it represents the number of customers served? Maybe they didn't have a two available to start the number with? Is the number on the sign honestly what we should be focused on?"

"I was merely curious."

"Curiosity is always a good thing unless you're a cat."

Pain climbed out, headed to the front door, and missed his partner's reply. "Curiosity killed the cat. Satisfaction brought it back."

She caught up to him in time to hear the tinkling of a bell as he opened the door and whispered, "Is a tinkling bell some kind of secret SISTER handshake?"

"Welcome to Buckman's." The young woman behind the counter greeted them with a friendly smile. "I'm Joni. How can we help you?"

Not this routine again. Pain was not in the mood to go through the same ruse they had endured at the Little Angel. Agony had ended up with her heart set on buying a swiveling rocking chair circa mid-1980s. For all he knew, she would want to trade Bertha in for a *Wayne's World* style AMC Gremlin they had stored out back. There was no telling which direction her tastes would go in.

He borrowed a line from Harry T. "The Esther Chongrak-mobile—don't waste my time."

The clerk smiled, came out from behind the desk, and opened the door leading into the main garage. "Johnny! Someone here to see you."

Johnny, in his early-forties and dressed in a classic mechanic's attire of a t-shirt and overalls, appeared a few moments later. He wiped his hands on a dirty rag and used it as an excuse to not shake any hands. Pain couldn't tell whether it was because his hands were truly dirty or because Agent Hollund had forewarned him to keep a slight distance from the dangerous duo.

The detective did his best to reassure the man but also wanted to get down to business. "We aren't here to hurt anyone. I only want to inspect what is left of Agent Chongrak's car."

"Agent Hollund informed me that you were rather direct. Joni, how about you track Jake down and try to help make our customers welcome?"

He led them through the garage to the end stall where a car stood under a tarp. Agony brought up the rear. *Johnny, Joni, and Jake?* She was rapidly losing respect for SISTER agents' creativeness when it came to cover names.

The tarp was removed with extreme care from what was left of the car. Johnny took a few steps back but did not leave. "If you don't mind, I will remain right here to answer any questions you might have."

"And to make sure I don't tamper with anything?"

Fortunately, the man seemed to take no offense. "Those two goals are not mutually exclusive."

Agony stood at his side and they both watched her partner conduct his inspection.

"Sugar cookies?" She turned as Joni appeared at her side, holding out a plate of what seemed like home-baked goods.

"Or would you prefer chocolate chip?" Jake made an appearance with an offering as well.

Johnny took a sugar cookie as Agony helped herself to one of each. She could be ambidextrous when the appropriate occasion required her to be.

Joni set her plate on the hood of a Toyota in the next stall. "I forgot the milk. Cookies are always better with some milk. I'll be right back."

"We always try to keep a family feel here at Buckman's," Johnny explained as they watched her scurry away and Jake took a bite of one of his cookies.

Agony smiled. The cookies might have been sliced off a roll available in any supermarket's frozen section, but they were still warm so they were at least freshly baked and not out of a box. It was a nice touch if someone was stuck in a repair shop for a few hours—which, for all she knew, she might be.

There was no hood left for Pain to lift. He stared at the husk of an engine and unperturbed whether he hurt anyone's feelings, called, "Don't encourage them!"

"Encourage them to what? Simple hospitality? People are never nice to us and I am not about to get paranoid simply because someone offered me a cookie or two."

"How do you know the cookies in question aren't poisoned?"

"Johnny and Jake are both eating one."

"Look at the bottom of the cookie. It would be exactly like SISTER to have a secret stamp to distinguish the tasty from the deadly."

"He seriously is a paranoid one, isn't he?" Johnny snatched what was left of Agony's sugar cookie out of her hand and popped it into his mouth.

Pain straightened from his examination of the engine, stretched, and beckoned Agony closer.

"Don't eat them all," she instructed as she excused herself and joined her partner.

Keeping his voice low so he didn't upset the children, Pain spoke. "They could easily pull a bait and switch. How do you know that none of it is poisoned?"

"The same way I know that you and all your spy shit won't end with me being poisoned to death because of who you fucked a decade or two ago. So back off. When it comes to fresh-baked cookies, I'm willing to take my chances."

"I changed my mind. Go ahead and shovel them all into your mouth. Anything to stop you from talking. My next stop will be Miles and Ignatius, so I'm sure that bringing an extra dead body along won't cause them too much trouble."

"You're merely jealous because people are being nice to me. I haven't noticed anyone offering you a cookie yet."

"Maybe it's because I'm working here? Which is maybe something that you should be trying to do too?"

He returned to his inspection. She returned to the triple-J's, took a glass of milk that Joni arrived with, did a double-dip, and followed Pain's suggestion to stuff her mouth. With a smile, she nodded her approval to the J's.

Pain moved to the driver's side door, knelt, and after a few minutes, stood and waved Johnny closer.

Once the mechanic had moved away and she had swallowed her latest round of sugary delights, Agony decided she could at least try a little friendly interrogation. "So, I've considered a career change. How do you two like working for SISTER?"

"Sister who?" Joni was the first to answer.

"I don't have any sisters," Jake added.

"Good answers. My advice is to stick to the simple assignments and don't wander too far out into the field. Otherwise, you may end up the same as Esther Chongrak—or worse, my partner."

Pain had returned to his knees outside the door and once Johnny stood above him, he looked up. "Do you have any actual experience with automobiles or are you simply a front waiting for a more exciting assignment?"

"My actual field is electrical engineering. I'm helping to hold down the fort here until an assignment comes up where I can be more useful."

"Have you done anything more with this car other than cover it with a tarp?"

"My specific instructions were to cover and keep it covered for future inspections. I try to remain within the specific scope of my orders."

"Then come on down here, Johnny. It's time you took a walk on the wild side."

Johnny was inherently cautious but knelt beside the big man. Nothing in his orders stated that he couldn't get his knees dirty as long as he didn't touch anything.

Pain pointed to a charred wire that seemed to run from under the seat to the door panel circuits. "We're only having a friendly chat here so I won't hold you to anything you say. As an electrical engineer, do you think you can determine why this wire is here and what its purpose might have been?"

He might have been an order-follower supreme but it seemed like a long time since he'd had any kind of an electrical puzzle to solve and he simply couldn't help himself. It took him several minutes as he went from his knees to flat on his back and from that position asked, "Do you have your phone handy?"

"Why? Are you in the mood to order a pizza?"

The mechanic kept his voice low. "No. I need a flashlight and don't want to bring the other J's in on this to hand me one. Phone —yes or no?"

Since Pain had been the one to invite him to the inspection party, he slipped his phone into the agent's outstretched hand. Johnny found the flashlight function and squirmed for several more minutes beneath the undercarriage before he rolled out and handed the device back.

"We need to talk. Do you think you can drag your partner away from the cookies long enough to join us in my office?"

"By us you mean only you, me, and her, right?" He checked his phone to make sure the man hadn't sent any texts.

Johnny pushed to his knees. If they were standing upright, the detective would have had five inches on him. Being on hands and knees did wonderful things to level off the eye-to-eye-contact playing field. "Yes, only the three of us."

"What will the other two J's do?"

"Work on baking a batch of brownies? How the hell am I supposed to know?"

"But you're the boss."

"So thinks the teacher in every kindergarten room."

Pain was the first of them on his feet. "Hey, Cookie Queen. Johnny has invited us to his office to share some ice cream. Do you wanna come?"

The mechanic stood and glanced at Joni, who seemed particularly upset by the big man's announcement. "You've been holding out on us with ice cream? It's not fair that your office has a mini-fridge and ours doesn't, especially if you don't share!"

Johnny leaned closer to the detective and whispered, "She is not using code words. She's merely pissed because she and Jake always forget to stock up on ice cream in the break room fridge."

Agony snatched two more cookies for the road and after a quick thank you to the accommodation department J's, headed after the two vehicle inspectors. The agent entered his small, barely cluttered office, sat behind his desk, and gestured for them to take the only other two chairs.

Pain grasped a chair, swung it, and planted the back of it firmly against the door before he sat in it. So far, he liked the engineer and wanted to trust him, but he hadn't known the man very long and didn't want the other two J's to suddenly burst in with AKs.

Agony took the remaining chair, kept it in front of the desk, and answered Johnny's question before it could even be asked. "Yes, he is always this paranoid. For some reason, he always expects someone to sneak up behind him."

"I also sleep with a nightlight on. That doesn't make me a bad person. Why are we in your office, Johnny?"

The man dug in a pocket he hadn't been able to reach while under the bombed car and retrieved his cell phone. He placed it on the desk, speed-dialed, and put it on speaker.

"So, they were there?" answered the soft southern accent without any preamble.

"They were and still are, Chris. The three of us are in my office now and you are on speaker, so let's not waste too much time going into our debate about whether barbecue sauces should be tomato or white-vinegar based."

"Fair enough. Hi, guys. How were the cookies?"

Johnny cut in before Agony could give two thumbs-up. "I took the tarp off and stood back, Chris, as Pain did his inspection. But then he asked me for a second opinion. It was the first time I took a look at the car, and…well, a few questions came up that I thought it best to discuss together. If we talk it all through now, it will save all kinds of back and forth because you are the common link between them and me and the higher-ups at SISTER. Do you have time to talk?"

"Yes, it so happens that I do. What did you find?"

Sometimes, you simply had to trust—not an easy commodity for Pain, but his back was to the door and the phone was on speaker, so it wasn't as if anything said would be a secret. *I might as well take a chance.*

He kept his voice as unemotional as if he was giving a report. "It was overkill."

"Overkill how?" Agent Hollund sounded as if he might be taking notes.

"First off, the explosives were a professional job. From the scraps I saw, they did not come out of a bomb-building kit you could pick up online. Tell him about the wire, Johnny."

"Half of it was melted to the frame, Chris, and most of the rest of it was charred, but its path was clear enough. It ran directly from under the seat to the door panel controls."

"Which means?"

Johnny looked at Pain, who nodded for him to continue. The detective wanted to see if he had come to the same conclusion.

"It means, I think, that it was attached to a pressure switch under the seat. Once someone climbed in and sat, it would flip the trigger, override the door locks, and trap whoever was inside. I also found remains of another wire that probably triggered the bomb itself. Once you were in, you could never get out, even if you sensed something was wrong. It was too late because the doors wouldn't open."

"Pain? Do you agree?"

"As I said, it seemed like overkill for someone like Chongrak. The level of skill and expertise to wire it, not to mention that the actual bomb materials seemed like more of an incinerator style rather than a simple explosion, are close to what would be used to kill heads of state or cabinet-level targets. Esther Chongrak was neither. Either someone was showing off or they seriously wanted to make sure she was dead and possibly even unidentifiable once the bomb had done its damage."

"It's scary, Chris. The new Havoc certainly means business and has connections who are not scared about getting their hands dirty." Johnny leaned back with a frown.

"Thank you, Pain and Agony. I feared something like that. Are you headed to the body now?"

"Not that I think there will be much of it left, but yeah." The detective nodded, even though Hollund couldn't see him.

"Again, thank you. Please keep in touch."

The engineer sighed. "I'll show them out and call you back. We need to try to get ahead of this."

"Roger."

When the call ended, Pain stood and spun his chair back into place. Agony, having had nothing to do during the visit other than make small talk with the baking J's, was glad to leave. It would have been one thing if she had been able to get anything resembling useful information out of them, but at least she felt good about being able to offer the two young agents some valuable career advice.

Johnny led them out. Pleasantries were exchanged and the partners entered their vehicle for the trip to the merry mortuary. The engineer went inside but before he replaced the tarp, he took another look at the undercarriage with his flashlight. Satisfied that he and Pain had both come to the same accurate conclusion and since he was already in position, he decided to inspect it a little more.

He didn't find anything extraordinary but did confirm the two-wire theory from the pressure plate—one to the door controls and one to the bomb location. His expression somber, he replaced the tarp and called Chris to let him know that he had no second guesses and to argue a little more about barbecue sauces.

CHAPTER FIVE

Having put Buckman's Auto Plaza and the triple-J's behind them and despite their shared reluctance, the partners headed to Miles and Ignatius, the funeral home for the dead and maybe dying. Agony hoped that once they arrived there, she would still be able to keep her cookies down.

"You were very adamant about the overkill. Do you care to elaborate a little more?" she asked, as much out of real curiosity as a distraction.

"It's merely something I've rarely seen before and that alone is enough to give me pause. Let's say you wanted to sabotage a small airplane while it was in the air—or a big one for that matter."

"It's not on my to-do list today, but okay."

"You could set a bomb to blow off one wing and that would do the trick. Or you could blow the tail up. Either one would end in a fiery crash. This would have been like blowing up both wings, the tail, and the cockpit."

"Could it be a matter of simple redundancy?" She felt honor-bound to find the most logical explanation. "In case one bomb didn't go off, there would still be two others for back-ups?"

"Good point, so maybe that was a bad analogy. But they only had one bomb. The door locks are what bother me the most. If they were going for redundancy, why not two or three bombs, each with a different trigger? Instead, they chose to lock the doors. It's almost as if they wanted the subject to know that something was wrong and then suffer fear and panic for a few moments before they died. I wonder if her seat belt was in place?"

"Because, of course, no one would want to be blown up while not being properly buckled in."

He sighed. "But that's part of my point. The first thing anyone does these days is climb in, buckle up, and start the engine."

"Some people start the engine and then buckle up."

"Okay. Forget the seat belt."

Before they had time to dig deeper into the mystery, Agony's phone rang. She glanced at the caller ID, cursed, and found the closest parking space. For a quick call, Pain didn't mind if she drove while talking hands-free and on speaker, but for anything like an in-depth conversation, he always preferred it if she didn't drive while distracted.

After she'd parked, she put the phone on speaker and answered.

"Yes, Eva. How can we help you?"

"You can help me," the grating voice screeched, "by telling me what the fuck you did to Miss Missy!"

Evangeline Boyer was the name of the Pomeranian's owner and she was currently in the lead when it came to Missy's custody battle, thanks to the partners having rescued and returned her the day before. Despite their success, this did not start sounding like a thank-you call.

She tried to keep her voice calm, professional, and reassuring. "We didn't do anything to Miss Missy, Eva, except rescue and return her. What seems to be the issue?"

"I'm not having any issues at all. But Missy is not acting like her sweet little self."

Agony turned the phone's volume down hastily so the screeching wouldn't shatter every piece of glass in Bertha. The windows were bulletproof but they had never had them tested for voice pitch. Plus there was the issue of the glass in the rearview mirror. It was hard enough to lose a pursuer without having to look through a spider web pattern to see what was coming up from behind.

Eva continued. "If I didn't recognize her sweet little eyes, I might think you brought me the wrong dog!"

"I can assure you, Eva, that we rescued the right dog."

She hoped that Pain might intervene and deal with the distraught bitc—client. He seemed to be suddenly focused on his fingernails, however, as if he was three days overdue for a mani-cure and wondered if he could hold off for another day or two until his favorite nail technician returned from vacation.

"Of course you rescued the right dog. I'm merely wondering what the hell you did to her. She is off her food and Missy loves the pureed chicken my maid makes for her fresh each day. And she is now yipping and yapping for no reason!"

"Your maid is now yipping and yapping?"

"Not my maid, you incompetent flamingo! Missy!"

"Flamingo?" Pain mouthed.

"I've been called worse," she whispered and shrugged the insult off. "So Missy has never been a yapper before?"

"Not until you two got your hands on her."

Agony wished she could get her hands on the dog again and wring its little Pomeranian neck. "I don't think it's fair to blame us for what might have happened to Missy while your soon-to-be ex was in possession of her. He is, after all, the one who dog-napped her and then had her for several days."

"Freaky-Freddy would never do anything to harm Missy! Me? Yes. But Missy? No!"

"Seriously?" As much as Agony didn't look forward to their visit to Miles and Ignatius, dealing with the dead and the wounded seemed like a big step up from dealing with Miss Missy's Mommy at the moment. She was vastly relieved that she had insisted on being paid in cash when they dropped the pooch off. "Then maybe you can explain to me why Freak Fred decided to toss her in the back of his SUV and take her on a joy ride when he and his friends started a gunfire-filled chase and tried to end our lives?"

"Missy's been on car rides before. She's even used to a little gunfire—wait a minute! You didn't shoot back, did you?"

"They started shooting at me first." Agony saw Pain smile and immediately realized that she had gone for the they-shot-first defense. Damn, he could look smug when he was right.

"But you shot back! Why shoot back? Missy wasn't armed."

"No! But every other fucker in the SUV was."

"That's no excuse for shooting at an unarmed dog."

"I wasn't shooting at the damn dog. If I had been, we would have returned a very dead dog to Mommy Dearest. And even if that was the case, it was Freak Fred's fault for getting the mutt involved in the first place."

"Miss Missy is not a mutt! She has papers that trace her lineage back for four generations."

"Then maybe you stopped one generation too soon because she certainly has some…some…" Agony tried to come up with an appropriate breed to use as an insult but remained blank until inspiration struck. "Dachshund in her!"

"Missy? Part wiener dog? You take that back or I will sue you for libel!"

"Wiener, wiener, wiener," Agony sing-songed.

"That's it! Not only do I demand my money back, but I expect you to pay for whatever doggy shrink Missy needs. Then I will find a lawyer to sue you for defamation of doggy pedigree."

"Oooh, now I'm scared."

"You will be! Freaky-Freddy isn't the only one I have gang connections through. With only a couple of phone calls, I can rain fuckin' vengeance on you harder than a ton of boulders dropped from the top of the North Pole, you trigger-happy bitch!"

"Bring it on, Missy's mommy. We returned the pooch safely and you paid us in cash. I wouldn't waste too much time waiting for the postman because there will most certainly not be a refund check in the mail any time soon. And as far as the bangers go, we can bang back equally as hard."

"Oh, you, you—" Agony hung up before Eva could decide on the proper insult.

Pain finished studying his nails. "Handled like a true professional."

"No one stopped you from chiming in any time you wanted."

"This is true. My only concern now, though, is that Eva knows where our office is and I truly don't want to have the door replaced again. I've grown very fond of the new font in the window."

"Okay, maybe I could have handled it a little better." She scowled but tried to look contrite around it, which did not work.

"And viewed from the moon, the Grand Canyon is only a little ditch. I guess it's all in the perspective."

"All right, all right. I'll give you thirty seconds to get all the gloating out of your system—starting now."

Agony began to count down —aloud—from thirty. He decided to try to act like an adult and managed to remain silent before he finally caved when she reached five.

"But Mommm, they shot at me firrrst."

"Was that satisfying?" she snapped.

"Very. But it's still early yet, so how about we swing past Kwan's before visiting Miles and Iggy? I think we're still in the green when it comes to who owes who a favor. Maybe we can use some of Ahjoomenoni's muscle to protect our office for a while, at least until Eva calms a little."

She had her doubts. "Do you honestly think she'll calm down?"

"I don't know and I don't have any desire to start a war over a dog. At the end of the day, we did our job so she is barking—excuse the pun—up the wrong tree if she expects her money back. And if it comes to intimidation, there's also nothing to prevent us from starting a campaign of our own."

"A campaign?"

"Only little things—like maybe mailing her envelopes full of dog fur mingled with a little blood."

"That would be subtle."

Agony redirected Bertha and headed to Kwan's Korean Restaurant to have a hopefully friendly chat with the owner, who was also the landlady to whom they paid the rents for their apartments across from each other on the second floor.

Ahjoomenoni, with strong ties to the Korean mob, was also one of the most dangerous people in the city and known for her mood swings that could go from genial to deadly in an instant. They hoped to at least start at genial.

They reached Kwan's before the dinner crowd arrived and were able to find a parking space directly in front. The establishment always had a uniformed doorman stationed on the sidewalk. He also doubled as part of the ever-present security sentinels Ahjoomenoni was never without.

Today's multi-tasker was a trim fifty-year-old named Ji-hun who had been in her service for over a decade. As the partners approached, Ji-hun studied Bertha's latest battle scars.

"Perhaps, Mister Pain, you should consider purchasing a tank.

Your gas mileage would go down, of course, but your life expectancy might rise."

Pain chuckled. The man had a point. "If you hear of any used ones coming on the market, let me know. Is she in?"

"You will find her at her table."

"How is her mood today?"

"So far, no deaths have been reported."

Ji-hun opened the door and the partners wound between the handful of early-dinner diners to the glassed-in reserved dining space at the back of the dining room where the owner usually conducted her daily restaurant-related business. Where she conducted her other business concerns was something Pain had never inquired about.

They reached the door to the cozy space, stood silently, and waited for an invitation to go in. Two men sat across from Ahjoomenoni at the table with what looked like ledgers spread before them. Another two who were solely on bodyguard detail stood at the door and bowed their greetings. The partners reciprocated but small talk was not forthcoming from the guards, so they all stood in silence.

The proprietor looked up after a minute and informed her bookkeepers that the meeting was over for the day. After the two men gathered their books and exited, one of the guards spoke in Korean.

"The inconvenient ones wish for an audience. Do you wish to see them?"

"I can already see them," she replied, also in Korean. "The proper question would be shall I let them in?"

"Yes. That would be more appropriate. Shall I let them in?"

"At this time, I believe it would be rude not to."

He bowed to his boss and stood aside. The partners entered, bowed to their hostess, and were waved to sit down.

"Miss Agony. It is always a pleasure to see you, whether with or without your friend."

Pain had known and known of Ahjoomenoni for well over a decade, dating back to when he was still with SISTER and she was still a higher-up in the North Korean Intelligence Community. She had been ruthless then and once she had broken free and set up her entrepreneurial shop in the United States, she had not softened to any great degree that he had noticed, except when it came to Agony.

For reasons he was still trying to determine, the two seemed to have formed a bond. In all honesty, for all he knew, they were the co-founders of the Let's Make Fun of Pain Club, but he was fairly certain that he would not have been offered an affordable apartment above the restaurant were it not for his working relationship with Agony. If their partnership ever broke up, he would be the one looking for new living accommodations, of that he was certain.

As was the custom, having taken their seats, they waited for their hostess to be the first one to speak. She kept her greeting short.

"You interrupted a session with my bookkeepers."

Pain responded with a polite head bow. "We would have been glad to have waited until your business was finished."

"And what? Forced me to listen to another two hours of idiots babbling about numbers? No, I thank you. Now, what do you want?"

He thought about saying something along the lines of, "What makes you convinced that we want anything? Can't we simply drop by to say a friendly hello?" but decided against it and let Agony do the talking. It seemed only fair since she had pissed Missy's mommy off and was the reason they were now seated there.

His partner drew a breath and began. "We seem to have acquired an unpleasant former client."

"No doubt due to your partner's less than pleasant customer-relations skills?"

She nodded, threw him under the bus, and wondered how long he would be able to restrain himself before he set the record straight. "Something like that, yes. So we wondered if maybe, perhaps in return for our assistance in ridding you of your Agent Buchanon annoyance, you would consider providing a little extra security for our office when we are not there? They would be mostly for show, but we have just gotten everything back into shape after our last unfortunate episode. Having a couple of guards to maintain a presence would go a long way toward discouraging any future vandalism."

Ahjoomenoni nodded. "That is no doubt true. So they would not be stationed to protect you, merely your office equipment?"

"Only some desks, a few file cabinets, and things like that, yes."

"And this will fulfill the return of the favor for the two of you having settled my Agent Buchanon problem?"

Pain interjected, "With all due respect, Ahjoomenoni, I am not sure that babysitting some office furniture is completely comparable to ridding you of a rogue federal agent."

Her voice took on a hint of a chill. "You wish to negotiate? With me? As long as we are negotiating, do you also wish to renegotiate the rent on your apartments?"

He backtracked immediately. "No, Ahjoomenoni. Your generosity regarding our rent has been very much appreciated. We will be happy to consider all debts paid in full if you would be so kind as to provide protection for our office."

She retrieved a small pad of paper, scribbled something on it quickly, and handed the note to his partner.

Agony took the note and looked at it. "I am afraid I have not had time yet to learn how to read Korean."

"That is okay. There is a Korean pharmacist on the corner. Take this to him and he will understand how to fill it."

"A pharmacist?" She felt like she had missed something but had no idea what.

"A pharmacist, yes. What I have written down is a prescription for Pain to take."

"A prescription for what?" He was as lost as his partner, especially since Ahjoomenoni did not have a medical license.

The woman smiled. "For a bottle of chill pills. You are very clearly in need of some."

"Gimme that." He snatched the note, read it, and hung his head. In Korean, the note was the equivalent of *Gotcha!*

The landlady laughed as she looked at Agony. "Ahjoomenoni yank Pain's chain good that time."

His partner looked at him and he rolled his eyes and chuckled. "She's right. She yanked it good."

"I tell what I do for you—not as a favor equalizer but because it was worth it to see Pain's face. I have a few nephews. They are young and not of much use yet. But they can stand around and look scary very well. I will have them keep an eye on your office until the threat is over. Is that agreeable?"

"Very," Agony confirmed.

"You may both go now. But please, use rear exit. If the accountants are still seated in the restaurant, I do not wish for them to know that our meeting is over."

The partners stood, thanked her, then bowed and slipped out toward the back, leaving Ahjoomenoni still chuckling about having hoodwinked Pain.

CHAPTER SIX

Leaving through the rear meant they had to walk around the block to reach Bertha. Pain had yet to relinquish his unease about being exposed on city streets when Oksana Baran was still lurking out there somewhere. The alley behind Kwan's didn't seem a likely place for her to stake out but he wouldn't put it past her. Phenomenal patience was only one of her many strong suits.

He asked if Agony would mind walking five steps behind him so it would take more than a second for Baran to fire, reload, and re-aim.

"That way, at least you'll have a chance to duck for cover if you see me go down."

"If separation is the goal, how's about you walk five steps behind me?"

"Because unless you've grown a spare pair of eyes in the back of your head, how would you know if I went down?"

"Look, I'm willing to go along with your avoiding the windows routine in places we frequent, but I am not willing to be ready to duck and cover while walking down the street in broad daylight. For all I know, that could make me so paranoid that any time a car backfired, I might take a leap in the wrong direction and get run over by a bus."

"Fine, live dangerously."

"And could you please walk in a straight line?" she added sharply. "Your listing from starboard to stern and back again is getting on my nerves."

"Starboard to port. Those are the sides of a ship. Stem to stern are the front and back."

"Whatever! I'm about to find a stem and port it right up your stern if you don't knock it off."

When they reached Bertha, they bowed to Ji-hun and drove to everyone's favorite mortuary. Pain's paranoia regarding Baran might have rubbed off on her because she often changed lanes suddenly for no apparent reason. They eased onto the freeway during early rush hour traffic, which eventually led to them being caught in a couple of slow-moving bumper-to-bumper situations.

At one point, she even began to wonder if there was an accident ahead that Baran had set up so Bertha and her occupants would be sitting ducks from the rogue agent's perch on a grassy knoll. They had to solve this situation quickly and get the bitch off their back or she would seriously consider a move to Louisiana to take up alligator wrestling for a living.

The traffic began to flow again and for sanity's sake, she decided to tough it out, choose a lane, and stick with it. Pain remained silent and for him, fairly un-fidgety, so she had time to think but came up with many more questions than answers. They were almost at Miles and Ignatius before she spoke.

"If you aren't the P in Chongrak's last text to Baran, then who is?"

"How am I supposed to know?" he replied with a trace of irritation.

"Not even a guess?"

"Not a one."

"We're not making much progress here, are we?" She scowled at the road ahead.

"Come on, we only started on it this morning and so far, we've located Christopher Hollund, inspected the car, spent quality time with Ahjoomenoni, and now get to visit our old friends Miles and Ignatius again. I think we're making good progress. Hopefully, Esther's body will give us another clue."

"From the way you made it sound at the auto shop, it doesn't seem like there will be much of a body left to provide any useful information at all."

"Probably not—but hey, look on the bright side. At least you found an over-priced piece of furniture you don't even need and now can't live without."

"There is that."

"Speaking of Agent Hollund…" Pain pulled his phone out and dialed the number the man had given him.

"Agent Hollund."

"It's Pain."

"Have you finished at the mortuary?"

"Not yet. We had to make a side-stop but we're pulling up there now."

"All right. I believe it was Miles I spoke with. He's the former pharmacist, right, not the scalpel man?"

"That would be an affirmative."

"Okay, then. I informed him that you would pay a visit but I should warn you, he sounded as if he had been sampling his wares so I can't guarantee how much of our conversation he will be able to recall or his actual state of…uh, shall we say, aware-ness, when you see him."

"We will keep that in mind. Harmless, useless, and stoned is essentially his SOP. Will you still be at the consignment store?"

"The store closes at nine, but I'll remain for another day or two and will sleep in the back, so call when you get here."

"We should be there well before closing. I doubt if we'll find much here. I merely wanted to make sure you'd be around."

"Come on in, I'll be right where you left me."

Agony parked and fixed the funeral home with a weary look. "How about we don't and simply say we did?"

"She was a fellow agent and at one time, a damn good one. I owe her this."

"She was a fellow agent to you. To me, she was simply another federal pain in the ass. How about I stay out here and guard Bertha while you go in and fulfill your SISTER obligations?"

Pain unbuckled his seatbelt and shook his head. "You're not getting off that easy. I might need you to stop me from making a very bad mistake."

"She's already dead and either all blown or burned up. How bad a mistake could you make?" Her tone was impressively reasonable given the circumstances.

"The mistake of crashing the proprietors' heads together so hard that I'll need to call all the king's horses and all the king's men to help put Humpty and Dumpty's heads together in the right order. We don't have the luxury of time for all the paperwork that would require."

She sighed, slid out of Bertha, and set the alarms before she followed him to the front door. Not for the first time, the front doors were neither locked nor alarmed in any way. He turned the knob that opened into a reasonably sized foyer and voiced his disapproval.

"You would think that with the number of drugs Miles keeps in stock, they would at least lock the front door."

"Your guess is as good as mine."

Straight through the foyer, a door opened into a long hallway. The first two doors to the right led to small but nicely decorated rooms where small viewings and memorial services could be held. To the immediate left was the open office and desk of Silvia, Miles' maybe-twenty-year-old former receptionist, office assistant, and secretary. The partners had decided that she chose not to file any charges of sexual harassment as long as Miles kept her snorting the fringe benefits readily available through a straw.

On their last visit, the ex-pharmacist had lamented having lost her to a couple of rappers who had injured each other and sought out Ignatius and his no-longer-licensed doctor skills to patch up a few gunshot wounds. Most of his business came from those without the compulsion to report said wounds to the proper authorities.

Sadly for Miles, Silvia had taken a liking to one of the wounded and had disappeared to seek her fame and fortune with one half of the dueling rappers, both of whom had more street-cred than musical skills or the ability to put together anything resembling a coherent sentence. Rap was not high on Pain's list of musical preferences, but he could still appreciate the intricacies and wordplay of some of the lyrics.

The first actual door on the left led to Miles' office. They didn't bother to knock and simply marched through the door. Douglas Miles was seated in his chair, his head face down on his desk next to an almost empty box of donuts covered in powdered sugar while he snored loudly. From the other vials scattered on his desk, it was clear that he wasn't only suffering from a sugar-rush crash.

The last time they had been there was to have Jules Ignatius bandage Agony's arm while Pain had spent most of the time with Miles in his office so he could use the man's computer to do some hasty research.

"He took Silvia dumping him hard and isn't over her yet," Pain told his partner, "because he's regained twenty of the eighty pounds he lost since she came into his life and has now put on at least another ten."

"I assume he'll be back to his usual three hundred within what...two, maybe three weeks?" she commented. "That's got to play hell with his heart."

He agreed but with the caveat, "You're assuming he has one. I haven't seen any evidence so far."

They backed out quietly and continued down the hallway to where they knew Ignatius had his body-prep room. This doubled as a surgical unit when the nightly rush of wounded made their appearances. They were halfway down the hall when a woman cried out and both detectives immediately froze.

Agony began to reach for her gun. "Definitely female."

"But is she being operated on without anesthesia or simply being tortured?"

"Oh God, oh God, oh God! Please, more! Please!" The cries were loud and energetic enough to leave no doubt.

She scowled and left her gun holstered. "I guess we overlooked a third option."

"Iggy having sex in his mortuary? I am mortified."

Agony resisted the urge to smack him. "Mortuary? Mortified? Humor, right?"

"Of a fashion," he admitted.

"Don't give up the day job."

Although she had no desire to witness Jules Ignatius doing the horizontal bop, they had a job to do and she wouldn't be shy about interrupting. Her partner caught her arm before she could rush forward.

"Hold on. Listen," he told her in a low tone.

"Listen for what? For them to finish and offer each other a post-coital smoke?" She snorted

"I think I recognize the voice."

She did as requested and ten seconds later, burst through the doors. Pain had been right. The two on the tabletop rolled off and scrambled to find their clothes. Silvia had gone from mid-moan to shrieking, but Jules Ignatius was able to muster a quick shout.

"What are you two fucking doing here?"

Agony was the first of the partners to find their voice. "The question, asshole, is what are you two doing fucking here? And who the hell screws on the prep slab where you drain the corpses?"

Pain was also upset, but his anger seemed to stem from a sense of betrayal between partners. "And with Silvia? Damn, man, where's your sense of honor? Couldn't you have at least had the decency to end your partnership with Miles before banging his girlfriend?"

The young woman had managed to get her top on and struggled to tug her short skirt up from around her ankles. "I ain't Miles' girlfriend! We broke up!"

"That's right. You left him for a rapper. How did that relationship not end with a happily ever after?"

"Because 'Fuck you, ho,' might be great for a song lyric but it gets old real fast around a dinner table when all I would do was ask him to pass the salt."

"So why not get back with Miles?" Agony interjected. "He very clearly loved you and was heartbroken when you left."

"Yeah, well." Silvia raised her index finger and let it droop. "His heart ain't the only organ that's broke now if you know what I mean."

She wanted to strangle the betraying bitch, but Ignatius had managed to get his shirt and pants on and she rounded on him. "Couldn't you two at least have used hotel rooms? He's right down the hallway!"

"Hey, she started it."

"That does seem to be the excuse *du jour*," Pain said in all innocence.

Agony was about to spin and take some of her disgust out on him but Silvia interrupted. "Can I go now? I thought it might be fun to fuck where dead people usually are but the top of that table is hard."

"Maybe for your next date..." Agony wanted to give her some

helpful advice. "You two can meet in a cemetery and spread a blanket on the ground."

"Oh, Iggy, that might be fun. Are we allowed to bring picnic lunches and a couple of bottles of wine into a graveyard?"

"We can discuss it another time, Silvia. But maybe you should head out now. I'm sure these two are here on business. Can I call you?"

"You can call, but I'm not sure I'll answer. It depends on my mood."

With that, she waltzed out. Agony stepped into the hallway to watch and to make sure she didn't make a side trip into Miles' office to pick up any happy pills on her way out. She returned to the prep room in time to hear Ignatius bitching at Pain.

"This had better damn well be important. That was the first time I had sex in over a year!"

"Well, there's always the graveyard to look forward to."

The mortician shook his head. "You don't understand. Miles is the one with the drug access. She'll end up back with him. But please do me a favor, okay? Don't tell him about this. We have a good partnership going and I'd hate to mess it up because of Silvia."

Agony begged to differ. "That's not how it looked ten minutes ago."

He shrugged. "What can I say?"

"Anything," Pain pleaded, "except she started it. I've heard that excuse too many times today."

"All right. So why are you here?"

"We need to visit your cold room. We're tracking a corpse down."

"It would have helped if you had called first."

"Someone did but Miles took the message. It would appear that he didn't pass it on."

"Has the stiff got a name?"

The detective winced at the term but answered civilly enough. "Esther Chongrak."

"You mean Esther Chongrak, the one who is not technically here?"

"That's the one."

"Follow me."

Ignatius led them across the room to where the drawers were. In earlier days, long before he and his partner had taken ownership, the cold room could hold up to eight bodies. These days, they seldom had more than two at a time and those were usually poor folks who couldn't afford more elaborate surroundings. On this day, Esther Chongrak was the only occupant and was in the top drawer of the second row. He slid her out—or what was left of her.

"What did they tell you when they brought her in?" Pain asked.

"They told me that who she had been was not my concern. My only task was to hold onto her until someone with the proper credentials came to claim her."

"And what would those credentials be?"

"I am sure you are quite aware of the answer to that question since they are probably the ones who must have sent you here. No one else knows we have her and I suspect that her death has not even been reported to the local authorities yet."

"That's a very good guess, Doc."

As much as Agony despised the late agent, it still was painful to see anyone's body in the condition she was now in. Burned to a crisp was the first description that sprang to mind. In her cop days, it would have been in poor taste but not out of the question for someone to mention, "Crispy critter."

"You used to be a medical examiner, Doc, and from what Agony tells me, you were a good one. Do you care to offer any of your expertise?"

"Obviously," Ignatius was quick to point out, "no one

requested any of my assistance in identifying the body. They brought her in, I opened the drawer, they dropped her in, I closed the drawer, and they left."

Agony had known the former medical examiner for a long time and knew how he loved to solve puzzles when it came to the cause of death. "Are you telling us you haven't snuck in at least a couple of peeks since then?"

The mortician hesitated for a moment but confessed quickly. "It's rare to see a body this burned and things can get very boring around here during our downtime so yes, I may have done a couple of cursory exams. That said, I assure you I did not touch or move the body."

Pain was curious to see how much of his skills remained. "You have our permission to touch it now. What do you see?"

"I see the result of an extremely high flash of heat in a confined space."

"How confined?"

"As a medical examiner, I preferred to know more before I offered an opinion, but if I was forced to guess, I would say she was in a car."

"Why a car?"

"Because when they brought her in, the body was in a seated position. They had to...um, unfold her to get her into a drawer. There are very few rooms small enough that if someone was seated in a chair when the fire occurred, they would not have at least tried to jump out and run. So, a car. How am I doing?"

The detective was impressed and said so. "Tell me more."

"Going with that assumption, I would then hazard a guess that it was some type of a bomb. That is because if she had been caught in a car fire after a wreck again, there would have been more movement as she would have tried to scramble out."

"She could have been knocked unconscious."

"I would say yes, except the burns are too severe for gasoline to have caused them. She isn't merely burned, she is charred.

Gasoline fires don't generate enough heat for that. Based on that, I will stick with a bomb, but not a typical car bomb as that would not have left the body intact. No, this would have been some kind of an incendiary device with such a high potency that if there hadn't been a limited fuel source, we would be looking at the ashes of cremated remains."

"Agony was right," Pain conceded. "You must have been a damn fine examiner."

Ignatius was pleased by the compliment. "There isn't much more the body can tell us, at least as far as identifying the poor woman goes. Dental records would be practically useless because the heat of the fire damaged most of the teeth, and saying that someone had two cavities doesn't do much to narrow the field down. But you said her name is Esther Chongrak. I am curious how anyone could make that firm an identification given how little there is to work with."

"They started by knowing she was in Esther Chongrak's car and worked backward from there."

Ignatius shook his head in disapproval. "It is very poor science to start with a conclusion. Maybe she was a friend who borrowed the car. For all we know, she could have even been stealing the car. Without knowing who the vehicle belonged to, there is not enough evidence to be able to identify her. Even her bones are cracked and warped so old broken bones would not be enough to go on since there is no way to tell if something is an old break or a new crack. Now, if she had an artificial knee or other pieces of metal in her body, at least that would be something to start with."

Pain had been right about the incendiary bomb but Agony still felt as if they were stuck treading water until her partner snapped his fingers.

"Wait a minute. You said metal?" he asked quickly.

"Rods. Pins. Something like that, yes. The serial number of the device would have melted but the metal itself might still be in place."

"We need to check her right wrist. She once needed to have some modeling done and I believe it took two pins."

Agony's hopes rose. "She broke her wrist? How long ago and how?"

"About a decade ago." Pain still had a fond memory of the day. "She was pissed and threw a punch at my kidney. It would have hurt like hell but that was back in the days when I still carried weapons and had a holstered sidearm under my sports coat that she didn't know about. She ended up with bruised knuckles, two breaks in her wrist, and a couple of pins."

"What did you end up with?"

"A smile and a new gun. She had bent the barrel enough that the damn thing never fired perfectly straight again."

Ignatius had moved the wrist in question gently and stepped aside so they both could see.

"Part of the pins have melted but there you have it. Definitely two pins."

The detective felt a sudden, unexpected sadness. "Enough for a positive ID?"

"I would be more positive if the serial numbers were still there but since it's all we have to go on, I would probably sign off on the remains having once been Esther Chongrak."

"So, Pain, would that be enough for SISTER to confirm also? They must have her medical records."

"One car and two pins? Yeah. In this case, it would have to be enough." He turned to Ignatius. "Thank you, Doc, we owe you one."

Ignatius slid Agent Chongrak's body into the drawer.

"Next time, knock—oh, and remember, Miles doesn't need to know about Silvia and me. I doubt if today's activities will be repeated. You two know your way out."

The partners left and Jules Ignatius stood a little straighter. He was still pissed about the interruption with Silvia but for at least a few minutes there, he'd felt like a real doctor again.

CHAPTER SEVEN

Agony slid behind the wheel and Pain called Agent Hollund to let him know they were on the way.

"Did you learn anything new?"

"It was more along the lines of suspicions having been confirmed than it was new discoveries. We'll be there in half an hour and will talk more then." He hung up and Agony noticed that he still seemed fairly shaken. While he might have had a loathe-hate relationship with Chongrak, they had both worked for SISTER. Like her checkered history with the boys and girls in blue, unless someone was utterly corrupt, it hurt when you lost one.

She tried to find some words of comfort but all she could come up with was, "At least she didn't suffer very much. I mean, it was a case of boom-gone, right?"

"Yeah, and her car seat was ground zero so there is some comfort in that. But still, it's not the way she should have gone."

Rather than say something to make things worse, she drove the rest of the way in silence and left him to work through whatever mixed emotions he felt. When they arrived at the half-vacant strip mall, she circled and they noticed no new vehicles lurking at the rear.

Satisfied, she parked out front ten minutes before the store was scheduled to close. Nickie, Matthew, and the manager—if you could call him that—Tony were again gathered around the front register, about to close up for the day. When the partners strode in and saw the looks on their faces, Agony wasn't sure which was more bruised—their arms or their egos.

"Do you still have my chair?"

Tony sniffed. "It doesn't have your name on it yet but yes, it is still here."

"In case I was too subtle earlier, there will be some serious damage done to all three of you if it happens to get sold before I am ready to buy it."

The two junior agents took a step back and let their superior handle the bitch. "You have ten minutes before we close. You can purchase it now and we'll help you carry it out."

"How about I buy it now and you put a tag on it saying sold?"

"Sorry. That is not the way things work here. We are strictly cash and carry. We don't want to be liable for any damages done to a piece between the time it is sold and the time it is retrieved, so we can't process any sales until you are ready to physically take it with you."

"That's a shitty policy, Tony. How about you put a pretend sold sign on it and I promise to return as soon as I can?"

"Again, that is not our policy."

"How about I tell you what my policy is and we work something out from there?"

Pain grasped her arm and tugged her toward the back office before she could cause any more actual damage to either bodies or egos. "You're scaring the children."

She shouted at them as Pain dragged her away. "They should be scared! That chair is mine and remains right where it is until I come back for it. Understood? I don't want to see even so much as another person's fingerprints on it."

None of the three workers acknowledged the threat but the glances they exchanged told her that at least she now had a fighting chance of having her chair still available until she was ready to claim it.

They knocked on the back door before they entered and Chris welcomed them in.

"Coffee?"

The detective declined. "Too late in the day for me."

Agony thanked him for the offer but also declined and they all took their seats.

"You said there wasn't anything new but you did get some confirmations. Do you care to elaborate?" Agent Hollund had his laptop open and typed notes in as Pain gave a concise report of the information they had managed to gather. It didn't take long.

"So the disgraced former coroner helped to inspect the body? Are you sure that was wise?"

She surprised herself by coming to Ignatius' defense. "At one time, Iggy was a very good coroner. If he hadn't gotten into trouble with his gambling, he would still be high on my list if I needed a go-to opinion. And I doubt there was anything he saw or learned that would be of any interest to his scattered mob connections, who are a fairly mismatched group of low-level goombas."

"Okay, so we don't need to worry about him blabbing," the agent conceded. "And he agreed that it had been a high-burn incendiary accelerant?"

"Very high-burn—cremation-level if it had carried on long enough," Pain confirmed. "Now I have a question."

"Fire away."

"Other than it being Esther's car, what did anyone on SISTER's side use to ID the body? Ignatius said it would have been almost impossible except for two little items and even then, he said he would have signed off on it but wouldn't have put it at one hundred percent certainty."

"You are referring to the pins? Nice work in thinking to look for them."

"I wouldn't have thought to even look for them if I hadn't been partially responsible for their existence."

Hollund smiled. "Just so you know, Esther still carried that grudge. But you are correct. The car and the pins were also all we could come up with."

"It's still flimsy."

"How about you, Agony? Did anything stand out?"

She frowned. "I've been very much a bump on a log all day. All I can do is attest to Pain's thoroughness. If he's satisfied, so am I. Hopefully, eventually, there will be something I can do to help the investigation along. Otherwise, I might spend the duration sitting in my chair to make sure no one steals it out from under me."

"Ah yes, the Queen Bitch's Chair, or so I have heard it has been dubbed. But there is some action coming up that should require some of your expertise and assistance."

"My heart went flitter-flutter." She grinned. "Tell me more."

"I will but first, I wanted to let you both know that Johnny —that would be Agent Johnny Williams who helped you examine the car—and I have worked together to set up some database searches. I am working on the hardware and who would have access to it but it's regarding the kind of pressure plate mechanism you found. These are not over-the-counter items."

"Not since Bombs-R-Us went out of business."

Agent Hollund made an effort to smile at Pain's dumb-ass joke. "Someone would need the components of the plate, the bomb itself, the accelerant, and the knowledge of how to put them all together. That should narrow the field down significantly."

Agony was ready to lean back in her chair and start counting ceiling tiles as her partner continued.

"And the wiring to the door locks?"

"Which, I am sorry to report, our agents missed, so we are very grateful for that. Johnny will handle that portion. Cars these days are essentially four-wheeled computers and the electronics are very intricate. It would take a certain set of skills and knowledge to be able to properly combine the devices to the specific fuses—knowledge that might very well not be part of a bomb maker's standard repartee. He seemed quite excited to be able to put some of his expertise to work."

"Gee, I wish I could say the same." Agony tried to decide if she should start counting each individual tile or merely how many were in each row and multiply by the number of rows.

"I am coming to believe that patience is not one of your strong suits, Ms. Agony."

She nodded toward her partner. "I am patient enough to be able to put up with him so don't sell me too short, Agent Hollund. I am good at patience. It's boredom I have a problem with."

"Well, I believe that we shall soon be able to provide you with some relief. While Johnny and I will be stuck behind our desks doing research, you two—if you would be so kind—can do some fieldwork for me and by extension, yourselves."

Having reached fourteen, she stopped counting the ceiling tiles. "What kind of fieldwork?"

"In this instance, I mean a real field or at least a firing range type of field."

"As long as we're not placed out in the field as the actual targets," Pain interjected.

Agony snorted. "With all the time you've spent practicing evasive maneuvers on the street to avoid becoming an easy target for Baran, you ought to do good on a firing range. At least there, you'll know which direction all the shooting will come from."

"She has gotten into your head, has she?" the agent asked with a raised eyebrow.

"He ought to charge her rent."

"I, along with a handful of others, have been busy gathering as much data as possible with the aim of identifying the new Havoc. As I believe I've mentioned, he is much more of a hands-on operative than the old Havoc was. He is a doer, not merely a provider. By now, he has probably gathered several troops around him in a type of coalition."

"Do you have any idea how many and if any of them might be former, or even current, disgruntled SISTER operatives?" Pain asked.

"Except for the amount of chatter, we have no idea as to the actual number. Our best guess is in the two dozen range of active associates and as far as current agents goes, except for Oksana Baran, all our operatives are accounted for."

"And former agents?"

"That line would begin and end with you, sir."

Pain accepted the mild rebuke and Hollund continued.

"With regard to what I called a coalition, for instance, I doubt if Havoc himself is the one who assembled and planted the bomb that killed Agent Chongrak, simply due to the set of skills involved. But I am also fairly certain that he provided the materials. If someone wanted Esther dead, Havoc would be the one they would most likely use to acquire the appropriate means. I do not believe that he is particularly fond of SISTER or her agents and so probably offered them a nicely discounted rate."

Agony put off her return to tile-counting long enough to ask, "You mentioned fieldwork but haven't offered any details other than a firing range. Why a firing range and what would we be looking for there?"

Hollund smiled his gentle smile. "Those are excellent questions. One of the few things we all agree on is that Havoc likes his guns."

"He sounds like my kind of guy. Excluding my partner, who doesn't?"

"We are also fairly certain that his main base is local. There have been two primary weapons used in the killings we suspect he has had a personal hand in. One is a Heckler & Koch HK417. The other is a Beretta 90-Two, chambered for a .40 S&W."

She pointed out that the Beretta 90-Two had gone out of production a decade earlier.

"True, but it must be a personal favorite because as I said, his is chambered for a .40 S&W."

"And what did you say the other one was?"

Pain surprised her by answering. "He said it's a Heckler & Koch HK417. It's a military-grade sniper special with a range between four hundred and six hundred meters depending on the caliber used. Is that where the firing range comes in?"

"Precisely."

"Precisely how?" It had been a while since she had been at a firing range of any kind and Agony was ready to saddle Bertha up and head out immediately.

"There are, of course, several indoor ranges where one can practice with the Beretta. The Heckler & Koch however, requires more space in order for one to be able to stay in practice properly. As Pain pointed out, it has a range of six hundred meters and there are only so many locations that can provide that kind of distance. Fortunately, one is within a half-hour's drive outside of the city limits."

"That close?" She was surprised.

"That close." Hollund smiled again. "The next closest is almost two hundred miles away."

She liked what she was hearing. "So if your assumption is correct and Havoc is locally based, he has a playground practically in his back yard."

"A sniper needs to keep his skills sharp, so we suspect that he visits the range on a fairly regular basis. Sadly, we have no photographs of what he looks like or we would have been able to work with facial recognition and bring him in. But knowing what his weapons of choice are and the proximity of the range to the city, we think our best bet is to send a couple of agents—or in this case, a couple of sub-contractors—undercover."

Pain thought it was a solid strategy. Time-consuming and possibly fruitless if Havoc wasn't local, but at least worth a try. "Eyes, ears, and feet on the ground. We find the weapons, we find the man."

"That is our reasoning. And his guns aren't overly common so should be easy to identify. You can alternate days inside the range while the other runs surveillance. It's up to you as to who goes in and who stays out on any given day."

"But what if he recognizes Pain? It's not like he is in any way inconspicuous."

Hollund shrugged. "I will admit that is a slight risk, but we have delved further into Esther's texts and what research we could find and are no longer convinced that Pain is the P she was referring to."

It was the detective's turn to scowl. "Has anyone passed that information on to Oksana Baran yet or is she still dark?"

"I am afraid she remains off the reservation. But remember, everyone at the range will be armed so it seems highly unlikely that it would be the opportune time or place for either she or Havoc if he is indeed aware of you to try to bring you down."

"Somehow, your words fail to reassure me."

"Oh, come on, Pain," Agony chided. "You still have your Wonderoos. All they've done is gathered dust lately. You can't tell me you haven't been itching to put them into action again."

"Wonder—roos?"

"Think of them as magical long-johns, only slightly more stylish—unless, of course, one is going for the mountain man look." She turned to her partner. "Do you have any actual long-johns, overalls, and cut-off flannel shirts you can leave half-unbuttoned to show off the latest fashion for the I-haven't-bathed-in-a-week crowd?"

He ignored her. "What does it pay, Agent Christopher Hollund?"

"Does the satisfaction of having performed a great service to your country and civilization in general do anything for you?" The man smiled.

"What does it pay, Agent Hollund?"

"How about playing a major role in bringing Esther Chongrak's murderer to justice?"

"What does it pay—Chris?" Pain kept his tone firm and his face stern.

"What is it worth to not have to worry about spending the rest of your life wondering if you are about to walk into the sights of whatever long-range rifle Oksana Baran is using on any given day?"

"You're getting closer."

"I can throw in three hundred a day each and a credit card in a false name that has enough on it to cover gun rentals and however much ammunition you can go through each day."

Agony leaned forward, whispered into her partner's ear, and leaned back and folded her arms in front of her chest to indicate that she had one more non-negotiable demand. Her partner looked at her but she sat immobile with nothing short of a final-offer look on her face.

"I am the only recognizable one facing the lion's den and that is your line in the sand?" he asked incredulously.

She stared straight ahead and didn't bother to acknowledge his question. Pain sighed and faced the agent who had met his negotiating match.

"Regardless of our success—or, as seems likely, our failure—and whether or not I beat the growing odds against my survival, there is a final condition. When she survives and returns, there had better damn well be a padded, swiveling, Naughahyde rocking chair with a sold sign and a tag with her name hand-written on it still waiting for her in the showroom."

"And if Agony, heaven forbid, isn't the one who lives long enough to claim it?" Curiosity seemed to have overridden the agent's common sense.

"Then I will be the only one who returns and will claim the chair in her name. She has given me the non-negotiable ulti-matum that she intends to spend the majority of what's left of her life in that chair. If her life is cut tragically short, her dying wish is to be buried in it."

Agent Christopher Hollund confessed silently that he had never taken the time to sit in the chair but came to two conclu-sions. It must be one hell of a chair or Pain's partner—who research had shown had been very involved in MMA training—may have taken one too many blows to the head.

He handed the detective the SISTER fabricated credit card, pulled out a notepad, and wrote, *Sell this chair and suffer termina-tion of job duties and possible death—not necessarily in that order.*

With the negotiations now completed to everyone's satisfac-tion, Agent Holland signed the note and led them out of his office and directly to the chair in question. He used the securest tape available that would not leave any residue that couldn't easily be washed off with the help of a sponge and tepid water and posted the note where Nickie, Matthew, and Tony would not be able to miss it.

Satisfied that the claim to her chair now had the official seal from the highest-ranking agent in the store, Agony thanked him and strode out of the door. Pain and Agent Hollund walked a little slower and paused as they watched her climb behind Bertha's wheel and give the dashboard a hearty slap.

"Be careful out there, Pain," the agent said in parting.

"Careful of what? Havoc, Baran, or my partner?"

Hollund didn't elaborate and chose instead to simply repeat his parting advice. "Be careful out there, Pain."

The two men shook hands and the detective walked out. He didn't look back but heard the snick of the door lock as Agent Christopher Hollund secured the Little Angel's Consignment Shop behind him, turned the lights off, and retreated into the back of this version of a SISTER safe house.

Pain slid into his seat. "You know, you could have driven a slightly harder bargain."

Agony didn't waste any time before she put Bertha into gear. "Why? I have an open card to rent guns and buy ammo and spend a few days at a range, and I have my new chair practically signed, sealed, and delivered. What more could a girl want?"

"Oh, I don't know. Maybe some kind of reassurance that SISTER would assign a couple of spare undercover agents to help cover our backs?"

"Sorry, but other than Johnny at the garage and Consignment Shop Chris, most of my experience with your still surviving former fellow agents has given me the impression that they are a dangerous combination of inexperience and incompetence.

"Then again, I have met a dozen others who at one time or another didn't hesitate to attack us, kidnap us, threaten us with torture, tazer us, and then leave us dazed and in tatters in a vacant lot as easy-pickings for early-morning street-cruising thugs.

"Have I forgotten any? Oh, right, I haven't had the pleasure of meeting her yet, but there's always your former fuck-buddy Oksana Baran, who from the rumors I've heard intends to shoot you on sight as long as she can do it from a safe distance."

"I guess you haven't exactly been exposed to the best and the brightest," he acknowledged regretfully.

"How the hell do you know that? You've been out of the loop

for a while. Maybe these days, what we have been dealing with is all that's left of the cream of the crop."

"I'll grant you all that but you haven't had anything to eat today since the cookies at the garage."

"Don't you insult those cookies. They were a damn fine batch."

"All I'm saying is that both of us are hungry and one of us doesn't function well on an empty stomach."

She scowled but it soon transformed to a hopeful expression. "So what are you suggesting?"

"I'm suggesting that we swing past our office and see if Ahjoomenoni's nephews have managed to protect it. Once we do that, we can visit Masha's, get a couple of fresh orders of healthy deli food to go, and go to our apartments and eat while we try to make some kind of sense out of this cluster-fuck we've gotten ourselves into before we head out in the morning."

"That may be the most useful thing I've heard you say all day. Masha's it is."

CHAPTER EIGHT

After inspecting their office the night before and before they called at Masha's deli, they had done a quick online search of the gun range and printed several aerial photographs of the layout.

Pain had the coffee brewed and the bagels as well as the printouts set out the next morning when Agony gave their secret raps on the door and strode directly to the coffee.

"Do I smell French Vanilla?"

"Guilty," he confirmed. "I was in the mood for raisin bagels and a couple of cinnamon and it makes for better dipping."

She poured herself a cup but went with the more traditional cream cheese topping. "Barbarian. Donuts are for dipping, not bagels."

"Says you. What were you able to find out about the Max-Bore Gun & Run history?"

"That all they had to do was paint over the *Culvert Construction* at the end of the name and replace it with *Gun & Run* on the building and they had a ready-made, macho-sounding name for a firing range. Seriously, is there anyone out there who is into guns and doesn't have wet dreams about having the maximum bore size? Hell, it wouldn't surprise me if they didn't have a tank out there somewhere for the Max-Bore fanatics."

"I'm not sure they don't but I'll save that until it's my turn. What else?"

"I only had the time to watch a few videos, all on the inside, but they convinced me that it is a weekend warrior's paradise. The factory itself is huge. Half of it has been converted into a full-time flea market, no weapons allowed, and after some serious renovations, the other half has been converted to an indoor firing range. Taken together, the inside is called the Shop & Pop and claims to have a little something for everyone. It probably offers a ten percent discount for anyone named Goober, Scooter, or Cooter." He shrugged and looked expectantly at her. "What did you come up with?"

"That for forty years, it was a very successful construction company specializing in concrete and metal culvert fabrication and installation. Then the federal money for infrastructure dried up. The factory closed and they were left with two square miles of outdoor storage space loaded with already fabricated culverts, beams, and supports of all sizes."

Pain spun a couple of the aerial photos to her and offended her sense of propriety when he tore a cinnamon in half and dipped it before he continued.

"The property also backs onto a good-sized quarry, so the yard is littered with dozens of piles of different types of gravel and a variety of vehicles ranging from graders to trenchers to excavators to dump trucks. It looks like they sectioned off one half of the yard for long-range target practice and moved the machines and gravel piles into the other half as a kind of tactical obstacle-training course—hopefully for paintball and not live ammo."

"I don't know. I'm always in favor of a little herd thinning."

"How very burned-out cop-like of you."

She snorted. "Are you going to sit there with a straight face and tell me that you disagree?"

"Am I allowed to lie?"

"No."

"Then I can't disagree." He ignored her smirk. "Do you have any idea how you want to work this?"

She sensed that it was something he had no desire to discuss or analyze so still hadn't mentioned the carnage Pain had caused with guns in his hands when he had gone into full-on berserker mode during their escape from the Moorfin Lodge a few jobs earlier. But this was a whole new assignment so she needed to know his current state of mind.

"Do you promise you won't take this the wrong way?"

Pain hated questions like that. "How can I promise something when I have no idea what you're about to say?"

"So, no promises. Is that what I'm hearing?"

"Your ears are perfectly functional, yes, although I'm beginning to worry about their connectivity to your brain's main processing unit."

"The thing is, we'll spend several days at a gun range. I'll be fine scoping out the shooters inside while keeping an eye out for the Beretta, but I'm not sure how well I'll fit in with the sniper crowd. Will you be able to square that with your no-guns rule?"

"I have no problem shooting guns at targets. I merely prefer the targets to be made of paper or cardboard, not flesh and blood. Don't worry. I'll be fine."

Agony assured him that she would do her best to not worry. What she didn't confess was a fear that he might have some kind of a flashback and forget that he was on a gun range and not in the middle of an actual firefight.

"You won't come up with some weird-ass ops name for this, will you? Because if you do, I claim full veto rights," she told him firmly.

"Not in the mood to go a-damseling again, huh?"

"How about we start with the basics? Do we know each other?"

"I would vote for no. It's easier to strike up conversations with strangers as individuals than it is as a couple."

She slid out a couple more of the aerial shots and studied them. "If you have a strong enough scope, I might be able to find a couple of places to perch on the top of the gravel pit to maintain surveillance while you're outside, but I'll be too far away to be of much use if something bad goes down."

"It's a shame we don't have a drone," he lamented. "That way, you could watch from Bertha."

"Yeah." She chuckled. "But even if we did, I'm very sure a dozen yahoos would start taking shots at it."

"Have you ever been to Sampson's Spy Store?" he asked

"I always wanted to, but no."

"Then that's our first stop. It will cost us our first day's pay, but for six hundred, we can get a pair of glasses with a micro-camera on each side. We'll trade off days of shooting and observing. When I'm wearing them, you won't be able to see directly ahead but you will be able to see anyone who might approach from the side. And they're basically one size fits all. Between those and our earpieces, we should be able to keep track of each other fairly well."

"And they'll pass for safety glasses when shooting?"

"They're graded out at A-20, so yeah. We can even pair them with our phones. One of us can watch from Bertha or even while browsing through the flea market, while the other does the scoping."

"Rock, paper, scissors for who gets to shoot first?"

Pain pouted. "But you always win at that."

"Fine. Odds and evens. You choose."

"Evens."

Agony got first crack at the action. She crossed the hallway to choose an outfit and returned half an hour later with black leggings tucked into electric-blue calf-high boots and topped with a checkered white-and-sky-blue tunic that stopped at mid-thigh.

The only argument they almost got into was at Sampson's. He favored gold-tinted shades, whereas she wanted pale-blue. She held her arms out and lifted a boot to show that blue was inarguably the color of the day.

He forked the cash over. "I knew I should have gone with odds."

"No one likes a sore loser."

"No one likes a gloater either." He might have lost the big battle, but at least he'd had the last-word sneak blow.

After all the times they'd played odds and evens, Pain had yet to determine how Agony usually won the majority of the time. She wasn't about to inform him that eight times out of ten, when he chose odds, he would come up with an odd number of fingers. When he chose evens, the number of fingers he laid out would also be even.

She wasn't sure what kind of subliminal message his brain sent to his fingers but since it usually worked out in her favor, she would keep that little tidbit of information to herself. When it came to rock, paper, scissors, she would look into the distance and make very subtle and seemingly unconscious hand motions. Pain, being the master body-language reader he was, would always display whatever option would defeat hers and she would adjust her real lay-down accordingly. Sometimes, she wondered how he had managed to live so long.

It was mid-afternoon when they arrived at Max-Bore and Agony parked in an empty space between two oversized pick-up trucks. This allowed them to exit Bertha without anyone being able to tell that they had arrived together. She donned her light-blue shades and they ran another quick check of the optics using his phone.

Satisfied with the glasses and their earbuds, she headed in

first, the thinking being that the gender-gap ratio would be ninety to ten in favor of men. Once they got a look at Agony, no one would pay any attention to another guy coming in shortly afterward. Was it sexist thinking? Of course, but they were willing to run with whatever it took to improve their odds.

Agony strode to the indoor range counter, used the credit card Christopher Hollund had provided, paid for three hours at a middle lane, and bought seven nine-millimeter magazines for her trusty Smith & Wesson M&P Shield 2.0. She could have had better value if she went with an extended magazine, but she didn't like firing with one she seldom used.

With her magazine plus the seven new ones, she would have fifty-six total rounds to fire at the targets twenty-five yards distant. If she took her time and fired one careful round at a time, she could easily stretch it to the three hours to enable her and her partner to study the other customers and their guns. They were looking for someone shooting a Beretta 90-Two. Everyone else was of no interest except to help her kill time by striking conversations up while trying not to be too obvious about her surveillance.

While Agony was getting set up, Pain wandered into the flea market side. He spent considerable time fake-texting as he strolled through the aisles looking for bargains. Spy toys could be fun and he was able to watch Agony's flanks without a problem. It had taken her twenty minutes to go through one magazine and retrieve her target. She used her thumb to engage the safety and inspected her grouping. Satisfied, she attached a new target, sent it down the lane, and popped in a fresh magazine.

Neither of the partners saw anyone with a Beretta of any model, but as her target settled into place, she heard her partner's voice in her ear.

"Coming up on your right. I'm surprised it took this long but you are about to get hit on in three, two, one."

"I don't believe I've seen you here before, ma'am."

Pain winced at the knucklehead's use of one of his partner's least favorite words and prayed she wouldn't blow their cover by beating the crap out of him. Well, their cover wouldn't be completely blown, but they wouldn't let her into the inside range anytime soon if her baton made an appearance.

To his surprise, her voice practically dripped honey. Although she still hadn't settled on which version of a southern accent she wanted to use at least this time, it was somewhere east of the Mississippi. As he listened carefully, he thought she might be trying to mimic Agent Hollund's soft drawl and didn't completely suck at it.

"Why no, sir, I don't believe you have since this is my first visit."

The stranger smiled and showed off teeth that were more acquainted with chewing tobacco than a toothbrush. "Then let me be the first to welcome you. My name is Russell J Peterson but my friends call me Rusty."

Agony scrutinized the less-than-handsome stranger. At a good two inches shorter than her and coming in at about the same weight as her six-foot-four partner, she wouldn't be surprised if rusty might also be used to describe his male appendage.

He did, however, know how to dress for the occasion. In range terminology, she chalked him up as a poser. Every item of his apparel was top-of-the-line and state-of-the-art, which meant he probably couldn't hit the broad side of a barn at a ten-yard distance.

His gun of choice was a Glock, which put him out of the running and she wanted to make a quick end to the conversation before she fell madly in love.

"It was a pleasure meeting you, Rusty, but I need to get back to my practice now."

The man showed no sign of taking the hint and backing out. "I can understand that. These lanes aren't cheap—but your practice will probably go faster if you released the safety on that S&W of yours first."

"You mean like this?" She gave in to putting the wanna-be chick-magnet in his place by thumbing the safety off and without waiting for him to move, emptied her entire magazine into the helpless target.

On his phone, Pain could watch the look on Rusty's face as the target was drawn in and she held it up to show a perfect score of seventy.

Ever so politely, she called the poser's bluff. "I'll step aside if you would like to show me how it's supposed to be done."

"That's quite all right, ma'am. I think I'll move along now."

He shuffled away with hunched shoulders and the detective almost felt sorry for the poor bastard, but he had survived a whole two ma'ams without suffering damage to anything but his ego. Even though he didn't know it, this was Rusty's lucky day.

Pain spoke in her ear again. "Did you have to empty a whole magazine to get rid of him?"

"It was either go all-in on the target or give Rusty a five-second head start to run before I unloaded in his direction."

"Are you sure you're in the right frame of mind for this?"

"I didn't pull my baton out, did I? I'm fine. Now shut up and let me shoot. Why don't you go look at some cowboy hats or something?"

He sighed and decided to do exactly that. After all, he'd always liked the way he looked wearing a cowboy hat.

Agony's three hours passed much too quickly for her and what seemed like forever to Pain, and all they had counted were three Berettas, two of them carried by women and one by a man, but it wasn't a 90-Two. They bought a couple of tacos from one of the food trucks on the edge of the parking lot and sat at a picnic table for half an hour while they ate and continued to watch the crowd before they finally called it a day.

Gun ranges weren't famous for catering to early-risers so they again aimed for a mid-afternoon arrival time and parked between larger vehicles. Agony headed to the Shop & Pop and Pain gave her a one-minute head start before he sauntered inside to the counter and paid for the time on the open range.

What he would have liked to have done was hit the tactical range, even if it was only paintball. The brochure stated that not only did the course have obstacles, it also had pop-up targets, some of them designed as bad guys and some good, with the object being to see how fast you could take someone down while not killing the good guys. The problem was both partners doubted that the new Havoc would hang out and mess around with paintball silliness, so the outdoor range was where he had to go.

He was relieved that Agent Hollund was footing the bill. Between the rifle rental and enough magazines to cover three hours if he took his time, he would have been out almost a grand. The rifle was a Remington 783 bolt action, an inexpensive model that was accurate up to seven hundred yards, but if you wanted to separate the men from the boys, could still be deadly up to thirteen hundred. He had to split the difference since the longest the range went up to was a thousand, which was where he headed.

As he walked from the shop to the range, he had the misfortune of sharing the path with a guy coming straight from the parking lot who seemed like he either wanted to make a new friend or challenge him to some kind of shoot-off. The stranger wasn't quite his size but seemed to be in decent shape. He didn't bother to introduce himself before he noted Pain's rifle and started the conversation with a brilliant observation.

"You got a rental, huh?"

The detective walked on but thought it would be rude to not

answer. "Yeah. I'm visiting some relatives and thought I'd kill some time."

"It's a shame they don't spend a little more on the rentals. That 783 won't let you go much beyond the five-hundred marker." He held up and patted his rifle case. "Now in here, I'm carryin' a Ruger 338 Lapua. I wish this range had more than a thousand max so that I could let this baby stretch its legs but hey, we gotta make do, right?"

His attempted pissing contest about whose gun was bigger having concluded and with the Ruger identifying him as not a Heckler & Koch guy and therefore likely a non-Havoc, Pain decided to skip the thousand-yard range and settle for the seven. This was mainly to make sure he didn't get stuck next to the guy but would also work out better for his purposes since he could probably keep a better eye out for Mr. HK417. A thousand yards would have been at the top of that gun's range.

Agony became bored with the flea market within half an hour of browsing and after another half-hour of deflecting advances made by several men and two different women, she decided to go hide out in Bertha and listen to some tunes as she kept an eye on her partner via her phone.

They had agreed that he should stand and stretch every half-hour and stroll from one end of the shooters' stations to the other. That allowed her to be able to identify any HKs without him having to turn his head. On two of his strolls, she noticed a couple of potentials and directed him to linger for a closer look. The two men were indeed using Heckler & Koch rifles but neither was a 417 and snipers in general stuck to the same model for practice as they used in real life.

Nonetheless, they wanted to be thorough so Pain kept an eye on both of them and alerted her when each was finished. That enabled her to leave Bertha and walk toward the end of the path to the range, thereby cutting them off while she looked confused and began her spiel, still working on her southern accent.

"I am sorry to bother you, but I was supposed to meet a friend here and my cell phone battery died, so I'm not sure if he is still here or not. Did you notice a big guy shooting? I think the gun he always uses is an HK417."

Neither of the men hit on her, which was a relief, and both acknowledged that they also used HK's, although not 417's. Even so, they would have probably noticed another HK man but sadly, they had not seen her friend.

"Thank you so much. Maybe he's running late. I'll go in and check at the counter."

After each exchange, she informed Pain that she doubted either of the men showed a temperament that would match what they knew of the new Havoc.

At the end of three hours, he returned his gun and met Agony at the food trucks, this time for good old-fashioned burgers and fries that they again ate while they continued their surveillance.

"How did the shooting go?" she asked.

Pain chewed and swallowed a large bite of his burger before he answered. "It would probably have gone better if I'd had the gold-tinted glasses instead of the blue. They almost made it too bright to see what I was shooting at."

"That good, huh? Come on, tell me. How did you score?"

"I don't know." He shrugged. "I left the target in place."

"What kind of a shooter does that?"

"Is there a law against it?"

"No—but still!"

He smiled at his partner's aggravation. He knew exactly how he had scored but had lied about having not retrieved his target merely to see her reaction. Of a total of twenty-six rounds he'd fired, each one was a kill-shot.

After drawing their dinner out for an hour, they chalked it up to another day of futility and left.

On day three, it was Agony's turn again. Pain spent an hour in Bertha, then an hour inside the Shop & Pop to stretch his legs before he gave in and bought a Stetson knock-off. He decided to take a short stroll to the viewing area of the tactical range. The yard was large and matched the description in the brochure.

Large mounds of gravel, a couple of dozen large boulders, several low sandbag walls, and construction vehicles of various shapes and sizes had been positioned strategically in the area. He checked his phone to keep an eye on his partner, silently counted to thirty while he studied the course, then glanced at his phone again.

At a guess, there were maybe a dozen players. It was obvious that a few had formed teams and he enjoyed watching their strategies unfold. What surprised him the most was that not only did the pop-up figures spring to life as targets, but those who were the designated bad guys would also fire a shot whenever someone passed through what must have been hidden lasers. He thought that was a nice touch.

Agony was only hit on once but quickly put the guy in his place. She watched him walk away and saw him connect with Rusty, who had watched the whole exchange. Both men shook their heads and wandered outside together. She wondered if they were comparing notes.

During the three hours of her time inside, she and Pain saw three Berettas, but none of them were a 90-Two. Since there were no apparent Havocs on location, they rendezvoused at the food trucks and the picnic tables. They chose tacos again and once seated, she tried and failed miserably to not chuckle at the headgear her partner now wore so proudly.

"How's it goin', Tex? Herded any cows lately?"

"Scoff all you want but the saleslady agreed that I look damn fine wearing this."

"Pay me as much as you paid for the hat and I'll compliment you too. But I'm wondering...how does a cowboy who wears an empty holster practice his quick-draw in the mirror? Do you simply pretend you have a gun, pretend to draw it, and go, 'Bang?'"

He made a management decision to never wear the hat again in his partner's presence.

They agreed to give the mid-afternoon one more try before they changed the hours and after breakfast, killed a little time by swinging past their office to introduce themselves to Ahjoomenoni's nephews.

The one who identified himself as Sang-Hoon seemed sad to have to report, "No action today, boss-man."

"But that's a good thing." Pain tried to encourage him. "It means you two are doing a good job, right?"

The other nephew, Sung-Ho, nodded in appreciation of the compliment but was also disappointed. "We try to prove ourselves but how prove when no action?"

"You simply need to stay alert," Pain instructed. "Sometimes, the most dangerous times are when there is no action."

The nephews nodded and the partners reached the Max-Bore an hour earlier than they had the three previous days. He called past the counter and walked to the range while Agony decided to avoid any other would-be Lotharios and remained in Bertha. Halfway through their three hours, she decided to buy a hotdog at the food trucks. It seemed like forever since she'd had one, but she wanted something to tide her over and chose a chili-dog, heavy on the onions. It was a beautiful day, so she lingered at the table and enjoyed the sunshine.

Pain decided to pause in his shooting and sat on one of the benches situated behind the stations. He watched as a shooter from the thousand-yard booth packed his rifle up—a Wilson Combat AR-10 if he wasn't mistaken—and passed him on his way out. A strong voice called out and the man paused a few feet past Pain.

"Hey, Billy-boy! Still happy with the Wilson?"

Billy-boy shook hands with the man.

"Love it! Thanks for the recommendation, Conrad!"

The newcomer slapped his shoulder. "I'm glad to hear it. It's a fine piece of equipment and I'm glad I was able to find you a used one at a very reasonable price."

Conrad came closer as his friend moved away. "Do you mind if I share your bench for a minute while I unpack?"

Pain slid to the end and the man made himself at home. "Appreciate it."

He was fit, maybe six-two, and hovered around forty in the age department. He was halfway through pulling his HK417 out of its case before he remembered his manners and held his hand out.

"Conrad. Conrad Ellis."

Pain managed to avoid staring at the 417 as he shook the proffered hand and thought that his new friend might be squeezing a little harder than required.

He still wasn't convinced that the new Havoc didn't know his name. He was also scrambling for a new M-name but decided to get it all out in the open at once to see if Conrad's response gave anything away.

"Pain. Maximillian Pain."

The man's voice took on a slightly different tone but his question took him by surprise.

"Maximillian Payne? Like Max Payne the game character?"

"No—wait. There's a game character named Max Payne?"

"You can't have any teenaged boys in the house." Conrad chuckled.

"I can't say that I do. How many do you have?"

"Me? None. Only nephews. I never cared for getting tied

down. I'm more of a man who favors action and a wife and kids and a house in the suburbs isn't on my bucket list."

Pain began to lean toward this guy being Havoc—a man of action who carried a 417 fit their profile.

"I've got an HK417 myself but left it behind on this trip. Not much hunting to do in the city."

"Oh, I never leave home without it. And there's a ton of hunting in the city if you know where to look."

He wasn't sure if he was talking about hunting for women in bars or hunting assassination targets. In an attempt to narrow it down, he kept the conversation going and hoped that Agony would speak her observations into his ear. She remained silent, however, and left him thinking that she might already be on her way.

After ten minutes of dancing around a variety of subjects, all of them related to tracking down targets of one type or another, he leaned heavily toward the assassination angle rather than the womanizing aspects.

Pain held his phone up and excused himself for a minute to make a call but never turned his back on the man. He pretended to dial and held the phone up to his ear as he spoke into his hidden mic.

"Where are you and are you hearing all this?"

"I'm out behind the food trucks and yeah, I've heard every word."

"Then you know he's got a 417 and he fits the alpha-male profile. Are you coming in for backup anytime soon?"

"I'm afraid that's not real likely."

"Oh, come on! You've seen what I've seen. Why the hesitation?"

"Because we may have been wrong about the male part of the profile."

"And you've deduced this how, exactly?" He scowled. This was not the time for conundrums.

"Because it's not a man who is holding a Beretta 90-Two a few inches away from my temple. She also, for my tastes, seems a little too eager to pull the trigger."

Someone from Agony's end spoke loudly enough for him to hear. It had been a long time since a voice had sent chills down his spine but that reprieve suddenly ended.

"How's it going, Pain, first initial M? Miss me yet?"

"I knew it was overkill."

"Speaking of overkill," Esther Chongrak informed him. "You might want to check your flanks."

CHAPTER NINE

Pain did as she advised and discovered that his flanks didn't look particularly good at that moment. As much as he wanted to rush to his partner's rescue behind the food trucks, that was not an immediate option.

Chongrak, back from the dead, already had her troops closing in around him. Twenty or so heavily armed men rushed closer from three different directions, which left the target range as the only way out.

Even with his Wonderoos and if he could get to the rental he'd left at his shooting position, he would still have no way to win if it came down to a firefight. Someone was bound to end up getting lucky with a headshot.

He also didn't want any of the civilians to get caught in the crossfire and did the only sensible thing he could do, which was to race away through the gun range. He did his zigzag running while he angled toward the wall that separated the range from the tactical course. Shots, none of them aimed at the paper targets, rang out behind him.

Conrad Ellis, being the alpha-male he was, also did the only sensible thing he could think of, which was to drop his weapon and dive to the ground while he shrieked like a five-year-old and pissed himself.

Other than the shrieks and pissing, all the other shooters mimicked him. If it was good enough for tough-guy Ellis, it was good enough for them.

Pain's main objective was to get to his partner as fast as possible, but he had to remain alive in order to do so. He gauged that the concrete wall separating the shooting range from the tactical course was about the same height as a basketball rim and hoped his legs still had enough of their dunking power. It was close enough and his hands found a hold on the top and he was able to hoist himself up and over. From where he dangled on the tactical side of the wall, he had less than a two-foot drop to the ground.

Half his pursuers ran behind him down the gun range and they fired wildly enough to not have a single bullet hit the six-foot-four moving target. They banded together and were about to start hoisting each other up and over the wall when Havoc gave the order for them to hurry back to join her.

The other half, having not been given the same order, continued their pursuit as they ran along the pathway that led to the entrance of the tactical area. The course sloped down for twenty yards before it leveled out with only a few gentle slopes scattered throughout. They sprinted down the hill with the utmost confidence after the unarmed object of Havoc's heart's desire. All of them loved having orders to shoot to kill, especially when they were the only ones with the guns.

The handful of paintball players heard a commanding voice shout. It came from a big man who had dropped down the wall and ran into the center of the course. "Drop your guns, run to the sides, and lay still on the ground!"

When he saw mostly confused looks, Pain tried again. "Terrorist attack force coming in! They're only after me, so drop your fucking guns and run as far away from me as you can and play fucking dead. They're using real bullets!"

The pretend warriors—six of them playing in two teams of three—had enjoyed an afternoon out of the office as part of their employer's team-building exercises and weren't sure if the big man was serious or merely seriously insane. Still, they unanimously decided they didn't want to have anything to do with whatever was going on and obeyed the command.

From his earlier observations, the detective recalled where most of the laser-triggered trip-lines were placed and therefore where he could snatch up a handful of paintball guns. Having a head start gave him enough time to trip four of the pop-ups while he ducked under the guns as they fired. He managed to rip three of the guns from them.

Cradling his bundle, he ran and dove behind the closest pile of gravel where he hurried to locate and scoop up as many of the smaller pebbles as he could find. From a distance, shots rang out in his direction, which gave him a sense of relief since it meant they knew where he was and would continue toward him and not randomly shoot at the prone and very innocent players.

Although paintball guns possessed a fair amount of firing power, no one considered them to be real weapons. As such, he didn't technically break his no-guns policy as he began to empty his pockets and stuff the muzzles with gravel.

He peeked out from behind the pile and estimated that slightly less than a dozen men had made it onto the course so far. None of them came from the side wall but those who had reached level ground seemed to split up and moved toward opposite sides. They were still far enough away that if he stayed in the center of the rear of the mound of gravel, none of the shots could score a direct hit on him.

His cover was being shredded, which worked to his advantage as the barrage of bullets hitting the gravel created a cloud of cover that allowed him an extra couple of seconds during which his movements were undetectable. Bent low, he raced as quickly as he could toward the back where the old excavation machinery was spaced out. He unhooked a couple of five-foot chains that worked as safety catches on a road grader's shovel and made a couple of knotted loops in each end. The result left him with two double ball and chain units.

Scrounging further, he discovered a solid scrape-shovel that he could use as a semi-helmet if he held it up at the proper angle to protect him from any headshots. He looped the chains around his shoulders and used one hand to carry the three paintball guns. With the other hand dedicated to keeping the shovel in place, he ran his zigzag patterns and adjusted his trajectory to his right. He used several of the obstacles as cover as he sprinted toward the area where most of the enemy fire had come from thus far.

His pursuers had semi's but none of them had the power needed to break through his suit. He sustained a few long-distant hits and if he lived, would be in some degree of pain the next day.

Secure in the knowledge that he wasn't armed, Chongrak's boys hadn't bothered to take cover. He finally cowered behind one of the sandbag half-walls and waited as they marched slowly forward, confident that they had the big asshole pinned down.

It was difficult to remain patiently in place when every synapse in his brain told him to run as far and fast as he could in the opposite direction of his pursuers. He gritted his teeth and forced himself to remain behind the sandbag wall. Once Chongrak's boys were close enough for the paintball guns to be used effectively, Pain stood and fired the three gravel-packed guns rapidly.

Aimed as nothing other than headshots, the stones were as effective as shotgun shells at close range. He hit at least four of the five squarely with the gravel and continued to fire two of his guns at the fifth man. Paintballs might not kill but they could certainly cause some serious suffering if one wasn't wearing a helmet, not to mention their splattered-paint blinding capabilities.

Pain had never been shy about crotch kicks and since his closest attackers now held their hands to their faces and left their naughty bits exposed and with him being in a hurry, he delivered five swift kicks and dove behind cover when shots now rang out from the opposite side. He thought about it but even if he'd wanted to, he couldn't get back to retrieve any of the AKs without exposing too much of himself.

Using the obstacles to good effect, he managed to move safely toward the machinery and sustained only one glancing shoulder shot. The group that now attacked made the same mistake the other half of their comrades had in assuming he had no weapons. They therefore didn't bother to take cover as they pursued and rapid-fired whenever he appeared.

The detective paused behind a faux wall where he knew a pop-up—now unarmed—had snapped into place. He ripped the metal figure off its hinges, leapt out, and flung it end over end, tomahawk style, at his closest attacker. Its feet met the man's forehead head-on and split his face half-open.

He needed better cover than a plywood wall, however, so he dashed farther back toward the machinery and dove behind a boulder, where he unraveled his chains and waited for his adversaries to close the distance.

Everyone paused as the sound of the dump truck starting up echoed off the back wall of the pit and over the course. Pain hadn't realized that any of the machinery was still functional or he would have tried it himself.

As it was, he used the moment of distraction to grasp the middle of the two chains, one in each hand, stepped out from behind the boulder, and went into a spin reminiscent of Bugs Bunny's Tasmanian Devil to release first one and then the other. The chains and their weights disabled three more assailants.

By his estimate, that left two, but he expected half of the original force that had followed him through the gun range to advance through the tactical course at any second now. He didn't want to take the time to fight through them and tried to work his way up the range, thereby delaying his race to Agony even further.

He had no idea who was driving the dump truck. At first, he thought it might be one of Chongrak's men and that it was loaded with more men in the bed and would plow through everything in the course as it tracked him. He changed his mind on that when the driver began to work slowly up through the gears and turned down the only road that led into or out of the range.

From their studies, Pain knew it ran to the outer edge of the parking lot and past the food trucks. Since that was where Agony had last spoken to him from, he decided to try to hitch a ride.

From behind, he wasn't able to even see the driver, let alone ask for permission to ride along. After a short sprint, he managed to swing onto the back bumper as the truck began to move in earnest and kicked a cloud of dust up. It left the rest of Chongrak's forces behind to stare while they tried to determine what the hell had happened.

Agony had certainly had better days. She was fast, but Chongrak was a professional who held a gun to her head and her chances of disarming her were low. The woman recalled some of her troops and the two remained behind the food trucks until almost a dozen well-armed men rushed up. Once her reinforcements arrived, the no-longer-dead agent ordered one of them to zip-tie their captive's hands behind her back.

She was then led to a row of five vehicles—three sedans and two SUVs—as Chongrak held her SISTER badge up and informed the curious that she and her men were federal agents and the woman in custody was a wanted fugitive. No one seemed eager to argue with her and Agony was bundled into the back of the last SUV in line with Esther seated next to her. The only good news was that the woman at least had the courtesy to not hold the gun aimed at her head as she started to explain.

"It doesn't much matter now," Chongrak began, "but I did not come here with my forces to kill either you or Pain. "

"Somehow, I don't follow your reasoning, what with my current situation and how you unleashed your hounds to go after Pain."

"While your deaths may be regrettable to some, the truth is that we were not tracking you. We were here on totally unrelated business. You merely had bad timing showing up today."

"So how shall I address you when I beg for mercy—Esther Chongrak or Havoc?"

"Esther Chongrak is dead. Everyone except you and Pain has accepted that as fact. Havoc will be fine, although Havoc 2.0 would be more accurate. I am the new and improved version."

"Define improved."

Agony wanted to keep the bitch talking as long as possible to give her partner a chance to make an appearance. She knew he was outnumbered and outgunned, but she also knew what he was capable of and didn't doubt for a second that he would come out on top.

"Speaking of the dead, Chongrak, was the once-living woman who was in your vehicle when the bomb went off anyone of consequence or did you simply kill a random stranger?"

"I didn't kill her and don't even know how she died. I broke into a med-school lab and stole a cadaver."

"A cadaver that happened to have the same metal pins in its wrists as you?" She snorted her disbelief.

"It's not hard to slip a couple of small pins into a dead arm and I needed the pins for identification purposes."

"Congratulations on your plan. As far as I know, Pain is the only one who still had doubts."

"That doesn't surprise me." The woman had the cheek to look smug as if she were somehow responsible for his abilities.

"But that still leaves the why." *Stall, stall, stall.*

Havoc—true to the trope of evil masterminds being eager to explain their genius to someone she should have already shot and been done with—elucidated.

"Simply put? I was bored with the perpetual futility of being a glorified janitor. Whenever a black op went sideways, I was the one responsible for going in and cleaning up whatever mess some dumb-fuck had left behind."

"How very tiresome that must have been."

"Try it for a few years and then get back to me."

"Give me a few years and I will," Agony retorted.

"If I could, I would bring Chongrak back from the dead and forward your application, but that would put a serious crimp in my plans to get out from under the deadweight of bureaucracy. Sorry, I plan to set up shop on my terms, thereby allowing me to get back some of my own on terms I can live with. Especially with SISTER in the process of being absorbed."

"Absorbed by who and why?"

"Who? Why? What? When?" Havoc mocked. "My, aren't we filled with questions today. Are you telling me that you and precious Pain haven't heard any rumors about that yet?"

Agony wasn't sure how much longer she could keep the woman engaged in conversation but was about to answer that no, she and Pain were completely out of the loop regarding any absorption rumors.

She never got to find out how far their friendly little chat might have gone because as she was about to open her mouth, a dump truck bulldozed into the entire back half of the convoy and Havoc's SUV took part of the blow and tipped into a sideways roll.

CHAPTER TEN

It wasn't a few bumps to her head that caused Agony's disorientation so much as it was having taken one and a half tumbles to finally land on her back as she stared at the floor of the SUV. Havoc lay next to her and although neither of them had been seriously injured, her captor returned to total awareness slightly slower.

She used the time, her limber body, and strange position, to at least get her zip-tied hands in front of her instead of behind her back. Outside, in the right-side-up world, she could hear a barrage of gunfire from Havoc's troops who hadn't been upended and now traded fire with whoever was on the other side of the dump truck.

Still upside down, it was hard to take in all of the action, especially when one of the men was shot and fell. She shook her head and fought to right herself as Havoc pushed through her fuzziness and came round. The two women cast about on the roof that was now the floor and both saw the Beretta at the same time and lunged toward it.

Even if it had been a fair fight, it would not have been much of a contest, and although her hands were in front of her, they were still zip-tied and put her at a distinct disadvantage. Another problem was that in the confined space, her height worked against her. Havoc was more compact and easily outweighed her by a good ten pounds.

Agony had to practically squirm across the floor toward the gun, whereas her adversary was able to crawl and barreled into her side, knocked her over, and landed on top. The detective was able to get in some good blows and wasn't above raking her nails across the woman's face and leaving deep scratches, but her opponent was no slouch when it came to close fighting and especially when she lay on top.

The end result was that as the fireworks continued outside, Havoc was able to crawl over her and beat her to the gun before she rolled over and leveled the Beretta at her. The only thing that prevented her from firing was the realization that someone had rammed her with a dump truck and that someone was most likely to be Pain, first initial M.

As tempting as it was to shoot, the woman knew that with Agony still alive, she would at least have something to bargain with. If she was dead, she would have nothing. And if she was the instrument of her demise, her partner would show no mercy when he exacted his revenge.

"If you want to live," she stated icily, "I would advise you to not run. Pain might take me down but not before I put a bullet into your back. Am I clear?"

The reply came through clenched teeth. "Perfectly clear. You always did seem like a shoot someone in the back type to me."

"I'm glad we understand each other. You get a door open. I'll follow."

Agony found a door that would still open on the side of the SUV opposite where all the firing had come from and with her in the lead, the two women scrambled out and to the front of the vehicle as silence fell. Two cars ahead, they could see two of Havoc's goons cowering behind a sedan's engine.

Havoc called, "I've got your bitch, Pain! It's time to talk."

With the gun pressed against her back, Agony stepped into the open. It infuriated her that the woman not only used her as a bargaining chip but also as a body shield. Her main regret—other than letting the bitch get the drop on her while she was enjoying a chili-dog—was that for once, she would have to thank Pain for having come to a damsel's rescue.

She expected the gun to be pressed even harder into her back when her partner stepped out from the shelter of the truck but instead, the weapon was withdrawn when Havoc's nemesis appeared.

Later, she couldn't recall what struck her first. The woman's eyes were such a pale shade of blue that not only did they have the look of ice, they also seemed as if they could turn water into ice with nothing more than an angry glance. The newcomer topped Agony by at least two inches, with broad shoulders and jet-black shoulder-length hair. She also had an impressive set of tits that even her bulletproof couldn't disguise.

She stared as the woman walked slowly toward them and had no doubt that this was her first glimpse of Oksana Baran. Agony didn't like being caught between the two women, neither of whom looked as if they would have any issue with taking her out of the equation with one quick shot so that they would have a clear line of sight at each other.

Given her options, she decided to take her chances with Havoc, who seemed to be so taken aback by the sight of the other woman that she had forgotten to return the barrel of her Beretta to her captive's back.

She dropped abruptly and spun with a scissor kick to take the woman's feet out from under her. Now out in the open instead of cramped in the SUV and with Havoc on the ground with her, she delivered her next kick at the gun-holding hand and knocked it a few feet off to the side.

The two women scrambled, reached the gun at the same

time, and fought for control as they rolled in a tangle of limbs. Agony finally wrenched the gun away but Baran now rushed toward them with her semi still in her hand. Out of sheer instinct, Agony fired and struck the newcomer in the middle of her chest.

Baran staggered but did not go down. With no sign of blood, she remembered her first impression that the newcomer wore a bulletproof vest. The woman slowed her approach but continued to advance.

"Why the fuck did you shoot me, you stupid bitch? I came for her!"

Agony stood and glanced at Havoc, who was now clearly terrified, then turned to the other woman. She had closed the distance and introduced her fist to the detective's face with a punch so hard that her feet left the ground for a brief second before she landed on her ass next to Havoc. Stunned by the punch, the next thing she knew was that Baran had kicked the Beretta out of her hands and now loomed above them both.

"Any last words?"

She wasn't sure which of them she was addressing, but Havoc made it clear. "None for you, slut! Go ahead. Put me out of my misery!"

It seemed Baran intended to do exactly that but Pain raced forward, tackled her from behind, and knocked the gun out of her hands as they both landed hard. Havoc wasted no time but scrambled to her feet and ran to the SUV that was the lead vehicle of the convoy. It was the only one that had yet to suffer any damage and she shouted orders for her last two remaining goons. "Waste them all!"

Ignoring Pain and Baran's struggle, Agony grimaced and managed to snap the zip-ties before she snatched the woman's rifle up, pushed to her feet, and aimed at the retreating Havoc. She cursed when she had to dive again and turn her attention to Havoc's men and eliminate them. The sound of an engine firing and the rise of parking lot dust from the front of the convoy told her that her quarry was now out of reach.

Hearing a commotion and cursing behind her, she spun to where Pain and Baran were now on their feet and exchanged blows as they grappled with each other. She wasn't sure if it was some kind of a mating ritual or brutal foreplay, but it didn't resemble any fight she had ever been in. She watched in strange fascination until the two broke apart, both of them roughed up, and gasped for air as they bent with their hands on their knees and tried to catch their breath before they resumed the fight.

"You're out of shape, Oksana. You never used to get winded this quickly."

"You should talk, Mr. I-need-to-catch-my-breath Pain. Your bitch shot me in the chest! What's your excuse?"

"You should know since you had a front-row seat to watch the hits I took at the tactical range."

"I should have swerved a couple of times to throw you off the back bumper for all the good you did here."

"You knew I was hitching a ride?" He seemed genuinely surprised.

"I felt the extra weight when you jumped on. What took you so long to join the fun once we got here?"

"Minor concussion from my head hitting the back of the truck when you came to such a sudden stop."

"Great! Now I'll have to pay for the dent you put in it," she snarked.

The sound of gunfire practically in their ears brought their little heart-to-heart to an end. They turned to where Agony lifted Baran's rifle barrel from the ground she had fired into and looked as if she was trying to decide which one of them to shoot first.

"All right, you two! Enough fuckery or I'll hose you both down."

At least the shouting stopped, if only for a moment.

"Do her first," was Pain's only request.

Having now caught her breath, Baran shouted again. "Why me? What did I do?"

"You were coming after me and by proxy, my partner."

"What the hell are you talking about? If you were my target, you'd be long dead by now. I was going after Havoc."

Her partner had been out of the loop so Agony filled him in. "The woman who was blown up was a cadaver. You were right. Chongrak faked her death and is Havoc now."

The tone in his voice matched the confusion on his face. "What? Since when?"

"Since you created a giant fucking power vacuum by killing him," Baran snarked furiously.

"Oh, so you're saying I shouldn't have killed him?"

"No. But you should have let me finish the job by letting me shoot Chongrak."

"How was I to know you were about to shoot her? All I saw was you standing over my partner with a gun."

"She shot me first!"

"I am so fucking tired of that excuse!" Pain turned to his partner. "Is that true? You fired first?"

"Do either of you know how to communicate with anything other than shouts and accusations?"

The two combatants answered in unison. "No!"

He was the first to lower his voice. "But it's true? You shot her?"

"Yes, I shot the Baran." Agony couldn't stop herself from adding, "But I did not shoot the deputy."

In the distance, they could hear the police sirens en route and no one was in any kind of mood to hang around and try to explain this.

"Happy life, Pain." Baran looked at the dump truck. It wasn't built for getaways. "I left my real car in the parking lot." She turned to Agony. "If I can have my gun back, I'll be on my way."

Pain nodded and Agony handed her the rifle. They watched her try to hurry away but after four steps, she staggered and fell onto one knee.

He rushed to her side and to his partner's surprise, the woman didn't fight when he lifted her shirt to inspect the bullet-proof vest and shook his head.

"You always were a cheapskate when it came to body armor," he commented bluntly.

"Okay, Dad! Help me to my feet so I can get to my car."

Rather than comply, he tugged a couple of Velcro strips open and lifted the t-shirt to reveal considerable bruising and a couple of small trickles of blood. The vest had stopped the round from completely penetrating but part of the jacket had dug in, which is where the bleeding came from.

"You're in no condition to walk, let alone drive. You're coming with us," he stated emphatically.

"The hell I am!"

"The hell she is!" Agony said almost in unison with the woman.

Finally, the women agree on something. "Sorry, you two, but she is. Help me out here, Agony."

She wasn't at all happy with the request but the sirens were getting closer so she moved forward and helped him get the woman onto her feet. With one of Baran's arms around her shoulders and the other around Pain's, they hurried to Bertha, loaded the wounded woman in, and managed to leave the scene while the sirens were still half a mile away but closing fast.

Their passenger was stretched in the small space between the seats and the cage where the partners stored a few supplies. Her breathing was steadier now but she still struggled a little. It hurt like hell but not enough to stop her complimenting the partners on their vehicle of choice.

"So, Pain, nice choice of rides. When did you become a soccer mom?"

He twisted in the passenger seat. "The cage behind you has enough room in it if you would prefer that."

"Thanks, but I'll pass. Am I allowed to ask where you're taking me?"

"To our apartments," he told her brusquely. "You need a place to rest and heal for a couple of days."

"You could simply drop me off at my place."

"Which is the first place Chongra—Havoc will look for you. No one knows how tough you are better than me, but you're not up for a fight right now and Chongrak—damn, how long will it take me to get used to the name change?"

Agony spoke from her experience. "It doesn't take long at all when she has a gun aimed at your head."

Baran spoke from her heart. "Hopefully, she'll be dead again before you have to."

Pain's voice took on a slight edge. "Will you please try to save your breath? We don't know what kind of internal damage you might have and wasting your energy talking right now will not help you heal."

His partner wasn't particularly proud of herself, but that didn't stop her from seizing the moment. "So, Agent Baran, tell me a little more about yourself. Where are you from? Got any hobbies? Read any good books lately?"

"Ignore her, Oksana. She'll get bored soon."

After a look from Pain, she shut up and decided to pout silently.

He pulled his cell out. "I would appreciate it if you two would both give me a moment of silence. I need to call a friend who owes me a favor."

Baran had to get one last word in before the hurt and exhaustion took over. "Oh, aren't you moving up in the world? You have a friend now?"

The detective ignored both smartasses and dialed. Someone

must have answered because Agony heard him make his request quietly but firmly.

"It's Pain... Yes, that Pain. Grab your medical bag. I need you to make a house call." A moment of silence followed while the person on the other end answered and he shook his head. "No, I'm afraid you don't have a choice. You show up, do what you can, and we'll call it even."

The friend must have agreed because he gave whoever it was his address and hung up before any further response could be made.

CHAPTER ELEVEN

The three continued in uneasy silence until they were within the city limits and close to Kwan's. Baran made an effort to remain still and conscious while the partners were lost in their thoughts.

Agony had mixed feelings about Pain's former associate. She flat-out didn't like the woman, but she had rescued her from Havoc before he made his appearance. That relieved her of the obligation of having to be the damsel who would eventually have to thank him. Thinking back, the only one he had rescued her from was the one person he should be thanking for having saved her.

She would still have to explain how she had come to be Havoc's prisoner to begin with but hopefully, that would slip his mind. Of course, she had never doubted that he would appear, which he did after having fought through however many of Havoc's forces who had been sicced on him. She also knew that he would have probably beaten Baran to her if not for the hard bump on the head he said he'd received when the dump truck had slammed to a stop.

With that thought, she had a sudden pang of guilt. "How's your head?"

He came out of whatever reverie he'd been lost in, raised his hand, and felt his forehead. "As hard as ever. It's still a little sore but I don't feel a welt coming up. How's your ego for having let the new Havoc get the drop on you?"

Damn! "Bruised. It may be a while before I can enjoy a chili-dog again."

He let it drop. Tempting though it may be, she was beating herself up enough without him adding insult to injury.

"I take it that your Wonderoos came in useful?"

"They did their job but I'll be hurting tomorrow." Pain smiled and shook his head. "I was so sure I had the new Havoc pegged at the range. He checked off every box on the score sheet."

"Every box except the one that said he could be a she, and we all missed that one. The southern gentleman will be in for a surprise. When do we call to let him know?"

"We're each being paid three hundred a day to track and identify the new Havoc. We have her identified so we're halfway there but haven't tracked her down yet, so I say we keep it quiet until we do."

"For three hundred a day, I can be real quiet."

They eventually reached Kwan's, but it was the dinner hour and no places were open on the street. She double-parked briefly and together, they managed to get Baran out and onto her feet. Agony left Pain alone to get her up the stairs as she swung and guided Bertha to her reserved place at the end of the block.

As she walked out of the lot, Game Show George called, "Did you lose the big fella? 'Cause if so, I got a second call-back for Wish & Win. My wish is gonna be for that week in Bimini I've been dreaming about. Wanna be my plus-one?"

Agony laughed. "I would, George, but the big oaf is still around. Besides, you can do much better than me."

"Not on this planet."

She bowed at the compliment and continued. When she was

almost at Kwan's, she realized she had just bowed. *The Korean politeness influence must be rubbing off on me.*

Unfortunately, she didn't get past the door to Kwan's before she was forced to give the politeness aspect a rethink. Ji-Hun wasn't the doorman on duty this evening. His place had been taken by two men who were new to her. One was dressed as a doorman and the other in business attire. She didn't recognize either one but the businessman recognized her. She nodded as she approached him on her way to the door that led to their apartments but the gesture was not returned.

"Miss A-go-nee." He struggled with his pronunciation of her name but not with his tone of voice, which was firm and formal. "Your boss would like to see you as pronto as possible."

The statement gave her pause. The "pronto" part was fine and perfectly in character for Ahjoomenoni, but the "your boss" rubbed her the wrong way. After the day she'd had, she wasn't in the mood to let anything slide and set the man straight.

While it was true that Ahjoomenoni had fronted the small loan to enable the partners to afford an office space while they set their business up, she was more of a silent business partner and had no part in the actual running of it.

"Ahjoomenoni is our landlady and a business partner, but she is not our boss."

The man shrugged. "Ahjoomenoni is what Ahjoomenoni is and she wishes to see you. Now would be a good time. Follow me, please."

She knew when she had been summoned and pulled her phone out to give Pain a quick heads-up as she followed.

"I've been waylaid by our landlady and will be up as soon as I can."

"Do you have any idea why?" He sounded weary and wary.

"Not a clue."

"Understood. If you're not here in half an hour, I'll send for help."

"What? Do you have an army in your back pocket you've never told me about? Oh—" She remembered her manners. "How's the patient?"

"She doesn't like to admit it but she's hurting. We're still waiting for the doctor to arrive."

"All right. See you soon, I hope."

Her escort led her through the crowded restaurant and past the private room with what she assumed were bulletproof glass windows where Ahjoomenoni usually conducted her business. They continued through the kitchen and turned right past the refrigeration and freezing units, which brought them to a closed door. She had never been in this part of the building before and began to worry, but they weren't late on the rent and as far as she knew, hadn't created any recent inconveniences for Kwan's owner.

Agony tried to convince herself that there was no cause for concern but with Ahjoomenoni, one could never be sure. Her escort opened the door, stepped aside as she entered, and closed it behind her while he remained outside. The activity in the room did absolutely nothing to calm her nerves or fears.

The first thing she noticed was what appeared to be a massage table covered by a white sheet.

That wasn't an issue in and of itself, but the second thing was that one of the two nephews she had met earlier that day when they had dropped in to check on the security detail at their office now lay on his side on the table. He bit down hard on a belt as a bullet was searched for and plucked out. One bullet and a little blood were already visible in a small metal pan next to the table.

And by far the worst, the third thing was that Ahjoomenoni stood to the side and appeared extremely displeased. She had been frowning before she looked up when the visitor entered and the frown showed no signs of easing anytime soon. Agony made her bow and noticed the second nephew seated in a chair against a wall. His face was mostly a series of bruises but the concern in his eyes was for his cousin.

The proprietor moved to the head of the table, knelt, and smiled at the patient. "You will live and grow stronger from the pain." She tugged the man's ear playfully before she stood and patted him on the head. "The door," she said to a man near Agony who she hadn't been aware of.

He opened the door and Ahjoomenoni did not so much as glance at her as she walked past her but did speak. "You will follow."

She took one more look at the two nephews who had seemed so young and eager for action only that morning before she turned and obeyed her landlady's command. Her escort from earlier was still stationed outside the door and led the way to the windowed room where the partners usually had their meetings with Ahjoomenoni.

Their guide opened the door and the Korean woman took the seat behind her desk. She waited until Agony was seated before she placed her palms together as if in prayer. After a moment, she leaned forward and rested her elbows on the desk while her visitor waited with dread for what she hoped would be only a stern lecture and not another eviction notice—or worse.

"Thank you."

Thank you? Okay... "Um...you're welcome?"

"Hah!" Ahjoomenoni smiled. "You thought you were in for a chewing of your ass, yes? Last time, I get Pain. This time, you."

She struggled with the woman's sense of humor but followed Pain's earlier lead and shook her head as she chuckled.

"Yes. Yes, you did."

"My nephews called me earlier today to inform me they had met you and Pain. They did not complain but made it clear that they thought they might be used better on an assignment where they could prove themselves to be more valuable than merely as babysitters."

"They seemed like very nice young men."

Ahjoomenoni nodded. "Nice they are. Wiser they are now. I do not know. Maybe they become careless and not pay enough attention to the approaching danger? What I do know is that this woman, Evangeline Boyer, is now associated with a gang that is almost as dangerous as the man she is divorcing from."

Agony shook her head again but this time, in disgust. "I don't understand how so much of a fuss can be made over one damn dog."

"Oh," the woman warned her, "you not let Mr. James Brownstone hear you say that. That is man you want to stay on good side of. People who love their pets can often not be rational. You not know this?"

Agony had absolutely no idea who this James Brownstone guy was but she took her landlady's word for it and made a mental note to Google him so she could make sure their paths never crossed.

"But you are sure your nephew who was on the table will be okay?"

"He will be fine. Maybe walk with limp for a while because of shot to leg and for sure, not sit down in comfort until butt-wound heals."

She had been so taken aback by the scene in the back room that she hadn't noticed that the bullet the doctor was extracting as she'd walked in had come fresh out of the nephew's ass. She was hesitant about asking her next question but worked into it.

"That is a relief... It's a shame they were injured because they were guarding furniture."

"Some furniture they save, some not. Tomorrow, you can inspect. I have been informed that the office door was not damaged, so office is now locked again. At this moment, I am much more concerned about the woman with the dog and a new...posse? I do not need more conflict, so I research her and her people. I could crush woman and her gang like bugs. Bugs not pets, so James Brownstone would have no problem, but I do not wish to become involved with more conflicts. Small conflicts often escalate to big conflicts, and they always complicate business. I do not need unnecessary conflicts."

Still seated, Agony bowed her apology. "I am sorry that this has complicated your business. If we had known, we would not have asked for your help."

"Is hard to know future. But we are now even in the favor department so I will not hold this against you. I also do not wish to run out of nephews, so I will no longer be able to help protect your office."

"I understand."

"It would be good to have these issues with the dog resolved before things escalate out of control. Would you not agree?"

"Yes, I would certainly agree."

"If my memory is correct, in the time you and Pain have been together, many little fires have been started. I would be disappointed if this little spark turns into a big flame and the flame turns into a bigger fire that burns out of control."

"Looking back on it," she confessed, "I'm not sure if the mischief with the mutt was ever under control, but I understand what you are saying."

"You are bright girl. I was certain that you would. Tell Pain I say hello."

With that, Agony was dismissed.

She walked slowly through the still-crowded restaurant, muttered a few curses under her breath about psycho-bitches and their fur babies, and wondered what they would have to do to get Missy and Mommy out of their—and therefore Ahjoomenoni's—lives. On impulse, she stopped at the hostess' station and asked what the Korean word for dog was.

The hostess smiled sweetly, perhaps sensing another puppy lover like herself. "Ah. That would be *gae*."

"How do you spell that in English?"

Another smile followed. "G-A-E."

"Do you have a menu I can glance at?"

"Certainly. All food here is very tasty."

With the menu in hand, Agony stood to the side and studied it carefully. Sadly, she found no gae-related items listed and made a mental note to remove *Steal back dog and give to Kwan's chef* from her to-do list.

She handed the girl the menu and stepped out the door. With the day she'd had, all she wanted to do now was to check in on her partner and whatever the hell Baran was and get to her apartment so she could begin to relax with a nice glass of Jameson—neat. She reached the door leading to the stairs and was about to enter when a voice from behind stopped her cold.

"Hold the door! Finding any parking around here can be a real bitch."

She hung her head for a moment before she turned to see the last person she needed.

"Hello, Iggy. Pain said he was calling someone who owed him a favor but he didn't mention any names. If he had told me, I might have suggested against it."

Jules Ignatius carried a fair-sized metal case.

"Yeah, well, I am none too pleased about it myself so I hope this won't become a habit."

"I could say the same thing with regards to what got you into this particular debt, but from the stench of Silvia's perfume, I assume you and the almost under-aged tramp are still going at it behind your partner's back?"

"She's twenty, almost twenty-one. That's nowhere near to being under-age."

"Unless you're a fifty-something adult. The age difference aside, she is still your partner's ex-girlfriend. Are you capable of learning any lessons or do you prefer to continue to be forever in debt to Pain and me for keeping our mouths shut about your dirty little secret?"

"Hell, go ahead and call Douglas right now and tell him the news. He's so stoned that he'll have forgotten all about it by the time he comes down. Can you please lead the way to Pain's apartment so we can get this over with as quickly as possible?"

"Is that what she said the last time you two were on the corpse table?"

"You are a singularly unpleasant woman." Any four-year-old would have been impressed by his pout.

"Only with singularly unpleasant people. So, shall we remain out here swapping shallow and false compliments, or shall we head upstairs to where your patient may be dying?"

"Not before I confess that as hard as it is to admit to, when Pain told me he needed my assistance with a wounded woman, I feared it was you and was not happy to hear the news. I was honestly relieved to learn that the patient was a stranger to me."

Agony often forgot that once upon a time, she and Iggy had been on friendly terms as colleagues and so she knew his confession was sincere.

"Thank you for that. Now let's head upstairs so you can put your superpowers to use for good for a change instead of helping to perpetrate evil."

CHAPTER TWELVE

When they reached the top of the stairs, Agony turned toward Pain's door.

"So this is where you live?" Iggy asked curiously.

"No. This is where Pain lives. Where I live is none of your damn business."

She didn't bother to knock, partly because her partner was expecting her and Ignatius but also because she didn't want the mortician to know they had a coded knock.

The couch would have made it difficult for the doctor-turned-mortician to get a good look at the patient, so Pain had pulled the cushions off and had lined them up on the floor, covered with a white sheet. Baran was stretched out and still and he knelt beside her when they entered.

"I hope you didn't hurt yourself by taking so much time to get here," the detective snarked without looking up.

"A pleasure to see you again too, Pain," Ignatius lied cheerfully. He knelt beside him and opened his traveling case. "What is the patient's name?"

"The patient is fully capable of answering that one for herself, you moron. My name is Oksana Baran, and I apologize for calling you a moron before you have had a chance to prove your uselessness."

"Is she always this pleasant?" Iggy raised a brow.

Pain snorted. "Only on her good days."

"I take the apology back. Only a moron would continue to talk to a third party when the patient is alive and conscious."

"My turn to apologize, Ms. Baran."

"It is either Oksana or Baran. If I had wished to be called a Miss, a Missus, or a Ms, I would have added the honorific title when I introduced myself."

"Again, my apologies." Ignatius had already been seriously pissed at himself for having answered the phone when Pain called and Oksana Baran did nothing to alleviate that. "Oksana, then. We'll start with the basics. I'll need to take your pulse and then your blood pressure."

Wanting to avoid any more reprimands, he reached cautiously for her wrist. Satisfied that her pulse was steady, he applied the cuff and hand-pumped it.

Baran tried to ignore the indignity of being inspected and turned her wrath on Pain. "You couldn't even find me a real doctor?"

"He is a real doctor."

"Real doctors—at least successful ones—do not make house calls."

"They do if the patient wishes to be able to avoid all the pesky questions that a visit to an emergency room would require the law-abiding staff to ask regarding the how, when, where, and who about how they acquired the gunshot wounds."

Ignatius, finished with blood pressure, removed the sleeve and agreed. "The authorities can be sticklers when it comes to information like that. Your pulse is steady enough but your blood pressure is a little low."

"It's always low. It is a job requirement."

He tried his hand at pleasant small talk as he looked through his case. "Oh? I have never heard of low blood pressure being a job-related requirement before. What kind of work do you do?"

"Wet—mostly."

With the icy look the pale-blue eyes gave him and knowing a little about Pain, he was fairly certain she wasn't intimating that she was a professional scuba diver. He happily broke eye contact and turned to the detective.

"I understand that this is your apartment. Would it be possible for you to provide me with a couple of towels? Preferably clean, if you have any."

He shrugged. "I only bathe once a year so yeah, I should still have a six-month supply somewhere around here." He stood and disappeared down a short hallway.

"Agony?"

"Yes...Doctor?"

"When Pain comes back, would you two be kind enough to find another room to occupy to allow me and the pa—Oksana, some privacy?"

That meant she would have to put the Jameson on hold a little longer, which gave her another reason to dislike the patient. "Sure. No problem."

Her partner returned with the towels and she accompanied him out to the hallway. She was tempted to simply go to her apartment but decided it would be rude to leave him standing alone like a lurker in the corridor.

"I don't know how long Ignatius will take. How about you fill me in on where we stand with Ahjoomenoni?" he said after a moment.

"Where do I start?"

"Your call. Chronologically? Alphabetically? First to last or top to bottom?"

"Top to bottom, you said?" Her eyes gleamed.

"I believe that is the term I used, yes."

"Then to hell with it. Don't go away, I'll be right back."

She undid her trio of locks and disappeared inside her haven but he didn't have to wait very long before she returned with two double-shots of Jameson. He knew they were Jameson because other than an occasional touch of vodka in her orange juice, the whiskey was the only booze she kept in her kitchen and she was very loyal to her brand.

They raised their glasses and drained them in two slow, satisfying sips. The warmth flowed and she felt at least within shouting distance of ever being able to smile again. She took the two now-empty glasses inside, rinsed them quickly in her sink, and returned to Pain.

"Our landlady and silent partner is having some mixed emotions," she said as an opening.

"Is this the part where you explain to me what emotions are mixed and why?"

"First of all," she told him cautiously, "her nephews will eventually be okay."

"I'm glad to hear that, but it leads me to believe that they're not okay now." He frowned at her, his tone impatient.

"They've been better. For that matter, so has our office."

"No one broke the window in the door, did they?" As soon as the words were out of his mouth, Pain realized how callous that comment was and apologized.

"No need," she replied brusquely. "Once I learned that the nephews weren't mortally wounded, it was the first question that sprang to my mind too. Of course, I took a little longer to inquire gently about it. I was told that the door is fine and the office is now locked. We'll have to swing past there tomorrow, but Ahjoomenoni said that as far as she knew, there was only minor damage to some of the furniture."

"I thought I was being overly cautious with the request for guards. In no way did I think the bitch would send any of her thugs on a revenge mission of vandalism." He paced a little and his frown deepened to a scowl.

"I have been informed that when it comes to their pets, people are rarely rational."

"You've been brushing up on your James Brownstone?"

"Who the hell is James Brownstone?" Agony rolled her eyes. "I've never even heard of the guy until today and now, both you and Ahjoomenonini have both mentioned him."

"Oh, he's merely a guy who loves his dog." He shrugged carelessly.

"Fine. Next time I'm at a PETA meeting I'll try to remember to track him down. By the way, Kwan's doesn't serve any kind of *gae*, which seems like a shame to me."

Pain often forgot that his partner wasn't much of a book reader. He could have set her straight right then and there and would probably live longer if he did but chose to let her find out on her own, regardless of the price he would pay for it later. Instead, he pursued the dog angle.

"Wait. You looked for *gae* on the menu?"

"A girl can always dream, right?" She sighed. "I bet some of those big fuckers could make a good roast."

"I can either pretend I didn't hear you say that, or I can set up an appointment for you to see a shrink because that is just wrong."

"Oh, c'mon," she protested. "You've been there. Are you going to tell me *gae* isn't popular on Korean dinner tables?"

He hung his head. "I wish I could tell you that you're wrong but you're not. It is very popular, although they're now looking into trying to discourage the practice. But it certainly won't become legal in the good old US of A in any kind of a future."

"It will if we ever start running out of food. Maybe we should get ahead of the curve and start practicing some recipes for our new restaurant. Benji Burgers. Lassie Lasagna. Cujo Ka-bobs." She honestly couldn't help herself.

"Will you stop it? Right now?"

Agony was on a roll. "Hey, how about Toto Tacos? I bet those would be a huge hit."

"I will not be part of this discussion any longer." Pain paced toward the opposite end of the hallway. When he reached it, he turned so he could face her, folded his arms over his chest, and waited until her fit of idiocy ran its course.

It didn't run its course so much as she ran out of names of famous dogs. She knew there must be many more but her knowledge was limited when it came to the four-legged fleabags. She waved to indicate that it was now safe for him to return. He wasn't sure he trusted her but they did have several items of business they needed to discuss so he took his chances.

She suddenly remembered something about Old Yeller and was sure there was a dog involved. Since she didn't want to scare him away again, she kept the concept of Old Yeller Fries to herself.

He approached warily. She resisted the urge to say something despite her good intentions.

After a long moment during which he regarded her suspiciously, he said, "Tell me more about the nephews."

"One of them had a face that was close to pulpy and the other had two bullets removed. One was from a leg and the other from his ass, so he'll be sleeping on his stomach for a while."

"On a scale of one to ten, how pissed is Ahjoomenoni?"

"Maybe a two?"

He frowned as he thought about this. "I thought she liked her nephews."

"She does. But she thanked us for giving them an opportunity to learn a few real-life lessons and insisted that they will be better off for it. But she also hinted that you and I need to get Missy and Mommy out of her life before little flames turn into a big fire and cause complications for her numerous business activities."

"Well, we did kind of get her into it," he pointed out reasonably.

"And she wants us to get her out. She also said she had no more nephews to spare."

"How would you feel about simply paying Eva what she's demanding and being done with it?" he asked tentatively

"How would you feel about trying to sandpaper an alligator's anus while locked in a phone booth?"

He sighed. "Okay. So no pay-off. Next?"

"I've been thinking that we aren't the only ones who have a beef with Eva and the mutt. Well, with Eva, not the mongrel. Freaky-Freddy loves that fur-covered yapping machine."

"All right. That's one more on our side."

"Are you sure? I doubt he'll be an easy sell. After all, we did destroy several of his gang's vehicles and who knows how many of his bangers we may have killed. And the Freakster never struck me as being a let bygones be bygones kind of guy."

Pain suspected she was right. "And I don't relish the thought of starting a gang war. We need some kind of an angle other than Missy misses you. The bottom line is that we need to convince Eva that we are the wrong ones to mess with but I'm not sure how to do that without resorting to violence."

"Violence that could escalate, which is the one thing that Ahjoomenoni made very clear she does not want to happen."

"So," he concluded bluntly, "we're left with needing to find a way to defang the bitch."

They paced the hallway a few times and each of them paused now and then as if they'd had an idea but rejected it before they bothered to share. Agony finally came up with what might be a viable option.

"Got it!" She stood between their doors and waited for Pain to return from the other end before she flung the idea against the wall to see if any of it stuck.

"We don't start anything. In fact, we may not have to do much at all except make a couple of phone calls."

"Don't make me beg," he said firmly. "Out with it."

"Thanks to Special Agent Buchanon and the Moorfin episode, we've added a new tool to our toolbox."

"One that goes by the name of Chief Chauncey Morris?"

"The old willie-waggler himself. I think it's about time we put our new bitch to work. Gangers know all about their rival's business, right?"

"You have to. The day you take your eyes off of something is the day that something decides to bite you."

Agony could see the plan clearly and Pain listened intently, so she pressed on. "Morris is big on clamping down on the city's gang activity. If we can get Freaky-Freddy on our side, he could give the chief the lowdown on most, if not all, of Eva's evil forces. Chief then busts most of Freddy's foes, including our former client, leaving Freak free to go in himself and get Missy."

Her partner was beginning to like it. "We met the security at Eva's house. Even if she's in jail, they will still probably be employed there and not one of them would raise a finger to defend the mutt if Freaky let them know he was coming for her."

She nodded. "I'll call our chief of police perv now and give him a heads-up that he may receive a call from a gang leader and explain how seriously he should take it."

"And I'll call Freaky-Fred after you chat to the chief."

"Why can't I be the one to call him? It was my plan so I should be the one to make the call. If it was your op, you would make up the names for different shit, but this is my op, so don't I get extra decision-making power?"

"Of course, but you need to take all factors involved under consideration. We both know it'll be a hard sell, but one of the issues with you calling the Freak is that he loves that dog. When you talk about pets, your voice gets all cold and borders on the edge of soulless."

"It does not!" She scowled at him

"The only time I've heard you sound excited when it comes to dogs is when you were creating a menu. We don't need you to be in the middle of negotiations with him and then start musing about whether coffee or milk would go best with Missy Muffins."

"Missy Muffins? Oh, I like the sound of that one."

"Thank you for making my argument for me." He folded his arms and looked smugly at her.

"Fine." She wasn't happy but he had a point. "You can call Freddy. I'll handle the chief right now."

Pain watched her move down the hallway, looking for a little privacy, and had no doubt that she would enjoy making the clown squirm. After several minutes of negotiations, she ended the call and gave him a thumbs-up as she returned.

"How'd he take it?" he asked.

"Like the whiny little bitch he is. But he did like the incentive of adding 'busted up a gang' to his list of accomplishments."

The detective was about to pull his phone out and walk down the hallway when the door opened and Ignatius motioned them in.

Oksana was still on the floor unconscious—at least Pain hoped she was merely unconscious and not dead. The sheet under her showed a few traces of blood but not enough for major concern.

"First of all, she'll live but will need time without any unnecessary activity for a few days."

Pain looked at her. "How did she react when you told her that?"

"I don't know how she'll react because I didn't tell her. I'll leave that fun part to you. She needs complete rest for the next several hours, or at least until the sun comes up. To help with the bed rest, I have her heavily sedated now."

Agony was impressed that the cold fish of a doc had been so considerate, but her partner frowned. "Crap, did you tell her you were going to sedate her?"

"I'm not stupid enough to have told her that either."

"I hope you have a strong fan because some serious shit will hit it when she finds out."

"I assumed that would be the case but I did what I deemed necessary and in the best interests of the patient. But I also needed to sedate her because some of the remnants of her bullet-proof vest had lodged beneath her skin and I had to do a little impromptu surgery to go inside and make sure they weren't causing any internal bleeding. I only made a couple of very small incisions that needed a total of six stitches—dissolvable of course—so keep them dry for a couple of days."

"What else do we need to know?"

"A heavy contusion and a cracked rib. Other than that, she's fine. If you two can lift her, I'll move the cushions onto the couch."

The partners linked hands under her and she remained unconscious as they moved her.

Ignatius already had his case packed. "This clears my debt as far as the favor is concerned, correct?"

Agony had been waiting for that. "Only if you promise to stop sleeping with Miles' girlfriend."

"She is a grown woman. I can't dictate her decisions."

"No." As an excuse, she wasn't buying it. "You can't dictate her decisions but you are fully capable of dictating your own. And if you were truly Miles' friend, you would help him to back off from some of the drugs he is self-medicating with, at least long enough for him to realize that he might still have a chance with her. So hands off the bimbo until you can bring us a note signed by Miles stating that you have his permission to pursue her."

Ignatius was not at all pleased with the irony of a doctor needing a doctor's note, but rather than continue with an argument he had already lost, he picked his case up and headed to the door, then turned as he opened it.

"Let's not do this again anytime soon," he said belligerently.

Pain shrugged. "Only on an as-needed basis."

"Then at least try, okay?" he muttered in frustration and vanished into the hallway.

The partners looked at the patient and wondered how long it would be before the sedative wore off.

Agony attempted to keep the sarcasm scaled down. "She looks so innocent when she's sleeping."

"Feel free to tell her that when she comes round." She rolled her eyes but he spoke before she could say anything. "Do you still have the Freakster's personal number?"

Agony scrolled through her phone and read it aloud while Pain dialed and put it on speaker.

Freak Fred answered on the first ring. "I don't recognize your number and if this is a sales pitch, I ain't interested so make it fast."

"This is Pain, Merlin Pain. My partner and I were in the minivan you and your friends chased and shot all to hell the other day."

"You're the fuckin' dog-nappers? I am sooo gonna put a hurt on you!"

"Go ahead and try. Maybe you'll come out better than the last time. And for the record, you were the one who was dog-napping at that time."

"What the fuck you callin' me for?"

"Do you want the dog back?" Pain asked bluntly.

"You have her? I will seriously kill you if you harm her in any way."

"No, we don't have her but we can tell you how to get her."

"You got two minutes to tell me what the game is. Then I'll decide."

"We have a connection who would be more than happy to take Eva's new gang out of circulation," he explained without adding unnecessary politeness.

"The Cobbays?" the gang leader responded doubtfully. "I dunno. Thanks to you two, I am down several rides and some of my men who aren't dead are still recovering. That means I have a manpower shortage and goin' to war is not in my best interests at this time. So you can take your offer and—"

"Hold on! I'm not done," Pain snapped

"I'll tell you whether you're done or not."

"You won't have to do any fighting."

"Those bitches ain't gonna go down without some fighting," Freak Fred pointed out.

"Under normal circumstances, I would agree. But they'll do their fighting from behind bars."

"I don't see that happenin'. The cops seem happy to let us keep our activities goin' as long as we stay away from any civilian damage."

"But we have one who has both the interest and the power to bring the Cobbays down. He merely needs some information about what activities they are currently running and he'll come down on them hard. Both the gang members and Eva."

"The bitch too?"

"If he has enough info to add her to the list, then yes. And don't tell me you can't come up with enough to give him."

"You askin' me to be the snitch? Nuh-uh man. The Freakman don't do the snitch dance."

"Oh, c'mon, Freddy. They'll never know who it was. And once Eva's in a cell, you can swoop in and rescue Missy. I know the security forces at her house would probably be willing to mail the dog to you if they had a chance."

Pain listened as the banger reasoned with himself out loud. "With them off the streets, even for a few days, it would give me some time to recruit... I'm gonna need some new wheels too."

He interrupted the thought process. "I'm telling you the truth now. We've heard from Eva. She is pissed at us because she thinks we caused Missy extreme emotional distress. She's not eating or drinking very much and spends most of her time hiding in a corner and whimpering. She needs her daddy to give her some tender loving care, big time."

"Shit. She's that bad off, huh?"

"She is indeed. That bad off."

The ice finally cracked. "It's gonna take me a few days to gather what the cops would call actionable offenses but yeah, I can get it. Who do I give it to?"

The partners high-fived and grinned at each other.

"You must give it to Chauncey Morris, the chief of police," he advised calmly.

"The dirty top-cop? Hell, what's his stake in this?"

"Let's say he owes us a favor."

"It must be a helluva favor. What did you do? Save the bastard's life or somethin'?"

"Something like that, yeah. We already told him you might call. Do you want his number or not?"

"Lemme have it. And you better be bein' straight with me."

"Missy is a sweet doggy and she needs her daddy," he assured him.

Pain read the number off and the call ended without either of the men offering any kind and sweet last words.

Agony nodded toward the couch. "And that only leaves us to deal with—her."

"And Chongrak. I don't want Oksana to wander off on her own. How about I take first watch so you can get some rest?"

"That works for me. I'll try to get in four hours. Call me if I'm needed."

"The bakery should be open by then. Before you come back, can you make a quick run after you get up?"

"You got it. Is there anything in particular you'll be in the mood for?"

"Make sure you have at least one Boston Cream with my name on, will you? Oh, and maybe a couple of plains for Baran. She doesn't care for the sugary ones."

She wouldn't have called it jealousy, exactly, but she was annoyed at the reminder that Pain had spent more than one breakfast with the woman on the couch. *It doesn't matter and is none of my business.* She trudged toward the door and wished it was still early enough for another Jameson. *It was a long, fuck-ass day.* She spoke without turning, not trusting her face to show the requisite none-of-my-business concern. "I'd say *mañana* but it already is."

Agony left and went across the hall. Pain realized that he hadn't eaten since breakfast the day before so he made himself a peanut butter and jelly sandwich. He stood in the kitchen and devoured it in three bites before he made a second one and carried it to a chair where he could sit and keep watch.

"Agony was right. You do look rather innocent when you're sleeping."

CHAPTER THIRTEEN

The bakery had only been open for half an hour when Agony entered with a yawn and immediately winced. Admittedly, she'd shot Baran, but her jaw was still sore where the bitch had slugged her. She bought a half-dozen donuts and hoped her partner would accept her choice without protest or questions. Maybe he would simply forget the patient's aversion to the sweet ones and that he'd specifically mentioned this. *Call me petty.*

Baran was still drugged and asleep on the couch and Pain sat at the table playing against himself on a small and very used portable magnetic chessboard. She put the bag down a safe distance from the board.

"Well, at least you have a fifty-fifty chance of winning. I'm going to make a pot of coffee. Should it be for two?"

"Thanks, but I'll hold off until I get in at least a couple hours of shut-eye. Let me know the minute she wakes up. She's likely to be pissed and there's no need for you to try to handle her alone."

"I think I could handle her, especially since she's wounded." Maybe the bitch would give her the chance to finish the job.

"Everyone knows the wounded animal is often the most dangerous," he replied logically.

She sighed. "I'll let you know the minute she starts to stir."

Pain headed to his bedroom as she wandered into the kitchen and started a half-pot brewing.

A little before nine—and with four donuts left—Baran began to come around groggily. The detective came out of his room seconds before Agony could summon him.

"Good timing," she quipped. "Did you feel a disturbance in the Force?"

He snorted. "Listen to you getting all nerdy on me."

Without further comment, he started a second pot and looked at what donuts were left. The good news was that two Bostons remained untouched. The bad news was that neither of the other two was plain. He fixed his best possible evil eye on his partner and she smacked her forehead.

"Damn! Sorry, I forgot."

It was too early in the day to call someone out for being a liar so he didn't pursue it. When the coffee finished brewing, he poured himself a cup and joined her at the table, and they noticed Baran watching them.

"I gotta piss. Which way is the bathroom?" She tried to stand but winced and sat again. "Shit! I may need a little help."

Pain provided some assistance and held her steady on her feet as he guided her to the bathroom before he stepped out into the room and stood where he could keep an eye on the door.

"I hope you don't keep any sharp objects in there." She studied the chessboard idly.

"Only a double-edged straight razor, a hatchet, and a chainsaw. We should be safe."

"I am not amused." Oksana came out of the bathroom but waved him off and shuffled slowly to the donut bag, peered inside, and frowned.

"No plain?"

Pain covered quickly for his partner. "She didn't know. I

didn't know she was going to get any so I didn't have a chance to tell her."

So much for him buying my excuse. "I can always go back and get you a couple." Agony was all sweetness and light.

"It's all right. I'm not real hungry yet."

They watched as she walked gingerly to the couch and settled into a seated position on the cushion closest to the end table.

"The quack doped me up, didn't he." It was not a question.

He took the heat for that one too. "We were out of the room at the time to let him work undisturbed. It wasn't until he was done that he told us he'd given you a sedative. I explained to him your unwillingness to ingest any drugs at all."

"So he knows I'll be coming for him?"

"I am very sure he has already managed to change his name and is probably four states away by now. He should be low on your list of priorities."

"Oh yeah?" Baran was certainly in wounded-animal mode. "And what, exactly, should my list of priorities consist of?"

"Do you want some coffee?"

"Yes. Unless you've already drugged it."

Pain stepped into the kitchen, talked while he filled a cup, and kept it untouched by such amateurish ingredients as sugar—or even worse, as far as Oksana was concerned, cream. "Let me repeat. We did not drug you and would not have let the doc do it either."

"I guess I'll have to take your word for that now, won't I?"

"The doc also stressed bed rest or at least a minimum of movement for a few days," he added casually.

"Yeah, like that'll happen. Thanks for getting me a doctor. Other than the drugs, he did a decent enough job with the stitches but his bedside manners suck."

Pain returned with the two cups and handed Baran hers along with a coaster before he sat again. "What can I say? Most of the people he works on aren't big conversationalists."

She took a sip. "You still got the touch with the coffee." She winced as she set the mug down. "Now, can you find a spare set of clothes so I can call a cab and get the fuck out of here?"

"Your leaving is not something we would like to encourage," he responded firmly.

"Are you telling me I am now a prisoner?"

"No, nothing like that but we only know one side of the story. We'd like to hear it from your perspective."

Another sip of coffee was followed by a seriously pissed-off sigh. "Shit. I might as well get it over with so I can get about my business. If I'm right, the one side of the story you know is complete bullshit."

"How much bull and exactly how shitty?"

"You tell me. How did you two end up at the gun range?" She paused and waited for an answer since the partners hesitated, unsure of how much to tell her. "Will you please stop it with the quizzical looks? I'll help you out by filling in the first blank. You were sent to the range by Christopher Hollund. If that isn't the case, there is nothing more for us to talk about because he is the only common thread here."

Agony leaned back in her chair and gestured for Pain to speak.

"Yes. We were there because Chris Hollund thought that was where we should start to track down the new Havoc. He knew the two guns Havoc favored, so we were on our fourth day, alternating inside and outside each day."

His partner interjected and explained how the agent had also sent them to inspect the bombed vehicle and the woman's body to see if they could find any evidence that his crew might have missed.

Baran uttered a half-snort. "Man, he reeled you in so slowly that you didn't even know you'd been hooked."

Agony slapped the tabletop so hard that if his mug hadn't already been half-empty, some of its contents would have spilled over the rim. "Damn! If you can't trust a man with an accent like that, who can you trust?"

"Help us out here, Oksana." He was capable of being charming if he put a real effort into it. "If only for old-times' sake. If we've heard you right, Hollund already knew that Chongrak was still alive. So why all the cat and mouse games?"

"Because that's the way AUNT wanted to play it," Baran replied and left it at that.

"We'll need a little clarification on this aunt bitch."Agony hated to be played and it showed in her tone.

"AUNT is no more a singular person than SISTER. A-U-N-T, the Agency for United National Taskforces."

Agony made her opinion of the spy world clear. "Can any of you people create any kind of an organization without resorting to acronyms? I hate fucking acronyms."

"Then stay out of the government game." The rogue agent shrugged indifferently.

Pain stopped short of begging but made direct, pleading contact with the pale-blue eyes.

"If Agony and I have any chance to survive, we will need a little more to go on and learn who we're going up against. We need you."

"What? No please?"

It was hard to sound sincere through clenched teeth but Agony did her best. "Pu-leeease."

The other woman finished her coffee and knowing how Pain hated having dirty dishes laying around, held it up for him to take and rinse out. She waited for him to sit again before she continued.

"There are numerous black ops programs that have gathered dust and rust since the end of the Cold War, we all know that. They limp around in an ever-swelling American bureaucracy and simply suck money up that could be used more effectively some-where else. AUNT was initially created to streamline the ops under a new umbrella. After identifying all the programs that had become nothing but sieves, they decided to deal with the biggest —and to them the most dangerous—first. That was SISTER."

Pain understood the strategy. "Strike the strongest, get them out of the way, then pick off the weak one by one."

"AUNT calls it absorbing. Officially, they absorb the agency and unofficially, go after the most powerful individuals left standing. The end result was that a handful of potent players eventually managed to centralize the power at the top of AUNT."

"So it's not too dissimilar to SISTER's behind-the-scenes structure." He scowled.

Baran looked like she wanted to give him a most-promising-student gold star.

"Chongrak and I—separately—eventually came to the same conclusion. While the ops might be absorbed, some of the operatives needed to disappear. Although most of AUNT's resources were focused on assimilating the ops, others had been directed to eliminate individual operatives, including many of those who had left the field.

"Which is where you come into the picture, Pain. AUNT doesn't care for loose cannons any more than SISTER did, and you are about as loose as they come. We all know why and for what it's worth, I was truly sorry to hear about Kip's death. He was a good man and an honorable agent. He deserved better."

"Thank you for that. Back to AUNT?"

Baran frowned. "Back to AUNT. Right. After Chongrak and I began to compare notes, the writing on the wall became very apparent so we started to make our contingency plans."

Agony thought she knew where this was leading. "The main plan being for Chongrak to become the new Havoc?"

"No. Esther devised that all on her lonesome. Although I didn't agree with it at all, I couldn't talk her out of it but I also wouldn't stand in her way. We do what we have to do and she was determined. She didn't tell me she intended to fake her death but once I heard, I knew it was so she could slip out of AUNT and assume Havoc's mantle full-time. I kept an eye out for signs of her activities as Havoc, and she was very active."

While the woman spoke, Agony tried to replay the conversations they'd had with Chris Hollund. "According to Agent Hollund, she had been very active. He had quite a file on her—or, him—but he didn't give any indication that he thought Havoc might be a woman."

"He's a sneaky son of a bitch, I gotta give him that. I don't know how, but he knew Esther was Havoc before you two even met him."

"That bastard." She vowed to never trust a southern accent again. The man she might have put on her list of kind of attractive in a gentlemanly way was now moved to a completely different list.

Baran turned her focus to Pain. "I assume he convinced you that I had targeted you?"

"It was a good angle for him to play," he admitted. "You and Chongrak were co-workers at SISTER. We all know what a checkered history she and I had, so it made enough sense to sound plausible."

"I promise you, Pain and your partner, that if I ever do come after either of you, I will at least give you the courtesy to let you know."

Agony couldn't believe these people with all their intrigues. "That's very considerate behavior, especially coming from an assassin."

Pain ignored them and voiced his next question. "So what was in it for him to set us up against each other?"

"Chris is now the head of the east coast branch of AUNT. He is an excellent organizer and can be very creative when devising his schemes, but he is not a warrior. He set you up against Esther and me as there was a good chance we could end up killing each other. At the very least, we'd be so distracted that

AUNT would have been free to continue to absorb more resources."

"Which would leave anyone left on the outside as lone targets that would be easier to pick off." Pain nodded but his expression mirrored displeasure and a little disgust.

Agony tried to put the pieces together in her head but began to feel like someone who was working on a jigsaw puzzle. The only problem was that the picture on the box was of a seascape featuring a lighthouse and the actual puzzle was animals of the Serengeti.

"But if you knew all this, why did you try to kill Chongrak?"

"Because Havoc, as a concept, was a dangerous model. One person having that much power is never a good thing, and I believed that Esther had passed the point of no return. A belief I still hold."

"So you went to the range to kill her?"

"I went because I wanted one last try to talk some sense into her. I have been in touch with one of her operatives who she is using to try to recruit me, and he told me she would be at the range. What the recruiter had forgotten to mention was that she wouldn't be alone. I got there a few minutes before she and her convoy rolled in. That left me with only a few moments to change my strategy, so I hurried inside and asked at the desk if the machinery in the tactical range was still functional."

Pain admitted he was surprised that any of them still worked.

"The clerk seemed quite proud of that fact. They keep them in at least minimum shape because that allows them to move the equipment around every month or so to keep the paintball players from becoming bored. I paid for my time and headed straight down the course to the dump truck. My thought was that if I could ram all the vehicles, she would have nowhere to go until I had a chance to talk to her. I barely had the truck ready to hot-wire when genius here barreled over the wall and Havoc's troops rushed toward him."

"The least you could have done was to offer me some assistance." His tone sounded a little affronted.

"Wrong. The least I could have done was what I did, which was to keep my nose out of someone else's business. For all I knew, they had a good reason for coming after you. Besides, I also wanted to see if you'd lost a step or two."

"How very Oksana of you." His sarcasm had little effect.

She adjusted her position on the couch but failed to hide the wince. "From where I sat, it looked like a fair fight. If I had joined it, the odds would have been drastically altered. And remember, I was after Esther as Havoc. Until fifteen minutes earlier, I didn't even know if you were still in-country or if you'd headed out again. Once I saw that she had unleashed her hounds on you, I knew she had already made the irreversible turn so I moved to my next option since I knew being able to reason with her was off the table."

"Would you have honestly been able to pull the trigger on your old friend and colleague?" Agony asked with genuine curiosity.

"Come on, now. Esther doesn't do friendships. But honestly? I don't know. In the heat of battle, I was ready but thanks to you, the question will have to wait for another day. Shit, after all that effort, the only thing I have to show for it—again thanks to you two—is the inconvenience of having to try to not bust a stitch."

"So the only problems Agony and I now face are SISTER, AUNT, Chongrak-Havoc, and lying-sack-of-shit Chris."

"I wish you luck." Again, Baran tried to stand but sat again quickly.

"The doc recommended several days of complete rest, but will you at least compromise and give yourself twenty-four hours?" He raised an eyebrow sternly at her.

Agony spoke as the woman thought about it. "Speaking of Chris, I know we planned to take a couple of days before we reported in but everything has changed now."

Baran lay on the couch with a grimace. "Make the call and put it on speaker—but I'm not here and you haven't seen me."

Pain nodded his agreement. His partner dialed and put the cell phone on speaker as requested before she placed it on the table between the two of them.

Three rings later, Christopher Hollund answered in the soft drawl she now loathed. "Agony, how are you? You didn't check in yesterday and I was beginning to worry. Any luck at the range yesterday?"

"I don't know. Maybe you should ask your sister. And if she doesn't know, then you can always try your aunt."

"I am sorry to sound confused but my father only had one brother and my mother, the dear thing, was an only child. I fear I have no aunts to consult."

"I find that almost amusing, Chris, given how you are the head-honcho in her east coast family—a family that seems to keep growing, I might add."

"You will have to clarify that for me because I am utterly in the dark here."

"Operating in the dark seems to be one of the family traditions shared between SISTER and AUNT."

Several seconds of silence followed before Agent Hollund decided to come clean. "Pain is there with you, I assume?"

"You assume correctly. Say hello to the snake-man, Pain."

"I'll talk to him in person soon enough," her partner retorted snidely

"Oh, people...people. You have no idea how much I'm hurting right now. I despised having to lie to you but I am new in my current position and had to make an executive decision."

"The decision could have been to not lie to us. Or is honesty too alien a concept for you spy-guys?" She injected as much venom into her tone as she could.

"Honesty?" The agent snorted. "I think I know what that word means but they made me check it in at the door so I'm a little rusty with its usage. Seriously, Agony, I like you guys, but when it comes down to a job, some compromises need to be made. You two should both understand where I am coming from. Speaking of honesty, I'm sure you have both done some things in your line of work that you aren't necessarily proud of. Try to see it from my perspective, will you?"

"I would have to get down on my belly and slither across the floor to see things from your perspective. Simply put, I do not enjoy being set up as part of a compromise."

"Okay, maybe compromise was the wrong word. I was faced with two problems...well, four. Havoc and Baran, plus you and Pain. I confess that I hoped you two would cancel each other out, but I suspect that's not likely to happen now?"

"That's how it's looking," Agony confirmed bluntly.

"Look, maybe I can make it up to you. You do accept apologies, right?"

"Depending on the sincerity—but that's another concept you probably haven't put into practice lately."

"You would be correct but I'll give it a try. How about you and the big guy take a little time off? You deserve a vacation. Spend some time in old Mexico or maybe the Caribbean. You two both look a little pale. You can blow off some steam, soak up some sun, and stay gone long enough for AUNT to get busy with something more pressing. Who knows? Maybe you'll slip through the cracks, which would make it safe for you to return."

She considered the suggestion for all of twenty seconds. "You've put our names, descriptions, and known aliases out to all the legit points of exit from the country, haven't you?"

Hollund practiced his sincerity with a warm chuckle. "That and some of the less than legit points of exit. But let's not pretend that any of that will matter to either of you. If you and Pain wanted to get out of Dodge, a few BOLO's won't hold you back."

"You are not wrong, but I have a hard time believing that you or AUNT will forget all about little ol' me, much less my three friends, Mr. Tall, Mr. Dark, and Mr. Brutal."

"Maybe. You two are unforgettable but you never know. Get out of the country ahead of us and stay gone long enough for a few election cycles, during which some bureaucrats retire. It doesn't always take long for the landscape to undergo some serious changes. Hell, who knows? Maybe someone else appears higher up the food chain and decides to send you and Pain after AUNT and me."

"That does seem to be the way the game is played," she responded acerbically.

"Big wheels keep on turning while the wicked world keeps on burning."

She snorted. "Is that your attempt at poetry?"

That drew a throaty laugh from Hollund. "Me? Poetry? Go on with ya. It's probably from a song I heard on an oldies station. But please, take my advice under serious consideration and make yourselves scarce for a while. I have another call coming in so I have to run."

"You damn well better run fast and far." Agony had spoken into a dead phone. She slid the device aside and faced her partner. "Okay. Thoughts?"

"I'm debating how many separate body parts I want to leave him in," he replied with a scowl.

"You'd have to catch him first," Baran interjected, "and he is one slippery bastard. That's how he managed to rise so high. It would be like trying to catch water with a spaghetti strainer."

"Maybe we should start with the basics?" Pain drew a slow breath. "Who is on our enemies' list?"

Agony counted them on her fingers. "The owner of the mutt, Agent Hollund, all of SISTER and AUNTIE, and Chongrak-Havoc."

She looked at Baran, who threw her hands up. "Don't look at me. I'm not even here."

He worked through the list. "Eva should be out of our way soon enough. I don't see SISTER being much of a threat these days but we can't take on all AUNT's agents ourselves, so that leaves us with only two individuals. How about friends?"

"That would be an even shorter list. Does Ahjoomenoni count?"

"I would put her down as a definite but it depends on the circumstances."

Again, she looked at Baran and received the hands-up reaction. "Like I said, I'm not even here. If I was here, someone would have thought to at least bring me a couple of plain donuts. But look on the bright side. You still have each other—at least on most days."

Pain tried to come up with some kind of an angle that would give them an edge, however slight, but the inspiration well was dry. "I hate to admit it but I can't find anything to latch onto."

"C'mon, partner. Think how excited you'll be if you come up with an op and could pick stupid names for it."

"Does he still do that?" The other woman smirked.

"Hey, you're not here, remember?" he protested

Agony was happy to fill her in. "Every single damn time. Damsels, dragons, maidens…" She faced him. "What was that one a month or so ago? Something about a cobra and a mongoose?"

"Wait until you get to a watery op and you'll be a mermaid while he's a dolphin. That one's fun. I damn near drowned him myself halfway through it because I've always hated mermaids."

Pain tried to voice a viable defense. "How can anyone not like mermaids?"

"Because they lack commitment! Water or land? The bitches ought to make a choice and stick with it."

"And you ought to decide whether you're here or not."

"Now, now, children." Agony was eager to get something—anything—accomplished. "We have it narrowed down to Havoc and Hollund. We need to get one of them on our side, at least temporarily, so we can work together to deal with the other. At the moment, Chris and AUNT pose the bigger of the threats, at least to us personally, which means we might have to play nice with Havoc."

Her partner was not pleased with that option. "After yesterday, Havoc will have fewer forces around her than Hollund can muster. It might be simpler to get rid of her first and work around to the agent with one less enemy after us."

"But if we can turn her from an enemy to an ally, she could be very useful to help us bring Hollund down. No one knows the inner-workings better than she does."

"Of SISTER, sure, but not of AUNT," he countered.

"Aren't all your agencies the same structurally?"

He granted her the point with a shrug.

"Plus," she continued, "we've seen some of the agents Hollund has around him. I don't recall being impressed with any of them."

Pain had grudgingly begun to come to terms with Agony's line of thinking. "Hollund probably expunged all the experienced agents. That would be a good plan for the future—to make sure everyone was on his side of the loyalty pledge—but short-term, he's not as strong as he imagines himself to be. He'll never be more vulnerable than he is right now." With a sigh, he turned to Baran, his expression deadpan. "If you happen to see Oksana, could you please ask her if she would be able to put us in contact with Havoc?"

CHAPTER FOURTEEN

Oksana decided that she was, indeed, present and accounted for.

"Those of us who were deprived of donuts are hungry. Does Kwan's have anything light on their lunch menu?"

"How about a few side dishes?" Pain provided the names in English. "Spinach, potatoes, and rice? I can order three of each so we'll all have our choices and I can put the leftovers in the fridge for later."

She was in favor of that option and Agony nodded her approval. He made the call and ordered three each of the Sigeumchi Namul, Gamja Jorim, and Bibimbap and requested that it be delivered.

Given Ignatius' advice to keep Baran resting, he fetched her phone from a bag in the kitchen.

"Where will you start?" he asked her.

"The only place I can—with the one who keeps trying to recruit me. Hopefully, he's not among the casualties from the little incident at the range." She made the call and left a carefully worded voice mail. "I will try to stand now. I promise to move slowly but I need to find out what I'm good for."

They watched as she pushed to her feet and made a couple of

slow circuits of the room while she tested the strength and range of motion in her arms.

"One to ten, how's the pain level?" Pain asked finally.

"For a mere mortal, it would be a nine. For me? I'd give it a six. I'd be fine with shooting but running and fighting might still be a couple of days away." She sat again, determined to not wince. "So shall we try some unnecessary and innocuous chitchat or sit in uneasy silence?"

"You and Pain were co-SISTER agents and briefly lovers. He and I have been strictly business partners and nothing more for a few months. I don't anticipate that ever changing and don't expect us all to start hanging out together, so I'm good with the silence."

He was rescued from having to answer by a knock on the door and their lunch delivery. It took only a few moments to bring the plates and silverware and Baran moved to the table as he laid out the spread. They were halfway through the meal when Oksana's phone rang and he scrambled to the end table to retrieve it before she put it on speaker.

"Hello, Henry. It's nice to know you survived."

"You could at least try to sound sincere. You did a fair amount of damage yesterday to both people and vehicles."

"Would you believe me if I said I only went there to try to talk to Havoc? She was the one who kicked everyone into combat mode."

"I can accept that. At the moment, I'm merely glad I was one of those running around after an insane man on the tactical range and not in the parking lot when you and your dump truck appeared."

"That's yesterday's news. There are still many opportunities to die left. I need to get in touch with Havoc. Will you admit you have her number and share it with me?"

"I will admit to having her number but no-go on the sharing. The best I can do is to pass a message on."

"Then pass it fast. Tell her that Pain and I need to see her today. We need to deal with an AUNT infestation before it gets any worse."

"I can let her know but can't guarantee that she will respond. She is still a little touchy about you being ready to shoot her."

"She'll get over it," she snapped. "But that is one of the reasons she should call me. We should not be shooting at each other and it's time we got that squared away."

"Like I said, I will pass that message along but I wouldn't sit beside the phone waiting for it to ring."

"That's all I'm asking. Thanks, Henry. And I am glad you're okay."

"I had to have half a dozen paint-covered pieces of gravel picked out of my face but it was only surface damage. All things considered, I'm fine. I'll make the call."

"That is all I ask. And please stress that whether she knows it or not, this is urgent."

The call ended, they finished their lunch, and Baran took her cell with her to the couch where she inspected her shirt.

"Agony, you probably don't have any shirts in my size, do you?"

"That would be a negative." It was honestly an easy question to answer given the woman's bold bustline.

"Pain?"

"I can dig something up," he responded.

"Then please do. Preferably something without bloodstains."

He rose, headed to his bedroom, and returned with a black snap-button shirt with two pockets.

Baran took it and excused herself to change in the hallway half-bath.

"Her rifle is still in Bertha, right?" he asked

Agony nodded." It seems safer there."

"Now, yes. But if we head out to see Havoc, I think we should bring it up to her."

She raised an eyebrow. "And you think that will be wise why?"

"Because I know her and if we leave her without a gun, she's liable to tear my whole apartment apart in an effort to find one. It's one thing to be laid up but being laid up without a weapon? She wouldn't take kindly to that."

"But it would be a waste of her time," she reminded him. "You don't do guns."

"We haven't seen each other in years so she doesn't know that."

"Yes, she does."

The partners turned to where she had stopped in the hallway on her way to the couch.

"We have been out of touch but that doesn't mean I have been out of the loop."

She settled again and seemed pleased with how well the shirt fit. It was a little baggy but at least the shoulders were broad enough to allow her a free range of motion.

"Remember, I worked alongside Havoc when she was still Esther. She told me about your inexplicable aversion to firearms. Have you talked to a shrink about that?"

"I haven't gotten around to it yet." He sounded a little defensive.

"Well, you should. It's simply not...natural. Maybe they have pills now for projectile dysfunction."

"That's all right. I'm fine with it."

"And you needn't worry about me tearing your apartment apart. That would be rude. But I will take my gun before you two go anywhere after I talk to Havoc."

As if summoned, her phone chirped. Again, she put it on speaker as the partners moved closer to listen.

"I did not appreciate having a gun in my face." The hard clipped tones immediately identified the caller.

"Will you keep going on about that?" Baran snorted. "I could have aimed it at your heart but since you don't have one, I didn't see the point. Also, Pain didn't appreciate you sending a goon-squad after him."

"You have me on speaker," Havoc stated coldly. "Is he there?"

Pain answered her. "Since we're in my apartment, I thought I had the right to be here."

"And the skinny bitch?"

"Present and accounted for," the skinny bitch confirmed.

"Good, then I can tell you all at the same time. Go to hell or at least stay the hell out of Havoc's way."

"It's never a good sign when someone starts to refer to themselves in the third person," he retorted smartly before Baran gestured for him to shut the fuck up.

"Will you hear me out or are we all simply wasting our time?" Oskana asked.

"Make it fast."

"We're going after Hollund and eventually, maybe all of AUNT, and want you with us. Is that fast enough?"

The pause that followed was long enough for Baran to think the other woman might have hung up. "Are you still there?"

"Whose brilliant idea was it?"

"That would be Agony and me," Pain told her, "but Baran also seems in favor of it. If we can set aside our little family quarrel long enough to join forces, we might stand a chance."

"If you recall, my forces aren't quite as strong today as they were yesterday, fuck you very much."

"And they're not likely to get much stronger if Hollund is left running loose," he countered.

"You're in favor of this, Oksana?"

"It was my idea to try to bring you in. Chris isn't operating at full strength yet. If we want to try to bring him down, now is the time to do it. AUNT will only get stronger from here on out."

Another long pause followed. "Do you know The Berwyn Café?" Havoc asked finally. "It's the coffee bar on Lexington and Fourth."

Pain looked at his partner, who shook her head in response. "We've never been there," he replied. "How's the coffee?"

"The coffee is excellent and they have a strict no-guns policy so you should feel right at home."

"Good for them. The last thing we need is a room full of overly-caffeinated people getting into shoot-outs over a latte versus cappuccino debate."

"How soon can you get there?"

He glanced at Agony to answer since she was more familiar with the city's layout than he was.

"Half an hour, give or take." She shrugged. "Forty-five minutes, max."

"All three of you?"

Baran nodded but Pain ignored her. "No. Only Agony and me. Baran will have to sit this one out. She's under doctor's orders to rest for another day or two."

"I'm well enough to handle a cup of fucking coffee," the woman protested.

"No, you're not. Sorry, Oksana. We need you healthy."

"Shit. Havoc, can you please send a squad to rescue me? I'm being held captive against my will."

"I find myself a little understaffed at the moment, so that would be a no."

Baran grew very creative with her expletives. Other than Pain's shirt fitting her, not much was going right for her.

"We're on our way." He moved to the table, gathered the few leftovers, and deposited them in the fridge.

"Let me run across the hallway to get my gun and baton," Agony told him.

"What about my rifle?" Oksana demanded.

"Right. I'll get Bertha and meet you downstairs with the gun. Not that I'm happy with the idea but I'd merely be voted down, wouldn't I?"

"That," the woman stated unequivocally, "plus your vote will be noted and held against you for reference in any future voting."

"Fine. I'll meet you downstairs in five. I might have to double-park so please be on time."

With that, she hurried to her apartment and retrieved her S&W, her baton, and a couple of antacids. She loved the food from Kwan's but sometimes, her stomach wasn't up for it and she didn't want to take a chance that heartburn might interfere with what they had to do.

When she reached the sidewalk. Ji-Hun was on duty, so she bowed her head in passing and continued down the block to Bertha. George greeted her as she slid between the lowered gates.

"Have you changed your mind about Bimini yet?" he asked cheerfully.

"Not yet but ask me again tomorrow."

She had reached Bertha when he thought to call, "Oh, and your friends were here."

The blaring of horns at a near accident drowned out what he'd said but since she was in a hurry and didn't have time for a conversation about what game shows he was up for, she simply waved to let him know she'd heard him. If she had taken the time to go back and ask him what he had said, she would have learned that four of her friends in a low-rider had asked him if it was her minivan they'd seen parked near the back.

She did have to double-park in front of Kwan's, but Pain was waiting and ran the gun upstairs while she stayed in the vestibule and checked her mailbox, only to find the usual flyers. While she never expected any letters since no one knew where she lived, a habit was a habit.

Her partner bounded down the stairs. "That is one pissed-off agent."

"When was the last time anyone at SISTER hasn't been pissed-off about something?"

He didn't bother to answer because he honestly didn't know

and simply held the door open and let her precede him to the sidewalk. She'd barely taken two steps when he snatched the back of her jacket and tugged her back into his arms and then behind him while he peered out and down the street.

"Are you fucking kidding me?" he muttered in disbelief.

Agony scooched forward enough to be able to look past him. "Love and hate are two sides of the same coin."

"We don't have time for this shit."

The shit he referred to was a convoy with Freaky-Freddie's SUV in the lead and half a dozen other vehicles—some low-riders and some jacked-up—that moved toward them with bass-lines thumping to announce their presence.

"Freddy doesn't have that many cars left."

"No," she agreed, "he doesn't but Eva does. Did the lovebirds make up or are the gangs teaming up to target a common enemy?"

Pain opened the door and they slipped inside again. "My guess is the latter. If Havoc and us can do it, there's no law against them having the same idea. They're not firing yet so I don't think they saw us."

"No, but they can see Bertha so they will know we'll be out there soon."

Even from inside, they could hear the thump of the music. To their dismay, it sounded like the convoy had decided to double-park behind Bertha while they waited for someone they could shoot at to make an appearance.

"Are you wearing your 'Roos?" she asked

"Like a second skin."

"Then you lead and I'll shoot."

He nodded. "Let me drive too so you can keep shooting if you have to." With a scowl, Pain pulled his phone out and called Baran, who answered on the first ring.

"Don't they have any noise ordinances around here?" she demanded.

"We need a little air support."

"Aim to kill or simply to let them know it would be a good idea to move along?" She sounded enthusiastic at the opportunity to participate in a little violence.

"Move them along. We don't need to draw any attention from the cops but if you can shoot the windows out of the lead SUV, that would be good. And let Chongrak know we'll be a few minutes late."

"Ground cover in three...two...one."

She opened fire as the lead SUV pulled out and around Bertha to block their immediate way forward. Agony hung back for a few moments while her partner sprinted toward the SUV. By the time he reached the passenger side window, there was no glass left and the armed thug in the shotgun seat was bleeding from the shoulder.

Pain jerked the door open, hauled the wounded banger out onto the sidewalk, and dove in fist-first. It broke Freak Fred's nose and knocked out one of his two front gold teeth. The detective opened the side door and emerged holding Missy in her cage in front of him as a shield. He kicked the goon on the sidewalk out of his way so he could lean in and push his face close to Freddy's.

"You and your boys leave now or you'll never see her again."

He kept the cage in front of him as he backed into the alcove of an apartment door. The rest of the convoy was too far back for Agony to be able to shoot at a good angle, but Baran continued to fire at the trailing cars and allowed none of the occupants a chance to get so much as one shot off.

Freak Fred hadn't counted on anyone being involved except the two who had tried to turn him into a snitch but he knew the odds were no longer in his favor. His gunman—minus his gun— was able to crawl into his seat and they led the escape. The other six cars pulled out and followed in their wake.

Ji-Hun, his sidearm at the ready, came out from the shadow of

Kwan's door, followed by four other security personnel. They were followed by Kwan's owner, who didn't appear to be her usual cheerful self.

Pain looked up and waved his thanks to Baran, who tipped her rifle up and blew on the end of the barrel as if blowing away smoke while the gun cooled.

His partner, disappointed that she hadn't been needed to fire even a few rounds, joined him on the sidewalk. She noted that he still held the pooch-in-a-pen up for protection as they approached the head-shaking Ahjoomenoni.

"Oh, Pain, Pain, Pain. Why does no one like you?"

"Everyone likes me. Some of them merely don't know how to show it. But look, I brought you a present."

Agony did her best to help the situation by pointing out that Kwan's should start offering *gae* as a menu option. From the deepening frown, she realized that their landlady did not find the comment amusing. Pain's look made it easy to see that he also lacked appreciation for her sense of humor.

Ahjoomenoni took a close look at the mutt.

"Is this the famous Missy everybody fight over?"

"The one and only. It seems they thought it was bring your dog to work day. Can you watch over her until we get back? We won't be long."

For once, Pain was pleased by Missy's behavior because the mutt whimpered softly but quieted immediately after the Korean woman spoke gently to it through the bars.

"No one like being in cage, do they, little one?"

They watched as she moved her hand to the door and a little red tongue stuck out between the bars and licked it.

"Dae-Hyun. Please take Missy into the back. Give her scraps —good ones. She had a hard day."

Her guard holstered his gun and relieved Pain of the cage.

"Ahjoomenoni must think again about best way to deal with bad dog owners."

"We tried." Agony stepped forward. "We truly did. Last night, we reached a deal with Missy's daddy but today, he broke the deal and decided to take a different approach."

"Then today, they make big mistake. I will think and let you know what I decide."

The partners bowed and since they knew better than to push their luck, they hurried quietly to Bertha while the dog-lover returned to her restaurant.

"I'll drive. Claim the gun the goon dropped in case they're waiting around the corner."

She snatched the pistol up and climbed in. "We should have fair warning if they are waiting up ahead. Who the hell goes to an ambush with the music blasting away like that?"

"They must have skipped class the day gang-school taught how to sneak up on a foe."

Agony readied both guns and Pain put the vehicle in gear. With a little green-light luck, they shouldn't be overly late to their meeting with Havoc.

"Will she wait for us?" she asked.

He shrugged as he made a U-turn. "Part of me hopes she doesn't."

"You need to start working harder on positive thinking."

"First thing tomorrow, I'll order some DVD's for instructional purposes."

CHAPTER FIFTEEN

They traveled a few blocks and no bangers renewed their assault. The partners wanted to be able to relax but that was difficult to do since they were on their way to meet Havoc.

Agony preferred to be in the driver's seat but she decided not to insist that Pain stop so they could swap places. Instead, she used the time to talk through some strategies.

"What are the chances that she's setting us up with this meeting?" she asked when her thoughts returned constantly to this possibility.

He gave it some serious thought before he answered. "Lexington and Fourth is not the kind of neighborhood usually associated with firefights, and a coffee bar seems unlikely to have many hiding places for any of her team to lurk in. My guess is we'll find her near the rear with her back to a wall."

"Well, I won't sit across from her with my back to the whole bar."

"Maybe we can arrange the seats so both of you can sit side by side and I'll be the one with my back turned to whoever storms in."

Even though they believed they were out of Freak Fred's range now, they both checked the mirrors constantly. Agony gave in to some wishful thinking. "It would be nice if they had mirrors on the walls."

"Nice, but I wouldn't get my hopes up."

"Why do you think she agreed to a meeting? It seemed almost too easy to talk her into it."

"She'd already read the writing on the wall when she faked her death. Whether she trusts us any more than we trust her isn't the point. She has the ability to be extremely focused on one goal at a time. She told you she wanted to set up an independent shop of her own and that is still probably her only goal. Now it's merely a matter of one step at a time to be able to reach it. One thing is certain, and that is she'll only use us in the short-term to help her achieve her bigger-picture dream. She won't have our best interests at heart. It is all about her."

"You're not helping my comfort level," she retorted petulantly.

"Good. Because the one thing you never want when dealing with her is to ever feel comfortable."

"I can do that."

The Berwyn Café occupied a storefront at the street level of a ten-story office building. On-street parking was not an option unless they wanted to circle the block until a space opened up. Already a few minutes late, they chose a parking garage—something they'd vowed they'd never do.

Having parked, Pain tried his Elmer Fudd hunting the wascally wabbit impression. "Be vewwy, vewwy quiet."

Agony snorted. "I don't think Havoc has the manpower to set up an ambush in a garage they couldn't guarantee we'd park in."

"True that. But it doesn't mean we won't land in the middle of another ambush."

She wanted to tell him he was being stupidly paranoid, but their history with parking garages stopped her. Their exit from the building proved uneventful and after a short walk, they stood across the street from the Berwyn.

"It looks harmless enough," she ventured after a careful scrutiny of the location.

"Did you read that somewhere on Famous Last Words.com?"

"It's purely an observation."

The café's front was all glass and even from across the street, they could see it wasn't very crowded.

Although they had the green light to walk, Pain was careful to look both ways as he left the sidewalk.

"You truly are on edge, aren't you?" she commented and resisted the urge to do the same.

"Chongrak—Havoc—doesn't do halfsies. Someone will get the better end of this deal and there is no guarantee it will be us."

On the inside, the counter was positioned against the wall to the left, another counter and stools were in place across the front window, and Havoc was, as Pain predicted, seated with her back to the far wall. The tables were all small and designed for two people, but they were free-standing and she had moved two of them together. They made eye contact with her, ordered their coffees at the bar, and studied the room while they waited for them to be served.

All counted, less than a dozen customers were present and none of them appeared to be any kind of a threat. Nonetheless, Pain sat across from Havoc while Agony slipped into the seat next to her. None of them had the energy to fake a smile and say how good it was to see each other again, but once they were settled, he took the initiative.

"We appreciate you seeing us."

"Yeah, well, time is precious," she responded waspishly, "so let's not waste any of it. You said you plan to go after Chris."

Agony had to fight the urge to deal with Havoc right then and there and settle at least one of their problems. Fearful that she might get carried away, she left her partner to do the talking, at least until he said something utterly idiotic. She gave him an over-under of five minutes.

"We've made no firm plans yet but we want to start with Chris and see if anyone else up the food chain is within striking distance."

Havoc regarded him suspiciously. "And you have no concerns about SISTER?"

"Between you, Chris, and Baran, we've been led to believe that no one is left with SISTER who is worth worrying about."

She nodded her agreement. "Speaking of Oksana…"

"She's recuperating at my apartment. At this point, I think a cracked rib is what is causing most of her discomfort."

"Oh, the poor thing." The woman did not sound even remotely sincere.

"Yeah, cracked ribs can hurt," he responded casually.

"I was referring to her having to stay with you."

"Oh."

"So…you want to go after Chris but don't know where to start and want my help. Is that about right?" The woman looked at each of the partners in turn.

"That is exactly right," Pain confirmed. "And since you are way ahead of us in that regard, do you want to help or should we simply pretend you are still dead and wait for your actual carcass to rot?"

"Esther Chongrak's carcass is nothing but a crispy critter now. Do you know how liberating that is? To be able to construct a life on my terms that I can be happy about?"

"But now that Chris and AUNTIE are aware of the truth, how long do you think your happy place will last?"

"This is why I agreed to meet you. I already had an op in mind and went to the range to do some rehearsal on the tactical course. I had the whole thing rented for a private party when you two and Oksana appeared. Some are now dead, others are injured enough to be out of commission for a while, and half simply decided they didn't want to be shot at and reneged on their commitment. They have all gone looking for other means of employment. It seems that not everyone enjoys being shot at."

"Hey, they shot first!" Pain cursed himself for using that phrase and wondered if it was contagious.

Agony's smarmy look told him she'd noticed. She also decided it was time for her to offer an opinion. "If you hadn't made an appearance and taken me hostage, Pain and I would have been out of there shortly. So you can keep the blame for that fuck up all to yourself."

Havoc conceded the point. "It wasn't the best decision I ever made. But what the hell were you two doing at the gun range to begin with?"

He cleared his throat. "In the interests of honesty, we were looking for you—I mean Havoc."

"Chris's doing?" She scowled.

"Good old Chris. First, he sent us to look at the car and then to the morgue. We now know that he already knew you weren't dead but he wanted to draw us in. He also told us that Oksana was after me for having killed you, so I had some skin in the game—I had to either prove you were still alive or that I wasn't the one responsible for the car going boom. I told him that while you might have been in the car, I still had my doubts. The pins were the only real indication it was you, but we now know how unreliable that assumption was."

"I guess I have you to thank for the pins in the first place." She smirked at him.

"Hey, you're the one who swung! I didn't do anything."

"I know. You were supposed to dodge, not stand there and let me break my wrist."

"Sorry. I wasn't aware there was a game plan."

Agony was ready to move the conversation forward. "Speaking of game plans?"

"Right." The other woman scowled. "If I thought I had enough time, I wouldn't even consider you two, but I am low on associates at the moment and I need to strike before anything changes."

"Oh, come on. You know how hard it is to find good help these days. Even if you have no crew at all, between you, me, and Agony, I'm sure we can make up in experience what we lack in manpower."

Havoc shook her head. "Even with the very best, we would need more than three people to be able to pull it off."

"What if we added a fourth?"

She scoffed. "Sure, sit tight and I'll go ask the coffee-jerk behind the counter if he's up for a little fun."

"I'm serious. Baran is also interested. Would the four of us be enough for whatever you have in mind?"

"Baran?" Agony was surprised at the suggestion and didn't see it as being very realistic. She turned to Pain. "That's a level of crazy I've never seen you reach before. She can barely move without wincing to make sure that everyone knows she has a little boo-boo. I don't see how adding her as a fourth would make that much of a difference."

Pain did his best to ignore her and keep his focus on the other woman. "What about it, Havoc? Would Baran being the fourth make it at least plausible?"

From the look on her face, it was clear that including the rogue agent in her scheme hadn't occurred to her. "Even at three-quarter strength, the bitch can be formidable. I'll have to reconsider a few of the objectives, but if we can pull at least part of it off, we might get AUNT's panties in enough of a bunch that it will allow us to catch our breath and come up with a more comprehensive way to fight AUNT in the future. It won't be a killing blow, but it might be enough to stall them and whoever is pulling the strings might be embarrassed enough to move their attention elsewhere—or hell, maybe even end up with a new face at the top with different priorities."

"Big wheel keeps on turning," Agony muttered.

"What?" It was now his turn to question her sanity, although he did have a vague recollection of having heard it before.

"Nothing. Merely something I heard recently."

"Are you sure she'll go for it?" Havoc asked.

"With Baran? Who the fuck knows what she might do? All I know is that she's itching for action and I'd rather her scratch that itch with Chris as the target."

Agony was slowly warming to the idea. "She does seem to hold Hollund in the lowest of regard. But still, I don't think she is even at three-quarter strength yet."

"Not today, no. But I can have her up to snuff by tomorrow." He nodded firmly.

She thoroughly doubted that. "How? Do you have some kind of magical boo-boo goes bye-bye juice?"

He avoided Havoc's eyes and lifted his coffee to take a sip while he mumbled into his mug, "Maybe."

The ex-agent leaned back. "You son of a bitch. How many canisters did you get away with?"

He continued to speak to his coffee. "Let's say I still have three left and leave it at that."

"She won't take it." Her voice carried conviction.

"She will if she wants in," he countered

"And if she doesn't, there's no point in talking anymore and this meeting has been for a lot of nothing."

Pain put his mug down. "Look, Havoc, it's not like we'll steal any of your ideas, so why don't you at least fill us in enough to be able to present something to her?"

The woman was silent for so long that they weren't sure if she intended to answer or simply get up and walk out. She finally gave in and shared.

"You've obviously talked to Hollund."

"We even got a tour of the consignment shop," Pain quipped.

"And we will go back there," Agony stated in no uncertain terms. "I need that chair."

"What chair?" Havoc frowned in confusion and irritation.

Pain sighed. "Ignore her. She's in love."

"Okay, then you know it's a safe house and I don't have to explain that part. But did you notice anything else about the building while you were there?"

The partners exchanged glances.

"There seems to be a ton of high-level security for a consignment store," he said.

Agony added, "And there's something off with the spacing of the units. You've got Little Angels in the middle and an empty space on each side, but the back doors don't line up."

Havoc made no attempt to keep the snideness out of her voice. "How very observant. You should be a detective or something." She smacked her head. "Oh, that's right. Those meany policemen don't want to play with you anymore."

"At least they don't want to expunge me like your friends do you," she retorted

Pain gave her a look and she kicked herself mentally for having said that because it brought back to her the fact that someone in the blue network wanted to do exactly that to her. She decided to not share that little tidbit with their tenuous ally and hoped her partner wouldn't either. He didn't and Havoc moved on.

"The tiny strip mall is a shambles. It has what? A Payday Loans office on one end that offers loans at thirty-percent interest and a nail salon at the other? The consignment store is merely a front for an extremely advanced high-level security system in the empty space to its left. So you are both right." The snideness in her tone suggested how surprised she was that they'd managed this.

Agony returned the snide with a smirk. "Yay for us."

The snide-score now even, Havoc filled them in.

"You can store all kinds of records electronically. They are all time and date-stamped and signed off on but no one can prove who gave them because they could claim they weren't in the office that day and someone else was able to hack into their computers. Shit, if a hacker is good enough, no server is fool-proof, even from off the premises. Thumb-drives, the cloud... there are dozens of ways to store them. But there's one thing an electronically stored item can't do."

Pain didn't waste time trying to guess. "And what is that?"

"I'll give you a clue. You know how SISTER operates. In some ways, they've been ahead of everyone when it comes to communicating between departments. But in one way, it is still very old-school."

"The basement?"

She grinned. "Give the boy a cookie."

"Give the girl a break and let her know what the fuck the basement is," Agony snapped.

"It's a file room," Pain explained. "Damn near every piece of paper produced is stored in boxes in the basement, mostly simply generating dust."

"Except that several of the most sensitive boxes have disappeared, courtesy of former SISTER operatives who got in on the ground floor with AUNT. And what information can paper copies give that an electronically stored file can't?"

Pain struggled with this one but Agony had the answer right away. "Fingerprints."

"Good girl. You get a cookie too."

His interest was on the rise but so was his impatience. "You will get to the actual op soon, right?"

"Inside the building, as you face the consignment shop, the space to the left of it is where the boxes of records are stored. Taking the place head-on as is would be inadvisable since I don't know how many agents might be holed up in the back at any given time. But if we can draw Chris out and whatever agents are there—perhaps for a meeting with a couple of high-value targets—another team might be able to get in quickly and come away with the records. Once we have them in our possession, we'll have some bargaining power."

Pain informed her that they had met the three clerks at the shop and weren't impressed.

"Trust me, there are more who are out of sight and their numbers vary from day to day. We want to have the building as unoccupied as possible."

Agony needed a little more information. "You said high-value targets. Do you care to be more specific?"

"In order of value, they go from me, to Pain, to Baran, to the ex-cop. Any two of those first three would probably be enough to light a fire under him. We can tell them we want to negotiate. Whether he believes that or not is up to him, but you can be sure he won't arrive without strong backup. My suggestion would be Pain and me. We'll only have to keep them all occupied long enough for you and Baran to clear out as many of the records as you can."

They all sat in silence for a minute and exchanged contemplative looks before Pain spoke. "I like it. Every plan has flaws, but the probability factor of success on this is over fifty-fifty."

His partner was still hesitant but saw it as their best option. "I would prefer odds that are better than a coin-flip, but count me in too."

Havoc smiled. "That's settled then. You two go get Baran back on her feet and I'll start working on Chris."

Agony decided it was time for one more question. "Why should we trust you?"

The other woman stood and left a small tip on the table. "You shouldn't—at least not one hundred percent. There is a lie in everything. You merely need to determine what part is the lie and base your actions on whatever is left."

They watched her leave and the view through the window revealed her turning in the opposite direction from the parking garage. Very sensibly, they gave her another five minutes before they walked to retrieve Bertha and for once, enjoyed a refreshingly unexciting exit from the garage.

CHAPTER SIXTEEN

The two partners debated about who to deal with first—Ahjoomenoni and the pooch, or Baran.

Agony stated her choice and the reason for it first. "If we can get past Kwan's door without being summoned, I'd say Baran. We know where to find Ahjoomenoni but we're not even sure if Baran is still there. Or what will be left of us after a visit with the doggy-sitter."

"Either way, neither of them is likely to be in a good mood. Let's try Baran. The chances are good that if Ahjoomenoni is well and truly pissed, she'll make sure the doorman stops us when we get close."

"I'm still not sure how you can get her back into fighting shape, even in a few days."

"Rest assured, she'll be fine." He showed no sign that he might elaborate.

"From what I gathered, you stole some kind of secret juice?"

Pain frowned and tried to decide how to word his reply without lying. "I didn't exactly steal it. It's more like…I relocated it from the possession of someone who didn't need it to someone who much more likely would."

She snorted. "In law enforcement, we call that theft."

"But is it stealing if the object in question doesn't technically exist?"

"How fucking experimental is this shit?" she demanded.

Again, he felt he needed to hedge around the complete truth. "It's had a few field tests and all of the results have been positive."

"This is probably a silly question but is the FDA aware of it?"

"I doubt they have been consulted."

"Good luck with it then," she replied. "Baran didn't want drugs of any kind, even when she was in bad pain."

He shrugged. "If it's a choice of either taking the medicine or missing out on the action, she'll go for it. Boredom does not suit her. And if that fails, I'll have to try a little charm."

"I've seen your version of charm. Let's hope we don't have to resort to you using it."

"There you go, being Miss Encouragement again."

"Sooorrrry." She tried to find something more productive to talk about. "When Havoc spoke about lying…what would you say the percentages were of bullshit versus the truth?"

"Well, we saw the security around the consignment store so I have to believe they're hiding or protecting something. If we could confirm that a few boxes from SISTER's basement have gone missing, it wouldn't be very hard to accept that they are now in Chris's possession. Beyond that? I honestly don't know."

With that thought and the sun nearing the horizon, she parked. George stepped out of his booth as they passed.

"We had a little action down the street after you left," he told them.

"Oh?" She played the innocent. "What kind of action?"

"I couldn't see it but I could certainly hear the gunshots."

"Gunshots? Phew. Whatever it was, I'm glad I got out before it all happened."

Pain nodded a greeting and they were ready to continue but George's next words gave them pause.

"Did your friends ever find you?"

"My friends?"

He nodded. "Yep. They came by a little before you did, said they were friends, and asked if the minivan was yours. I think they wanted to surprise you. That's what I was saying when you got to your van."

"Oh, them. Yes, they did and we were able to spend a little quality time together."

"I'm glad to hear that. It's good to keep in touch with friends. Hey, big guy. When I win my trip to Bimini, you wanna come with? I've been tryin' to talk Agony into being my plus-one, but she keeps turning me down. So how's about you and me? Between the beach, the babes, and the beer, we could have us a good ol' time."

"Heaven knows I could certainly use a vacation. Ask me again after you win."

"I can do that but think about it." The man grinned. "Blowing out of town for two weeks in the middle of winter? I even went and got myself a passport. I can't wait to get that sucker stamped."

"I'll make sure mine is up to date."

They left George to his Bimini dreams and managed to get past Kwan's with only a slight bow from Ji-hun. When they reached the top of the stairs, Pain rapped on his door and called, "It's only us. We're coming in now."

He flipped the three locks and they entered cautiously. Baran sat at the table, reassembling the rifle she had just cleaned.

"You're welcome," she muttered.

"Thank you." Pain pulled a chair out. "For the air support and for aiming at them and not us."

"It was a toss-up but I wanted you both to at least live long enough to tell me what Havoc is up to. Don't keep me in suspense."

Agony remained standing. "Why don't you finish with the gun first?"

Baran snapped the last piece into place and placed the rifle on the floor next to her.

"Happy now?" The woman raised an eyebrow.

Somehow, she resisted a retort and sat before they related everything they had discussed and left out only the number of operatives Havoc would be able to bring along. From her questions, it soon became obvious that she was interested. Having drawn her in, Pain brought up the manpower shortage.

"Shit, only the four of us?" She frowned in thought. "I don't see any problem with that."

He smiled. "If each of us is at full strength, we agree."

"It's the full strength part," Agony stated bluntly, "that we have issues with. As tough as you are, you're still a long way from being one hundred percent. I'm afraid I need a little more convincing before I sign on."

"But if I can get her healthy?" he asked.

"Then I'm in. But if not, you'll have to choose between her and me and still have to find a fourth."

"If you can put it off for a week, I'll be good to go, for certain."

Pain shook his head firmly. "Havoc says we don't have a week. We need you fully functional now. She is aiming for Saturday or Sunday so that only gives you two or three days."

"Shit! A week? Yes. A few days? No—damn! I want that son of a bitch!"

He excused himself to let Baran stew in her anger for a few minutes while he headed to his bedroom. After he had settled into the apartment above Kwan's, he had moved his trunk of gear from the sub-basement of the Imperial Palace to the floor of his bedroom closet. He returned a few minutes later and put his find on the table in front of Baran, who leaned back as if she feared the object would bite her.

"Is that what I think it is?"

"It's your ticket to being able to get in on the fun," he told her with a shrug.

"You sly bastard."

"That was Havoc's response too. She and I have a side-wager as to whether I can convince you or not."

Agony hoped for the best as she added, "I hope you'll take it without too much argument because otherwise, he will try to be charming and none of us want to be around when that happens."

To her, the item resembled the type of long lighter used on charcoal or fireplaces, only slightly shorter and with a fatter barrel.

"How did you get hold of it and what was your reaction when you used it?" Baran asked warily.

"I am not at liberty to say how it came to be in my possession, but I don't remember any time in the last decade that I felt better than after I took a dose, and I was in bad shape before. We'll be rolling this weekend, so now is the time for you to either take a hit or tell us to go find a different fourth to join our little party."

The woman lapsed into silence for several minutes and her gaze alternated between the lighter and the door.

"You had no side effects, either long or short-term?" she asked finally.

"Other than three of my toes rotting off and growing a third eye on the back of my head that only appears when there's a full moon, there have been no negative reactions at all."

"Shit...okay. How do we do this?"

"We do this by having you sit on the couch. You simply put the gun in your mouth and pull the trigger as you take the deepest breath you can."

With a sigh that would put any discontented four-year-old to shame, Baran snatched the item and stood. "Is there any particular place on the couch where I should sit?"

"Smack in the middle would be best," Pain replied and hid a smile.

She sat where directed, held the lighter up, and inspected it again.

"If I die, I will haunt every dream you have, so say good-bye to ever having another night of restful sleep for however long you live."

She pushed past her hesitation, thrust the barrel into her mouth, and squeezed the trigger while she breathed deeply. All she felt was a rapid intake of air into her lungs and she inspected the lighter before she looked at Pain in confusion.

"Nothing. Are you sure there's nothing more I need to do?"

He looked puzzled. "Well, you could always start singing the theme song to The Brady Bunch or simply count down to zero from five, four, three, two—"

Baran's face flushed suddenly and her body shuddered through two brief spasms before she passed out.

Pain rushed forward to catch her by the shoulders as she began to tumble off the couch. "Grab her feet," he instructed his partner.

Agony was fast and between them, they stretched the unconscious agent on the couch.

"What the hell is in that shit?" she demanded.

He shrugged as he moved to pick up the rifle and set it to the side. "Oh, the usual this and that, plus seven secret herbs and spices to give it that extra little tang. Do you wanna try it?"

She held her hands up and took a step back. "That would be a no. At least until I know whether or not you now have a soon-to-be corpse spread on your couch."

"Then I'll save the two cans I have left to use on an as-needed basis." He picked up the lighter from where it had landed when it fell from Baran's hand and returned it to his bedroom. "She'll be out for a while and when she comes to…well, let's simply say she'll feel better."

"If you are sure she'll be out, we might as well go and face the dragon-lady."

Kwan's was close to the end of its dinner rush when the partners were escorted to Ahjoomenoni's office. Their arrival was announced and they were waved in.

"For such a small animal, your dog is pain in ass."

"But probably goes very well with a side-dish of *cheonsachae* salad," Agony responded hopefully.

"This dog-humor of yours is very bad habit."

Pain bowed. "I am so sorry, both for my partner's behavior and for the inconvenience that watching over Missy has caused you. We can take her with us now and with your permission, will keep her upstairs while we resolve this problem."

"Ahjoomenoni already has plan to sort out issues, but must keep pain-in-ass dog with her until done."

"But we can keep her while you put your plan into action and bring her down whenever you are ready," he protested.

"I said dog must stay. Come look."

The woman stood, moved out from behind her desk, and pointed at the floor. The partners circled the furniture and gazed at Missy, who lay on a folded blanket next to a bowl of water and an empty entrée-sized plate. The dog ignored them but got up and sat at Ahjoomenoni's feet, looked at her, and wagged her tail.

"See? Mangy mutt eats now. Eats, drinks, and gets walk every hour. Must keep consistent so she stays with me."

"Okay, if you insist." Pain bent and scratched the dog's head, which produced a rapid tail wag.

"Thank you, Ahjoomenoni." Agony tried to duplicate her partner's movements but Missy growled and snapped at her hand as soon as it was within striking distance. She straightened and decided to not make any effort to pet the beast lest she upset the furry brat and the Korean woman as well in the process.

Pain nudged his partner gently toward the door, where they bowed and he spoke as if for both of them, knowing full well that he only spoke for himself.

"Thank you. If you need any help with her, please let me know."

They waited for a moment but realized that no response would come. Ahjoomenoni cooed at the dog and Missy returned to her towel as her new mistress sat again.

They wound between the diners and Agony stopped at the front door to look back toward the proprietor's office.

"Why doesn't the damn dog like me?"

He didn't have enough time to list all the reasons and settled for, "Beats the hell out of me."

In the apartment, Baran was still unconscious on the couch.

"She can't hear us, right?" she asked.

"She isn't even dreaming," her partner assured her.

"All right, then. How do you honestly feel about Havoc's personnel assignments?"

"Ideally, I'd rather you and I stayed together but she's right. She and I would be the best combination to get Hollund's interest."

"Putting aside the whole probability factor of us pulling this off at all, what concerns me the most is that we don't have any guarantees that once we're separated, they won't pull off some kind of treachery along the way."

Pain felt some hesitancy as well but he had already given the healing drug to Baran and she would be one pissed-off agent if she woke to find no action being planned.

"If we want to abort, now would be the time. Otherwise, we're spinning our wheels while nothing is getting done and our prospects dwindle."

Agony agreed but reluctantly. "It sucks but we need to move on this. The only thing I will insist on is that you and me are the only ones who are wired together. Baran doesn't have a voice-to-earbud device on her so other than using cell phones, they will be out of contact with each other. If they are planning any shenanigans, the plans will have already been made while we weren't in the happy huddle."

Pain headed to the end table at the head of the couch and picked Baran's cell up. "Don't rat me out."

He scrolled through the call list before he put the phone down exactly as it had been. "Anything?" she asked

"The last call in or out was the one she made to Havoc while we were here with her."

"So any turn-coating will be an on-the-fly decision. That makes me feel a little better."

"But not completely at ease. Neither am I. Do you have any specific safe word you want to use?" he asked thoughtfully.

"Havoc's planning on this going down over the weekend, right?"

"That's what she said." He nodded.

"Then we'll have to check the sports pages to see who's playing."

He frowned in bewilderment. "Who is playing what?"

"Anything, as long as there's a game on television at the time. That way, we can use 'shit, I forgot to record the game.' No one ever questions a sports fan's devotion."

"That works for me." Pain nodded. "Oksana's never been in your apartment so she won't know whether or not you even have a TV, and Havoc's never been in mine. For that matter, I don't know if you have a TV either."

"There should be some mystery in everyone's life, wouldn't you agree?" she asked with a smirk.

"The mysteries in my life are plentiful enough already. I'll simply assume that you don't and move on to the next great unknown."

"All right. I've had about all the fun I can handle for the day. Breakfast. Donuts or bagels?"

"Bagels. She loves bagels."

"Does she have a favorite?"

"She does, but I certainly won't tell you. Covering for your stunt this morning was hard enough as it was, so I won't give you two days in a row."

"Spoilsport. *Mañana*." She moved to the door.

"Call it noonish, and *mañana* it is."

He watched her leave, still not sure if they were on the right track with Havoc and Hollund. While his mind worried at their plans, he raided his fridge for the leftovers from lunch, microwaved them, and sat at the table so he could keep an eye on Baran while her body healed rapidly.

Pain was familiar with Agony's style of noting time, especially when she was anticipating an op, so he knew that when he'd said noonish, she would interpret that as any time after eleven-thirty-one. With a bag of bagels and three different cream cheeses in her hand, she knocked on the door promptly at eleven-thirty-four and entered. No one was in the living room, so she put the bag on the table as Baran emerged from a room down the short hallway.

On the left side of the hallway was a door to a half-bath. On the right was the door to Pain's room and the full-bath. Oksana, her hair still wet, came out of the right door dressed in a sweat-suit that must have been Pain's.

The women nodded a brief, wordless greeting and Agony stepped into the kitchen to retrieve plates and cutlery. She multi-tasked and filled a cup with Pain's latest preference, a Sumatran light-roast with a touch of vanilla.

When she returned with the plates, she noticed that Baran now moved with ease. She didn't wince and showed no hesitation as she dug into the bag, took a poppy seed, and sat as Agony put a plate in front of her and brought out the cream cheeses.

The detective chose a blueberry and went for a light touch with the cheese, whereas the other woman layered the shit on hers. They were both about to take their first bite when Pain emerged from the bedroom, also looking freshly showered. If his apartment matched hers, there was a toilet, a sink, and a claw-footed porcelain-enameled cast iron tub with a shower nozzle mounted on an end wall and a tub-surrounding curtain rod hanging from ceiling mounts.

It would be a tight fit, but two people could use it at the same time if they were determined and didn't mind close bodily contact. While she immediately checked it off as a don't-ask-don't-tell situation, that didn't mean questioning looks were completely off the table. She tossed one at him as he moved to refill his mug before he sat while the others remained silent.

Having chosen a bagel, he was halfway through spreading the cheese when he realized that so far, no one had said a word.

"What? Did I miss something?" he asked with a small frown.

"Usually." Her comment managed to draw a slight smile from Baran. "No word from Havoc yet?"

"Radio silence so far."

Agony looked across the table at the other woman. "You seem to be moving more freely today. I guess the magic potion worked?"

"I hate to admit it, but I feel fine and ready to go."

"It's better living through chemistry," was Pain's response.

Baran took another bite of her bagel. "I merely wish I had somewhere to go to. I do not enjoy having to kill time."

He looked at his bagel as if rethinking his choice. "One thing we ought to do is go and retrieve your car from the shooting range. It's been a couple of days and hopefully, they haven't had it towed yet."

"Shit." The woman snatched her phone up and called. When she'd been assured that her car was still in the lot, she returned to her seat.

Agony again noticed no sign of her hurting anywhere and

turned to Pain. "How do we manage this? Until we've dealt with Hollund, I'd rather none of us be left alone."

Baran was not pleased with the sound of mistrust. "Except for you and your apartment. At least you have a bed to sleep on."

"Yes, I do. And I also don't have to worry about being alone because I am not looking to possibly sabotage anything or make some other arrangement behind your backs."

The woman pulled a sad face out of her repertoire. "Aw, did we wake up on the paranoid side of the bed this morning?"

"She's right, Oksana." Agony was pleased by how quickly Pain came to her defense. "You and Havoc are the only wild cards in this. I don't mean any offense but there is a definite trust issue here."

Baran did take offense. "So I'm now under house arrest?"

He didn't like it any more than she did but he nodded and was firm. "It's the only way this can work. No phone calls unless we're together and no wandering off on your own. Well…you can, but your first call should be to Havoc to tell her the op is off."

"Some choice," she muttered belligerently.

"It's only for a couple of days but if you want Hollund, that's the way it has to be."

"I had forgotten about how big a dick you can be." She scowled at him to emphasize her point.

"Thanks. I work at it. So it's settled. We'll all ride there together and Agony can ride back with you.

"Why me?" his partner demanded

"Why her?"

"Why not?" His question was met with withering stares. "Look, you two will work together so don't you think it's time you started to at least practice talking to each other?"

"Fine." Oksana folded her arms petulantly.

"Fine. But I get to drive there." Agony fixed him with a look that dared him to argue.

CHAPTER SEVENTEEN

"I'll be on the show in two weeks," George was happy to announce as they passed his booth on their way to Bertha. "I can comp you some tickets if you want to be in the audience."

If they were in no hurry when they walked into the lot together, they would often stop for a little chitchat with good old Game Show George, who led a simple life. He watched the cars while he listened to sports-talk-radio, and TiVo'd his favorite game shows. Each evening, he watched them while eating whatever take-out he'd bought on the way home.

Every Thursday night, he had a few friends over but only his most trusted friends—those he could trust enough to not cheat and watch the games when they were being broadcast. While they consumed pizza and beer, they would watch and bet quarters over each answer. They always ended the night with Jeopardy with all money in on Final Jeopardy. The next week, whoever had won the previous pot would be responsible for paying for the pizza.

George was content with his unpressured lifestyle and the partners often envied him. When in a hurry, their pattern was to alternate who would pause for a quick moment to apologize.

That day, it was Agony's turn. "I'm sorry, George, but we're on a complicated case right now so we'll have to pass."

"That's probably for the good. I might get nervous if friends are watching."

"Let us know when, though, so we can at least send some good vibes your way."

"I can do that." He nodded to Pain and Baran who were halfway to Bertha. "Hey, your new friend—has she ever been to Bimini?"

"I'll ask her George. I gotta run."

"You all be good, now!" he called after them. "And if you can't be good, try not to get caught bein' bad."

Agony thought that was excellent advice.

The drive to the shooting range was mostly in silence. All of them were anxious to hear from Havoc but it was at the range where a little trouble made an appearance. Pain was not surprised when Baran directed them to park next to her late-model muscle car in a non-factory metallic silver color.

"Nice ride," Agony conceded.

The other woman hopped out. "It functions."

They watched as she popped the trunk and made a quick inspection. She closed the trunk with a look of satisfaction and slid behind the wheel. For a few moments, the partners thought the battery was completely dead because nothing happened when she turned the key. They caught on at the same time and looked at each other.

Pain didn't know what his partner would come up with but he could condense all his thoughts into one word. "Sweet."

"Shouldn't it make at least a little noise when it's running? How do you get one that quiet?" She scowled at the vehicle.

"Military-grade baffles." Baran left the car running in park and stepped out. "Other than the sound of the tires on gravel, you will never hear it coming."

He was in love. "That could be useful. How about the trunk?"

The woman was happy to report that her weaponry and her suitcase of clothes were still there.

"No, I meant the cubic space. How big?"

"It's always about how big with guys, isn't it?" Agony handed her partner Bertha's key reluctantly. The only consolation was that she got to ride in the car. "It's a shame we don't have enough time to shoot off a few rounds."

Baran jumped on it. "Who says we don't?"

Pain did not want to encourage that line of thinking. "We're waiting for a call from Havoc, right?"

"No." Agony moved to stand beside Baran. "We aren't waiting for a call from Havoc. You are."

"And," the other woman was quick to point out, "we shoot guns, while you…uh, don't!"

Agony continued the barrage. "So we can all go back to your place and sit around all edgy and serious, or Baran and I can do some of that girl-on-girl bonding you wanted us to do."

"Or like she said, we go back to your place and play read any good books lately as a silence breaker. Yay, that sounds like a boatload of fun."

Oksana didn't bother to wait for an answer. She spun and strode to the trunk. It took her a minute to open the gun safe and find what she was looking for, but she returned with her favorite pistol, a Magnum Desert Eagle.

Agony voiced her approval. "How much money do you want to put down?"

"I'm up for a Franklin. Two out of three?"

"That sounds good."

Their business concluded, Agony turned to Pain. "All right, bucko…truth time. Who are you putting your hundred on?"

Please, ground, swallow me now. "I'm a little short this week so I think I'll pass on the big-money wagers."

"Tell me, Baran, did he have cowardly moments when he worked with you?" his partner asked.

"Never. I guess he's getting wimpy in his old age."

He was determined to not be baited into answering. In the long run, he would be wise to keep his partner happy by betting on her. In the short run, he believed he would be out a hundred if he didn't bet on Baran. Whichever one he put his money on, he would have to deal with the anger of the snubbed party. Nope, his reputation of courageousness would take a hit but he was adamant that he would sit this one out.

"Best two out of three, right?" he asked. "No deciding later for three out of five. That's all I ask."

"You used to be much more fun, Pain." Baran taunted.

"I hear that often these days."

Agony had everything she needed for the contest. "Maybe you should go to the tactical range and play paintball with all the other little kiddies. Baran and me will do some serious shooting now."

Pain watched them stride away and disappear into the building. *Girls and their guns.* That thought led him to start singing quietly to the old Cyndi Lauper hit, "Girls just wanna have guns." This led him to Bertha where he could sit comfortably and listen to some tunes while he avoided whatever drama would unfold inside the range.

His main fear was that they might end up shooting each other —in which case, the op with Hollund would have to be put on hold while the arrangements for one or two funerals were attended to. His secondary fear was that they would team up and shoot whatever idiot asshole tried to hit on either of them. When all this was over, he would have to seriously consider George's offer of two weeks on Bimini.

They returned an hour and a half later, having been very bad girls since they opted for the best three out of five. If he had been curious about who had won the wager, he would have set himself up to be seriously disappointed. Having let off some destructive steam, they were both all smiles and determined not to tell him when he asked.

Agony explained it somewhat bluntly. "If you wanted to know so badly, you should have had some skin in the game. We'll keep this a secret between us gals."

Agony and Baran becoming friends? Pain felt his universe slowing as if it might come to a complete stop and start rotating counter-clockwise. He wished he had something solid to hang onto during the transition. His partner slid into the car's passenger seat and he followed them out of the parking lot and tried to look as if he wasn't tailing them in case a disagreement came up between the women that might or might not be followed by gunshots.

When they reached the lot and parked, he let the women lead the way past George. He was too far behind to hear Agony softly tell Baran to let George down easy, even if she had to resort to lying. She was pleasantly surprised when the woman showed a tender side as she approached the booth.

"So, you are the famous, Game Show George I've heard so much about?"

He extended his hand and Agony was pleased to see the other woman shake it and George not try to be all gallant and shit and try to kiss the back of it. "Well, I am a George, and I do love my game shows, so I guess that would be me."

"It's a pleasure to meet you, George. Agony told me about your Bimini offer, but I'm afraid I am already spoken for. Otherwise, I would gladly accept your offer."

"If you got a good man, I'm happy for you. But if he starts doin' you wrong, you know where to find me if you ever go lookin' for a replacement."

The women walked on and left George with a smile as Pain passed.

"You are one lucky man, Mister Pain, to be hangin' with two such lovely ladies."

"You don't know the half of it, George."

The man gave him a knowing wink and he moved on before he could give in to the temptation to simply chill with him for a while. He had a different perspective on exactly how lucky he was and it certainly didn't match George's.

The call from Havoc finally came a few minutes after they entered his apartment. They were on for Saturday afternoon. Now, all they had to do was get through the evening and the next day without killing each other before the sun rose on Saturday.

Friday passed without any casualties from friendly fire. The only damage was to Pain's ego as the women continued their bonding exercise by talking about the one thing—other than both being taller than most women and their love of guns—they had in common. Unfortunately, that was him.

When he couldn't find an excuse to leave the apartment—if only for a few minutes of relief—he felt as if he were attending a dress rehearsal of his wake. Agony's memories of her time with him and Baran's memories, both seemed to follow the same theme.

Was the theme how brave he could be? No. Was it how dangerous? Another no. Could it maybe be how good-looking he was when the light struck him in the right way? That subject never even came up. How stupid he could sometimes be? He should have guessed that would be the winner.

"Geez, to listen to you two talk, it's a miracle I've managed to live as long as I have," he protested.

Agony admitted that it could be a miracle if one believed in such things.

Baran added, "Or pure dumb luck if you're of more the atheist mindset."

For him, the time moved with aching slowness. For the two women, their let's-make-fun-of-Pain party helped it to pass way too quickly. Eventually, however, night fell.

"I'm going to bed now," Pain announced. "Feel free to go to Agony's if you two want to continue with a pajama party."

"So early? Come on, we're only getting started." To Oksana, his partner said. "Wait until I tell you about the swan dive from a balcony at the Lascivious Lodge."

"A swan dive?"

Agony laughed and nodded. "Buck-naked."

"Hey, I was drugged!"

"So there we were, undercover, and I had escaped a deadly encounter and was running to find support from my partner when he hurtled out of the sky and into the pool."

Baran snorted a laugh. "Was it head-first into the shallow end of a kiddie pool? Because that would explain so much."

Pain gave up and pouted as he left the room, tried to ignore the giggles that trailed behind him, and closed the bedroom door. For good measure, he slid his dresser in front of it. He didn't need them to sneak in and take pictures of him sleeping, especially if he was snoring with his mouth wide open—which was what they would hope to capture and was something he'd been informed he sometimes did.

―――――

By the time Saturday finally arrived, they had managed to do some actual strategizing when the women took a break from making jabs at Pain and they had refined the op to a point where they were all confident with it.

Pain would take Bertha and join Havoc a block away from the plaza at the park where they were to meet Chris and company. The women would be in Baran's car to stake out the consignment store. They planned to wait in the distance for Hollund and his gang to saddle up and leave for their meeting with the others.

The choice of vehicular assignments worked out well as Hollund was fully aware of what Bertha looked like but had no idea what kind of car Baran drove. Their only problem was to find an inconspicuous place to park since the lot at Little Angel's was mostly deserted. They settled on the parking lot of the church across the street from the side of the strip mall, where they could keep an eye on both the front and the back of the building.

Once in position, all they had to do was wait for the building to empty or at least be left with only a skeleton crew. The women didn't have to wait for very long before the activity started.

Pain heard Agony in his ear.

"A large extended-cab van pulled up in the back. I couldn't get a solid headcount of the agents who came out and loaded in, but my guess is easily a dozen."

"Roger that," he replied.

"Oh, and three more cars from the parking lot pulled out behind them," she added. "Don't have too much fun without me."

He frowned as he considered the numbers. "We'll try not to. You take care of yourself. Remember, our main objective is to have all of us come out of this alive. It would be great if we end up with some bargaining chips but if we don't, we'll be no worse off than we were when we woke up this morning. So try not to die by doing something stupid."

"Please remember to tell yourself that too. Out."

Pain had left the apartment after the women so he only reached Havoc when Agony finished her report.

"Your estimate of Hollund's manpower may end up being on the woeful side of short," he told her bluntly.

"How short?"

"From Agony's report, we may be facing Hollund plus two dozen of his aunties."

"His, aunties?" She snorted. "Did you come up with that all by your lonesome?"

His smug smile was all the answer she needed for that question. They gave their plan one last run-through before they walked the block to the plaza.

"I have to tell you, Havoc, if he's bringing two dozen, it doesn't feel like a simple little meeting-of-the-minds chat."

"Chris has always tended to be overly dramatic."

"Two dozen is a shitload of drama," he retorted. "If things go south and we get split up, where do you want to rendezvous?"

"Certainly not at the plaza. If we end up on the city side of the plaza, I'd say every person for themselves and we can hook up later."

Pain agreed and made a last-minute double-check-inventory of the assorted toys he had stashed on his person. "If we end up in the park, I noticed from the satellite photos that there is an old playground in a small meadow near the middle. I don't think it's used much now so it should be safe enough to not lead to any civilian deaths."

"I remember seeing that. Good choice. The swing-set didn't even have any swings left on it. I assume you're not carrying?"

"I'm armed enough."

Havoc shook her head. "That is not very reassuring. I liked you better when you were more into mayhem."

"I got the better of your goons at the tactical course, didn't I? So I can still cause a fair amount of mayhem—hey, Mayhem Pain. That has a nice ring to it, don't ya think?"

"Maladjusted begins with an M too," she snarked, "in case you wanted my input."

"I'll save that one for a future time. Still, regardless of how many aunties Hollund brings with him, the plaza is a very public place and on a day like this, it should be crowded. I don't see how much of a threat they would all pose with the number of civilians who'll be present."

"But the number of civilians can also be problematic for us because it will make it easier for him to seed his people into the crowd," she countered.

"Still, it will be a crowd of innocents. That's good for us because it's never ideal for a gun-heavy battle."

"Normally, yes," she agreed but remained wary. "But what if he pulls out his federal credentials, orders everyone to the ground, and yells, 'Federal investigation,' or worse, 'Domestic terrorists?'"

"Then we are screwed. Damn, that didn't even occur to me. And if he pulls something like that, it's shit-for-sure he's already greased the wheels with the city's finest boys in blue network. We'll be nothing but sitting ducks. He has all the authority on his side. I don't have a badge of any kind to flash and you are—officially at least—dead. This does not look good for the home team, folks."

With Pain, Agony and Baran had studied the outside of the building from a variety of angles using as much information as they could find online. None of them had come up with any foolproof methods to gain entrance yet, let alone how to do it stealthily. Pain believed that the security cameras were not connected in any way to the police department. He reasoned that the last thing Hollund and AUNT wanted was to have the cops arrive and start nosing around.

"That," he had said, "at least gives you two a fighting chance to get close without drawing anyone's attention. They might have a dozen cameras but no one can keep an eye on them all the time. Of course, if they do have someone doing that, forget the suggestion was mine."

On their earlier visits, the partners had noticed that the window in the front of the storefront that was their objective showed the empty hollow of a seemingly abandoned front showroom. They didn't know at the time that the empty space was merely a front for where the real goodies were kept and so didn't take a closer look to see how many doors led from the front to the back. Since the store was narrow, they all assumed there was only one.

Agony had no way to be sure but her opinion was that there was probably only one door and that they had it securely reinforced and locked. "They don't want some idiot vandal to shatter the front window and stroll in to see if anything of value has been left in the back room."

Pain nodded agreement. "And they don't even have to be idiot vandals. They could simply be scroungers. There's a ton of money to be made with stripped wire and copper plumbing."

The back of the store had two doors, one as an entry for human access and a larger, roll-up door for deliveries. It didn't seem to be much of an option to stroll up and knock on the entry door. Baran finally came up with the weakness. High on the back wall were two small, barred, and probably screened ventilation openings, each one the size of a standard building block, but that didn't deter her from voicing her thoughts.

"Even if they didn't have any bars, neither of them is large enough for one of us to be able to squeeze through."

"And that's a bad thing." Agony pointed out the obvious with a frustrated edge to her tone.

"True, but they can be shot through. If the boy with all the toys has anything resembling a stinky bomb, maybe we can smoke them out. Let's say Agony's right and there is only one very thoroughly secured door to the front, if we can get a canister in there, they will all head to the quickest, easiest exit."

"Which is where we'll be waiting for them."

The two women looked at Pain, who hung his head. "I was saving them for a special occasion."

The women looked at each other and Baran left the answer to Agony. "I think we are special enough."

He brightened. "Very much special enough. I'll be right back." He stood and moved toward his room but stopped and turned to them while still in the hallway.

"It might take a few minutes to find them. Maybe you guys can try to track down a couple of pictures of the back of the building, especially the window vents. We want to be able to estimate the space between the bars so we can be sure the canister will fit."

Pain disappeared long enough for them to agree that the opening between the three bars in the window was about three and a half inches each. When he returned, he carried a bulky pistol that at first seemed to have a silver silencer much like a bullet-shaped can of whipped cream.

Baran whistled. "Whooo, that is one seriously stinky smoke-shell. It's outlawed now for civilian use, isn't it?"

Pain wobbled his hand. "Eh, that's mostly true. But as long as you promise not to use it, if you can find access to it, you can buy and sell it all you want."

"You gotta love America. How many do you have and did you cross your fingers behind your hand when you promised to not use them?"

"I've got one and four canisters and in this instance, I won't be breaking any promises because I'm not the one who will use them." He smiled as if he had gotten away with something naughty. "Did you make any progress on the windows?"

"Yea. Baran and I both agree. Each window has three bars. Subtracting the size of the bars from the total, we came up with three and a half inches for each opening."

"That could work—but it would be a hell of a shot. The canister is three on the nose, so you'll only have a quarter of an inch of play on either side of dead center." *Oh—oh, this will be fun.* He held the gun up. "I, the giver of gifts, have been led to believe that you both know which of you is the best shot, and the best shot gives us the best chance of pulling this off. One gun and two bullets in case you need a second shot. To whom shall I present the gun?"

"One gun," Agony addressed Pain, "but two bullets, correct?"

"Correct. There is one gun for the best shooter, and two bullets for the one who came in second to carry. So, who gets the gun?"

The women exchanged a look that men would never come close to understanding.

"Go ahead, Baran. You take the gun and I'll take the bullets."

"Who wants a stupid gun? The bullets are much more fun. You take the gun."

Agony stood firm. "I don't want the gun. Come on, be a sport and take the gun." She turned to her partner. "Pain! Make her take the gun!"

"He can't make me do nothing. You take the damn gun!"

He dropped the damn gun and the bullets on the table and changed the subject.

The partners had agreed to keep their earpieces on but their mics off unless there was either an emergency or if one half of the mission had been accomplished. It was hard to concentrate on something when someone talked to you about something else. Once they watched Hollund and his backup head out, Baran left the church parking lot and passed the front of Little Angels. They noted that the store was closed for a special event. She parked in front of Payday Loans.

Three empty storefronts stood between the Loans' and the one on their side of Little Angels where Havoc assured them the safe with the documents was. The question they now faced was how to get into the storage space and how many guards the agent had left to guard the safe.

Now, all geared up and seated in the car in front of Payday Loans, it was showtime. With Baran at the wheel, Agony climbed out with the smoke gun in hand and slid into the back seat on the driver's side.

The car started and Oksana pulled out quickly and around the back in a clockwise direction. She braked sharply and shoved it into park when they reached the first window. The detective hopped out and took a shooter's stance, lifted the smoke gun, and steadied her aim by crouching and resting her forearms on the car's roof. She had two canisters but didn't need the second. A quarter-inch of play on each side proved to be sufficient.

They hurried to the hinged side of the door and grasped the three gagging agents as they emerged, whirled them around, and pounded each one head-first into the wall. While Agony zip-tied them together, Baran stepped inside far enough to locate the switch for the roll-up door and opened it to hasten the dispersion of the smoke and stench.

Once the interior was clear, they dragged the agents in and closed and locked the two doors rapidly. They wandered around the space for a few minutes and noted the various objects being stored, including a small cache of weapons. After five minutes, there had been no sign that an alarm had been triggered and they met in the middle and looked at the reason why this location must have been chosen.

"That is one big fuck of a bank vault," was Agony's observation.

"This is your city. Is there a dynamite store nearby?"

"Shit. We may be here for a while. Let the scrounging begin."

CHAPTER EIGHTEEN

The plaza was about as crowded as they had expected when they reached it. If it had an official capacity limit, Pain guessed it would be three-quarters full. They wound slowly to the fountain in the center.

He had never found anyone who could explain why the centerpiece of the fountain was two polar bears who faced each other on their hind legs while they looked up and spouted water high in the air from their mouths. The city was on the east coast, so he could understand if the centerpiece was whales or something aquatic but as far as he knew, polar bears seldom made it south of the fiftieth parallel—or was it the sixtieth? He would have to look that up.

"Do you have a quarter you can lend me?" he asked.

"Grow up, Pain," Havoc snapped.

"Come on. It might be the last wish I ever get to make."

She took her eyes off the crowd as she dug in a pocket and handed him a quarter. He took his time to decide on the best wish, let fly, and watched with a satisfied smile as the quarter ricocheted off of one bear's nose and hit the other's before it fell into the water.

Hollund suddenly appeared beside him. "Nice shot."

Havoc cursed herself for having missed his approach. "Hello, Chris."

The agent had lost a couple of pounds since she'd last seen him and had developed an eight-o'clock shadow look. "Death becomes you, Esther."

"I am rather enjoying it."

He turned to Pain with a slight smile. "Pain. I'm glad to see you're still alive."

"Save it. Just talk to the walking dead and pretend I'm not here."

"Was he this grumpy when he worked for you?" Hollund asked Havoc.

"No. He's managed to lighten up since then. You should see him when he's seriously grumpy."

"Let's move away from the fountain, shall we?"

The agent didn't wait for an answer but turned and headed toward the benches along the left side. He must have realized that his suggestion had not been taken as he turned and looked at the two who hadn't budged from the fountain.

Havoc called that she liked the other side better. That provoked nothing but a shrug as he walked toward them. "Sorry, I may have become a little too accustomed to giving orders. Please, lead the way."

She walked to the edge of the plaza that backed onto the park and they followed her to a circular concrete table with two attached concrete half-benches that provided seating for four. The hole in the center of the table held a large umbrella for shade but the day was crisp enough to not need it open. Chris took a seat that left him with his back to the park and his eyes on the plaza and waited until they were all seated before he started the conversation.

"Thank you for inviting me here, especially on a lovely day such as this. The world moves so fast sometimes that taking a little time to sit back and relax is like a deep breath of fresh air."

Pain left the talking to Havoc, determined to not speak unless necessary. Half of his brain considered the order he would like to strangle them in. The nod went to Hollund. With the woman, the various intrigues had always been business as usual with the odd minor flare-ups of dismay and mistrust. With the man, all his interactions with him had involved the agent knowing more about the situation than he did. One person always having the upper hand rapidly grew old. He merely hoped his adversary would reveal a little more of his hand.

"We are not here to relax, Agent Hollund. We are here to negotiate, not to catch up on lost time."

"But Esther, I've missed you."

"It is Havoc now. You can either get used to that or I'm out of here."

He sighed heavily. "Okay, Havoc, let's get down to negotiating. You hinted on the phone that either one or maybe both of you were considering coming in from the cold."

"That all depends on how hot it is, but we're willing to listen."

"All I can say is that since you jumped ship, the temperature has remained very warm with regard to you or whatever persona you choose to adopt at any given moment."

"So what would have to be done to lower the temperature?" Her expression was hard and unyielding.

He shrugged. "I am not completely sure there is anyone who desires to do that. You burned many bridges."

"I also did considerable dirty work and know where most of the bodies are buried. You need to start taking me seriously here."

"What are you bringing to the table, Pain?" the agent asked him.

"Moral support. Other than that, I'm merely waiting for you two to finish with the main course so that I can decide what might be appropriate to serve for dessert."

"The main course?" Hollund smiled sadly. "I doubt we'll even have time to finish the appetizers."

That comment was enough to make both Pain and Havoc stand.

"We came here in good faith, Chris," she told him coldly.

The agent remained seated and unconcerned. "You came here because the creek is rising and you don't have a paddle. You taught me to never exchange anything in trade for something you can simply take. As I see it, my only consideration is how much I want to take."

They felt and saw a sudden shift in the dynamics of the plaza. Slowly, those who had come for pleasure edged toward the street while others threaded through the crowd to the table.

"You son of a bitch," Havoc snapped and glared balefully at him.

"You taught me well, Esther. Maybe too well."

Pain didn't wait for further conversation. "You will want to be behind me, Havoc."

With that, he bounded onto the table, yanked the umbrella up and out of its hole, and opened it as he made another leap, this time up and over Hollund's head. For one brief moment, she had a surreal vision of him doing a Mary Poppins impression as he held the colorful umbrella over his head and floated down to land behind Chris.

The agent had heard tales of Pain's abilities but other than the escapade with the dog had never seen him in action. He sat stunned and motionless until the detective yanked him out of his seat and used a near stranglehold to keep his captive tightly against his chest. With deliberate calm, he lowered the umbrella and used it for cover as he began to walk slowly backward toward the trees.

If they tried to shoot him, they would fire blindly into the umbrella and the bullets would have to pass through Hollund's body before they reached their target. Havoc caught onto the strategy quickly and rushed to get behind him. She was two steps away from the shelter of the umbrella when a bullet struck her shoulder. Although she staggered a step, she managed to step into position behind Pain.

"How bad?" he asked her brusquely.

"It grazed the left shoulder. There's some bleeding but nothing is broken, and it's my non-shooting arm. My legs work fine."

Pain tightened his hold on Hollund. "We'll let you join us for a little stroll through the park now, Chris. I hear a nature walk can be quite soothing."

With her good arm, Havoc grasped the back of the detective's shirt and turned to face the woods. She walked forward and acted as the guide while he and the agent walked backward behind her.

They reached the trees as Hollund's agents spread out strategically. Some advanced toward them while others sidled to the sides and into the trees.

"They'll try to circle us, Pain. We can't outrun them with you walking like that and dragging Hollund."

He was in the mood to simply snap the agent's neck and be done with him. The problem was that since he had him under control, he couldn't legally claim self-defense. Behind the shelter of a large oak, he closed the umbrella, released the man, and took a step away, which left the agent expecting a bullet in the back.

What he got instead of a bullet was a hard thwack as Pain slammed the umbrella between his legs and into his tender parts. He doubled over and felt the detective's boot land solidly against his ass before he shoved him hard enough to send him head-first into the oak. With the agent now stunned, Pain turned and raced after Havoc who, although wounded, had made good time in her retreat.

She ran with her gun drawn and as Pain caught up, cursed

him for not being able to do the same. "One fucking gun! Would it kill you to carry at least one fucking gun?"

"I could carry a gun but I'd leave dead bodies behind every time some joker stood in front of me and took five minutes to order one fucking cup of coffee. So no, it wouldn't kill me but I might leave too many widows behind."

They chose a winding path into the woods with no initial strategy except to run and run hard. Their trail would not be difficult to follow but the goal was to gain some distance before they tried to hide or retaliate. Regardless, they would eventually be caught up with. Havoc moved okay but the blood loss would soon become a factor.

Pain tried to pull up some mental images of the park. "Can you make it another quarter-mile?"

"Probably." She panted between words. "But not much farther."

"All right. That's about how far the meadow with the playground is. Unless they've remodeled, there should still be a couple of cinder-block bathrooms. Each of them only has one door and no windows. A vent comes out of each roof. Grab a roll of toilet paper or anything else you can find and try to block the vent from the inside in case they try some kind of smoke grenade. If you can get into one of them, you might be able to hold them off until I can catch up with you."

"You're leaving me? Where the hell will you take off to?" She glowered at him in indignation.

"Overland. First, I will try to slow them and give you at least a fighting chance. Then, I'll sneak through the woods to see what kind of damage I can do to tilt the odds a little more in our favor."

"All right," she conceded, "as long as you don't forget about me. I appreciate it, Pain. I'll be waiting and will try to give you as much cover as I can."

"And Esther?"

"Now what?" Her breathing was getting heavier.

"Thank you for not walking me into an ambush. I wasn't completely convinced you weren't setting me up."

"Trust can be a bitch, can't it? But I had a slug go through my shoulder so that should count for something in my credibility ledger."

"It certainly counts as something. See you at the shithouses."

Pain disappeared into the trees and she ran on and wished she had been setting him up. Her shoulder hurt like a son of a bitch but this was no time to stop to see if she and Hollund could try to come to some kind of an agreement. She had trained the fucker too well. He had all the chips and would not share or forgive.

Shit! I should have stayed dead!

While Oksana scrounged through everything in the vault room, Agony ran to the car and snatched up her small travel bag. Yarn, needles, mini-binoculars, and a first aid kit were only a few of the items. Along with a couple of spare magazines for her S&W, it had everything a minivan-driving soccer mom needed.

She slammed the door shut and paused. *Engines?* Definitely engines and from the sound, they were coming fast. She raced inside.

"Baran! Company coming!"

"Shit!" The woman rushed from the front to join her at the back door, where they both saw two cars coming, one from each direction in the back alley. "Still no word from Pain yet?"

"He must be busy."

Baran popped her trunk remotely, sprinted out, and returned with her rifle. She pointed toward a small pile next to the free-standing safe.

"I found a few odds and ends but no dynamite. Pain said you

spent a year on the bomb squad so lock the door and see what you can do with the vault. I'll head to the roof."

The woman slung her gun over her shoulder and ran to the side wall where a bolted ladder led to the latched door on the ceiling. When she emerged on the roof, she raced toward the back. With the door between the front showroom and the side door that had been made for easy access to the Little Angels' space both secured, she didn't need to worry about the agents coming in any way except through the back.

The pedestrian door was solid enough but if they were determined, nothing would stop them from revving a car and trying to crash through the roll-up door. Once they bulldozed through that, the only thing in their way would be the zip-tied bodies they had dragged in and deposited on the floor just inside.

The two non-descript sedans squealed to a stop nose to nose, and three agents scrambled out of each and assumed shooting stances as they surveyed the scene. *We don't want paperwork,* she reminded herself, *and we don't want unnecessary attention.* She decided to at least try to aim to maim but not to kill.

The alley being clear, one of the agents circled her car and reached for the passenger side back door. From above, a single shot rang out. Below, an agent screamed in pain.

"It's only your big toe, ya wimp!" someone yelled.

Baran fired a rapid burst that made them scatter for cover while she ducked behind the parapet. She moved quickly to the roof above Little Angels, straightened, and fired another few rounds from a different angle that forced them to duck on the other side of their vehicles. They returned fire in a very haphazard manner.

She remembered that many of the best agents had been expunged in one way or another, so she wasn't up against elite forces. That and the fact that Hollund had probably taken the best of the rest with him to the plaza led her to believe that she was pitted against basic amateurs. Satisfied with the probable odds, she ran a hundred feet in the other direction and fired another barrage.

The change in direction of where her shots came from might not convince them that there were more people than only her on the roof, but it would at least give them pause since they had no idea where the next blasts would come from. She liked the angle she was shooting from now, so she set her rifle to single-shot, positioned it on top of the parapet, and aimed at the roof of the closet sedan before she squeezed the trigger.

The bullet did its job and pierced the roof before it continued through a door and out. From the short scream, it was clear that it had found flesh when it exited the sedan. She had the agents pinned down securely. Their only choices were to climb in the cars and drive away or else climb in the cars and head to opposite sides of the building where they could climb up the exterior ladders and attack her from different directions.

The distant sound of fast-approaching sirens threw a wrench into everything. She was a sniper on the roof of a building she had no authority to be in. Her expression grim, she switched to automatic and fired another volley. Again, her intention was to do the cars some minor damage but not to take either the cars or the cowering agents out of commission.

She was on her knees while she considered her next options when both sedans started again and raced out with tires squealing. It seemed the agents didn't want attention from the authorities any more than she did. With the rifle slung over her shoulder, she ran to the hatch and descended the ladder in a fireman's slide into the back room.

"Sirens?" Agony looked up and shouted.

"Coming our way! Don't blow anything up until I have a chance to deal with them."

With the safety on, she slid the rifle across the floor to the detective and pointed at the three agents on the floor near the door.

"Oh, and keep them quiet."

Agony nodded compliance and Baran rushed to the back door as the sound of the sirens reached the alley and went silent. The woman took a deep breath, opened the door slowly, and stepped out cautiously as if she was nothing more than a curious shopkeeper.

Two police cars and four cops were outside. She tried to look like a businesswoman and raised her hands.

"Whoever was doing the shooting," she called, "it wasn't me."

She stepped farther away and closed the door behind her as the lead officer approached. "Did you also call it in?"

"Me? No. But I did hear some shots a few minutes ago, which is nothing new given the neighborhood."

She needed to get rid of them without letting them in—three zip-tied bodies would not go over very well. Not only that, but she also had to move them along before they noticed any agent's blood that might have dripped onto the pavement.

"Someone reported gunfire in the alley, ma'am. We're merely following up on the call."

"Well, I'm the only one here and I didn't call anyone. Maybe one of the neighbors?"

"The first call came from a house around the corner and I already have a car there. Before I join them, though, do you mind if I have a look inside?"

"I mind very much." Thankfully, her SISTER ID card was still valid, so she presented it. "I am Federal Agent Oksana Baran and this is a federal safe house. There are items stored here that are not for public consumption. The number of security cameras alone should confirm that."

The officer's gaze followed to where she was pointing. What he saw was inarguably overkill.

"So you would need a warrant, officer, and a federal warrant at that before I could allow you access. If you manage to find a federal judge who is willing to sign off on one—and good luck

with that— you will be free to go through all our security moni-
tors. But I'm telling you, I know this neighborhood and the way
sound travels. I can assure you that the gunshots came from
farther away than this alley."

The officer inspected her credentials. "SISTER. I never heard
of it."

"No one had ever heard of NCIS either until the TV show—
and please don't ask me what it stands for. It's somewhat embar-
rassing."

He was skeptical but the ID seemed legitimate and he didn't
need the headaches involved with interfering in anything federal.
He handed it back. "Well, thank you for your time, Agent Baran."

"No problem. If any other questions come up, feel free to
knock. I'll be here for at least a few more hours."

"I doubt that will be necessary. Whoever was shooting didn't
leave any bodies behind—at least not in the alley—and is long
gone by now. Life is too short and crime is too heavy to waste
time on wild goose chases." The officer turned. "Around the
block, boys. Let's get this done without wasting too much time."

Once inside again, she locked the door and Agony stooped to
pat the agents' heads as she spoke in a strange voice.

"Were you good boys? Yes, you were. You were very good
boys."

"What the fuck are you doing?"

"Practicing my puppy-talk. I have been told that I need to
work on my canine communication skills."

Baran shook her head and faced the vault. "Did you come up
with any ideas?"

Agony caught up to her. "I can't do anything with the lock. It's
not my area of expertise, so I think our best bet is the hinges.
They're a little rusty but the acetylene torch you found should do
the trick to cut through them. With a little luck, we should have
the door off in twenty minutes."

"Who's on torch duty?"

"I would volunteer but I'll be busy. We overlooked the alarm panel."

She pointed out a covering the size of a playing card on the vault side of the door's handle and lock and picked up the screwdriver she'd put down to stand guard over the agents. Deftly, she removed the cover to expose a small inset box containing wires and some kind of switch.

"I assume there is a bomb inside, so if you want to start with the hinges, I'll get to work on disarming this bad boy."

Baran snatched the torch up and donned the safety goggles that were strapped to it with Velcro and studied the hinges. She ignited it, adjusted the flame, and got down to business.

The good news was that the wiring wasn't very complicated but the bad news was that so much was crammed into the small box that isolating one wire from another was a difficult task. Agony found a small pair of wire cutters in the pile that Baran had scavenged—primary tool number one. She searched through her bag and congratulated herself on using plastic knitting needles instead of metal.

Using a triple-zero and a double-zero-sized needle, she was able to sort through the wires and managed to wiggle enough slack to be able to isolate the violet and the slate wires. She honestly missed the days of the simple red-green-black wiring schemes.

"Baran? Can you give me a hand for a second?"

The torch was turned off and she approached. "What do you have?"

She handed the wire snips to the woman. "I have these separated but I need both hands to keep them apart. Could you please give the slate wire a little nip and tape the ends?"

Baran made the snip and Agony deftly kept each end isolated with her needles while the tape was applied.

The detective stepped back and surveyed their handiwork. "That should do it."

"Should does not instill much confidence."

"I'm either right or wrong but it's my best guess. How are the hinges?"

"Five more minutes."

They turned their focus to the hinged side of the door. Agony saw that the top hinge was already severed and only two more cuts on the bottom were needed. She stood to the side and watched as the other woman fired the torch up again.

She had finished the middle bolt and was about to start on the final one on the very bottom when Agony turned the propane torch off.

Baran was pissed and she spun toward her. "What the hell are you doing? I'm almost through."

"Yeah, I know. And so is the door!" She caught the rogue agent's arm and dragged her as she dove a few feet to the side. They landed hard as the vault's door inched slowly away from the corner where the top hinge had been. The weight dragged it down and if she had cut the wrong wires, whatever was inside would blow.

"Just in case, the safe's walls should protect us," she muttered in what she hoped was reassurance.

From their angle, they could see the hinge side lean away from the vault until gravity and torque forced the one uncut bolt to snap. The corner of the hinged side struck the floor first, followed by the opening side. Once on the floor, after a brief wobble, it crashed loudly and the doorway gaped.

Agony had cut the correct wire so nothing exploded, but the force when the door met the floor shook the whole room and they could feel the vibration where they sheltered.

They pushed to their feet and studied their handiwork and the treasure they had been sent to retrieve.

"Nice job on the wiring." Baran sounded relieved.

"Thanks. You did some serious rocking on the hinges."

"Thank you. Yeah, give a girl a torch and let the party begin. I don't think we'll be able to put the door back, though."

"Not by ourselves, at least," Agony agreed.

They scanned the contents of the vault in silence. When they located the twelve by fifteen-inch cardboard boxes, they counted hastily. The bottom two layers were each four rows across and four deep. The third layer up was stacked against the back wall and was four across and three deep. The fourth was four across and two deep and the top layer was only one row of four across.

Some quick math confirmed that they were looking at a total of fifty-six boxes, all of them clearly labeled. The stacking layout formed a type of staircase, the result being that the boxes and their contents in the front row of each level were visible.

"Crap." Agony expressed her frustration with a scowl. "There is no way we'll get all of those into your car."

"We'll have to hope we get lucky. We don't have the time to rent a truck and I think we'll only be able to squeeze in about twelve."

"The labels give the dates. Do any memorable dates spring to mind?"

"November."

"Can you be a little more specific?"

"Anything that's from a November. In SISTER's cycles, November was the month where they evaluated the cash flow and dreamed big for possible upcoming ops. If we need to make a decision—which we do—my vote is solidly for any November we can find in the front few rows. We don't have time to dig too deep."

They loaded the car and ended up with eleven cases of files. For good measure, when they were done, they dragged the three agents away from the back door where they might be heard by someone on the outside to the front of the shop and zip-tied them to a large water pipe.

At the exit door, Agony looked back and sighed.

"Damn. We're leaving so much behind."

Baran slid behind the wheel and when the detective took her seat, she headed out. She'd gone no more than ten feet when she braked sharply and they both turned to look behind them. The blast blew the roll-up door across the alley, followed by a huge whoosh as a dozen or so boxes followed it, their contents a snow-flurry of paper.

"I guess I didn't get the ends taped up thoroughly enough and far apart," Baran muttered.

"Ya think? What about the agents we left in there?" Agony demanded.

"They were out of the blast zone with the vault between them and the explosives inside. They should be fine. We, on the other hand, will not be fine if Officer Friendly and his cohorts are still in the neighborhood. We gotta go."

Without waiting for a response, she accelerated sharply. Once safely away, Agony's thoughts went back to the consignment shop. She managed to convince herself that her chair was far enough away from the blast to not have suffered any damage. At least she hoped so.

It was time to update Pain.

CHAPTER NINETEEN

Fortunately for Pain, the path that led to the playground where Havoc would attempt to defend her chosen bathroom was no more than six feet across, barely wide enough for two people to walk or run on at a time. The overhanging branches often formed a canopy over the trail and offered an abundance of protective cover, so even with the large multi-colored umbrella, it would be hard for those rushing forward to notice him.

From the sound of the running feet and the shouts, he estimated that half of Hollund's forces had stuck to the path while the others spread out in a straight line through the woods to make sure their quarries didn't try to double-back. If he had been in charge, he would have done the same thing.

It took him a few precious minutes but he finally found a useful tree and used the branches to climb ten feet to reach the limb he wanted. It was tricky but he managed to inch along a large limb that extended over the path. Once in place, he found a footing solid enough for him to maintain his balance—unless he looked straight down, in which case, he knew a little vertigo would set in.

He held the closed umbrella and a small but fast-acting smoke grenade behind him but only had a short wait. As expected, Hollund had thought the same way he had and ten agents advanced down the path two by two. They moved at a jogger's pace and scanned the ground cover on each side as they hurried forward.

Yeah, you don't want anyone coming at you from the side. Pain was a big fan of aerial assaults. The two in the lead were directly beneath him when he lobbed the grenade ten feet ahead where it detonated and engulfed the first four or five men. He opened the umbrella, held it upside down, and leapt, and while in the air, he placed his feet on opposite edges of the umbrella's frame. His aim was good and his timing perfect as the pole came down in the center of two marching pairs. The canvas covering ripped between the frames and four agents were suddenly caught in the tangle of canvas and the metal frame.

With a firm grasp on the end of the handle, he spun and the four men had no choice but to try to keep their feet as they stumbled in a circle. After one full revolution, he released his hold and his captives tumbled into two agents who had turned back instead of running forward in an effort to get out of the smoke. The four caught in the umbrella swept two others with them in a jumble of arms and legs.

Pain yanked the umbrella up and away from the bodies, snapped it closed, and jammed it tip-first into every leg he could find. He had roughly five more seconds to disappear before the smoke cleared and he raced through the trees on the right, not caring if the right-side sweepers knew he was coming or not. He knew the path had a curve to the right a little farther ahead and used it to cut to the brush on the left-hand side. It wasn't much as far as subterfuge went, but it was all he had at the moment.

The four or five agents made no effort at all to maintain stealth as they moved steadily onward. They beat the brush as if they expected him to be flat on the ground, hoping no one would notice him if he could simply remain still and quiet long enough.

He had never been a fan of still and quiet, however, because they were never as much fun as chaos and battle.

When Hollund—who had trailed a good ten seconds behind his agents, heard the skirmish on the path ahead, he slipped quickly into the woods. An onlooker would be forgiven for being confused about whether the motivation was to try to sneak up on their quarry and attack him or to avoid him at all costs. He did manage, however, to get a glimpse of Pain as he rushed ahead and to the right.

The danger now passed, he hurried to the path to see what kind of damage had been caused. He found six agents with painful but non-mortal wounds but out of action for the rest of the hunt, and two more coughing to clear their lungs.

Wasting no time, he radioed to let everyone know that their prey was now on the right side and moving forward. Pain tried to judge where the left-side agents would cross the path and beat them to the place with ten seconds to spare. He crouched low behind a thick shrub. Hoping he was right in his guesstimate of the numbers, he counted four. The next one was his.

He attacked as the agent passed him and caught the man by his shoulder with one hand. His other hand covered the man's mouth as he swung him head-first into a tree. Gunshots rang out from up ahead. He assumed it was Havoc firing at the two who had run forward when the grenade had been thrown and who had now reached the playground clearing.

The agents in the trees stopped their brush-beating and rushed toward the sound of battle. He was able to catch up and disable three of them before the trees came to a sudden end on the edge of the clearing. His senses alert, he crept closer and peered around an oak as the men took cover the best they could behind rusted metal rocking ponies, a merry-go-round, and a concrete water fountain.

They were too spread out and he had no cover between the trees and the equipment on the playground. His Wonderoos were very effective when it came to five or six rounds, but a dozen automatics aimed at him wasn't his idea of a good time.

Pain didn't hang around to watch but as he moved rapidly through the trees, he could hear Havoc and the agents exchange an occasional shot. There didn't seem to be any urgency on the agents' part. He assumed there would not be any kind of a full-frontal assault—at least not until their boss appeared and gave the order to sacrifice themselves, as long as one of them survived long enough to capture their quarry.

Hollund did eventually reach the end of the path and stepped into the clearing. His voice boomed. "Cease fire! Cease fire!"

The order took everyone by surprise until they caught sight of the lead agent. Pain was behind him with one arm around his neck and his other hand holding the point of an eight-inch knife at his throat. Once the man had drawn everybody's attention, the detective took over.

"Listen carefully! No one has died yet today and no one needs to. You have wounded agents up the path and three in the woods to the left going back. Those men need medical attention and you all need to go and help them get it. Agent Hollund and I and my teammate will finish the talk we were having earlier. If anyone circles back, your boss will never know how the conversation ends because he won't live long enough. Am I clear?"

Pain must have asked too difficult a question because all he received in response were puzzled looks. He whispered in his captive's ear. "You try."

"Listen to what the man said. Leave immediately and get your fellow agents the care they need. That is an order!"

A grumpy group of agents withdrew from the playground clearing to tend to the wounded along the path.

"Olensen!" Hollund called to one of them. "Call Medical and let them know we're bringing a few in. Then have everyone else meet at the safe house."

The detective tightened his hold on his neck while Agony

spoke in his ear and gave him a quick update on the safe house. She ended with, "There may have been a little explosion."

"Roger that. We'll be done here soon. I'll let you know."

Good old Chris's day won't improve anytime soon.

Havoc came out of hiding, her shoulder field-dressed as best she could, and they all met at a bench near the merry-go-round.

Pain offered Hollund a smile he usually saved for when he was about to take a knife and fork to cut into a bloody-rare prime rib. "Now, where were we?"

"I believe," Havoc responded, "the word is negotiating."

"A nasty word, that is." The agent made his feelings known with an edge of dislike in his tone. "But as I recall, you two have nothing to offer except yourselves and currently, we already have our allotted share of turncoats and Neanderthals. So, since no federal agents died, shall we part ways and gear up for the next round? I am sure we all learned some valuable lessons today."

The detective reached a hand out to stop him from simply walking away. "Before school is dismissed for the day, you will probably want to know that the safe in your safe house is not as safe as you would like to believe. In fact, I'm afraid the poor thing is now in two different pieces."

Oh, how he loved to see blood drain from faces.

"Did…did they destroy the boxes, or steal them?"

"Some were missing when the safe accidentally blew up. The saved files are now in the possession of our associates who are awaiting word from us as to whether they should simply toss them."

"What boxes do they have?"

"No, no, no." He shook his head. "We won't take all the mystery out of it. I know they took about a dozen. Which dozen is something you can only find out after our negotiations are finished."

Havoc was down to one good arm and flinched when she

stood up from the bench. She stepped slowly in front of Chris and leaned into his face.

"A dozen. My, my, think of the possibilities. How much trouble can twelve boxes from the basement cause? How much do you think they are worth and what are you willing to pay to have them returned?"

She straightened and circled behind him.

"Chris? Look at me."

Hollund craned his neck to look back at her, and even though, deep down, he knew he shouldn't have been surprised, he was taken aback by the sight of Havoc, one shoulder covered in blood and her good hand holding her Beretta tightly against the back of Pain's head.

"I don't think she likes you anymore, Pain, first initial M."

The detective responded with a what-can-you-do shrug. "It happens."

"I am now in possession of the boxes or will be as soon as I notify Oksana. What can you offer me?"

"I can guarantee you a place at the table," Hollund replied. "What you do with it once you are in…well, that will be up to you."

"Pain? Are you willing to walk away and pretend I'm still dead?"

"I don't like to make promises I can't keep."

"You are down to two choices, Esther. Shoot Pain right now and get him permanently out of my way and I'll bring you back in. Or walk away knowing we will always be coming after Havoc —as will Pain, I'm sure."

"I honestly thought you might have changed, Esther." The detective sounded disappointed.

She smirked. "Leopards and their spots, Pain. Leopards and their spots."

Pain didn't respond and merely held his head high and steady. He had faith in his ears—and in his abilities when it came down to basic math—and sincerely hoped his ears hadn't let him down. Granted, if they had let him down, he would never know it since his brain was about to be shattered by a bullet from Havoc's Beretta, a gun that had a very distinctive sound to it.

If his ears were to be trusted, however, they had heard her fire nine rounds, which left her gun empty. The sudden appearance of the two men in the clearing had ended the shooting but with her wounded arm, she would not have had enough time to reload before she left the bathrooms. It saddened him to know that someone he might not have gotten along with for a decade but was once almost a friend would go so far as to pull the trigger.

He heard the first snick of the firing pin, followed by a click, then by Havoc's response. "Mother-fucker!"

"Oh, poor, poor psycho. Did you run out of bullets?" he snarked.

The flick was so fast that he didn't see it coming, but she had spun the gun and smacked his cheek hard with the butt. In one swift move, he leapt up and over the bench, wrenched the gun from her hand, and fought the urge to smack her in return.

She looked past him. "He's getting away!"

Pain turned and sure enough, Hollund sprinted toward the path through the woods. He turned to the wounded woman.

"A Havoc in the hand is worth an agent in the bush." Even though it was empty, he used it to guide her toward the path everyone had traversed on their way from the plaza and clicked his mic on as he went.

"Agony, I lost Hollund because Havoc turned on me. Big surprise, huh? She is now our prisoner. How is it going on your end?" *Three...two...one.* "Agony. Are you there? Respond, please."

More silence followed and he frowned.

"Aw, did we lose a little girl?" she snarked viciously.

He didn't have to strike her to be able to apply some hurt. All he had to do was grab the wrist of her wounded arm and twist, an action that evoked a scream of pain as she fell to her knees.

His expression hard, he leaned down and spoke slowly and carefully to make sure she heard every word.

"If she comes to any harm, I—will—kill—you, and I promise that you will not enjoy it, nor will your body ever be found. There won't be any missing person's file opened for you because you are already dead. So, did you and Baran plan the betrayal together?"

The detective gave her arm another slight twist of incentive.

"No. Ow! No, we didn't. I haven't talked to her since the shooting range but I know how she thinks. She is not the sharing kind so if she has a chance to have it all for herself, she'll take it."

"Agony. If you're listening but can't speak, can you manage to turn your mic on and scratch something against it?"

Again, silence was the only response. He confirmed that his comm device was turned on and operational and frowned. Taking hold of Havoc's good arm, he yanked her onto her feet, slid her gun behind his back, and tucked it under his belt so only the handle showed.

"We'll take it nice and easy back to my ride," he told her calmly. "Then we'll get your arm taken care of."

"Shouldn't you be focused more on the danger your partner is in than on little ol' me?"

"I've seen her in action. I'm not worried."

The truth was that he had seen her in action and she was very, very good. But he had also seen Baran in action so he was worried—very worried. But if he let Havoc go to rush to Agony's aid, even though he didn't know for sure that she needed him, she would berate him mercilessly for having captured and released their enemy.

With his hold firmly on her arm, Pain dug in his pocket and pulled out a small round bulb that fitted into the palm of his hand. A half-inch needle protruded from the end of it. He held it up for Havoc to see.

"What's it loaded with?"

"You don't want to find out." He stabbed the needle into her bicep, held it in place, and looked for all the world as if he used both hands to help steady her as they walked. "The juice won't kill you but it will fuck your nervous system up big time. The main trouble, though, is that it's still so experimental that they can't direct it to affect a specific nerve. So it might be the optic. It might be something in the spine...or maybe something in the brain."

"In other words, I could end up blind, paralyzed, or lobotomized?" Her voice had taken on a much sharper edge that might have been fear.

"Those seem to be the systems it has affected the most but maybe you'll get lucky and only be left with a twitchy pinky finger. I honestly don't know. So please, give me one reason to squeeze and we'll both find out."

Hollund's agents were long gone by the time they reached the plaza. Fortunately, so were the police who had spent a minimum amount of time interviewing witnesses whose responses to their questions were useless. Someone might have fired a gun. It might have been a car backfiring. People rushed everywhere but no one knew why.

It was merely another Saturday afternoon in the park.

They reached Bertha and Havoc stopped at the front passenger door.

"Not today." He dragged her forward and popped the rear hatch. "Today, you get the special treatment and ride in the cage."

"Let me make this perfectly clear, asshole." She glowered at him in suppressed fury. "No cage."

"Yes, cage."

"We are on a city street now. Do you want to learn how loudly I can scream?"

Pain withdrew the needled-bulb gently from her arm, stowed it safely, and threw a roundhouse right that knocked her off her feet and into the cage. He closed the hatch and climbed behind the wheel. Once he'd activated the sound buffer between the front seat and the rear, he tried to contact his partner again.

He had begun to develop a sincere hatred of silence.

Baran drove down the alley to the cross street and swerved into the church's parking lot. The street side had enough bushes to give her some cover and she climbed out without an explanation.

Agony unbelted and followed her. "Do you seriously want to maintain surveillance? Shouldn't we—not point guns at teammates?"

The rogue agent's Magnum was a foot from her face. "Maybe you should start walking and forget any of this ever happened. I'll drive away with the boxes and you can walk back to Pain. I know, I know. I'll get the better part of the deal, but I need to get out from under all the SISTER-AUNT shit and those boxes are my ticket. It's nothing personal, you understand. If it were personal, I would simply shoot you right now."

Agony spread out her arms. "Then fucking shoot."

Baran mimicked the gesture and mocked the statement. "Then fucking shoot, she says."

Agony had drawn the hoped-for scenario, which was to have the gun pointed somewhere other than directly at her. She flashed a roundhouse kick that launched the weapon five feet and into the bushes.

She grappled for her gun but didn't manage to draw it before the other woman was on her. Her MMA training had boosted her already well-formed fighting skills, but Baran had her by both size and weight. In their first clinch, she learned two other things. The rogue agent was still energized by the healing-juice Pain had given her and she fought dirty. Very dirty.

Shit, she thought at one point, *she probably learned half of her moves from Pain.* Speaking of which, he was now in her ear.

"Agony. I lost Hollund—Havoc turned— big surprise—now our prisoner—you there?" Scattered phrases were all she was able to make out as she rolled on the ground with her adversary.

At close quarters, Baran knew how to use her height and weight advantage. Agony received mostly elbows and knees and wasn't able to get enough distance to put any power into her punches. She directed most of her effort to fight off the attempts to force her face down on the dirt. If the woman ever got on top, Agony knew she would end up as nothing more than a punching bag.

The fight never left the dirt. Agony was able to use her speed and agility to dodge several blows and did some damage but in the end, Baran's size and weight combined with Pain's juice was too much. She delivered one last knee to a kidney, which doubled the detective up before she scrambled away and retrieved her Magnum from under the bush. The detective froze when she saw the barrel aimed at her.

"You don't get it, do you bitch? I don't want to kill you. You might end up being a valuable asset to someone someday. All I want you to do is walk away. It's what I am going to do, only I'll take the car. Make sure you tell Pain that I let you live but can't promise the same the next time."

Agony, bloodied, bruised, and still on the dirt, watched her walk toward her car and took some satisfaction in seeing the bitch limp a little. Baran opened the door, paused for a second, and spun with her gun drawn. A second later, a bullet ripped through her armpit. The Kevlar vest might have been a good one, but it ended at the shoulders and from Agony's angle on the ground, she had been able to shoot at an upward angle.

Bleeding and her shooting arm now disabled, the woman dove into the car and screeched forward, leaving her gun behind. Agony fired a couple more shots before Baran spun the wheel and roared directly toward her. She managed to roll away barely in time and fired a couple more rounds as her adversary raced out of the parking lot with all of the boxes.

"Agony," Pain said in her ear again. She had heard him talking during her entire scuffle with Baran but this was the first time she was able to listen in peace. "I need you to talk or make some kind of noise to let me know you're alive. Shit!"

She fumbled gingerly for her comm switch. "I'm alive, Pain. Not happy but alive."

"And Baran?"

It hurt to breathe, let alone talk, so her voice resembled a stuttered string of gasps. "I am sad to say that Baran is gone."

"Gone?"

"She pulled her gun and turned on me. We got into a fight. She won but I managed to get a shot off."

"And you killed her?"

"I didn't say I killed her. I only said I shot her. She's not dead-gone, she is gone-gone. Gone with the car. Gone with the files. Gone to wherever the shit isn't constantly flying, the lucky bitch."

"Are you hurt badly?"

"I feel like an orange that's been dropped from a hundred feet and lost its battle with the ground but I'll live. It would be nice to have a ride, though. I'm in the parking lot of the church across from where they are holding my chair hostage. I don't want to linger here in case someone reported the gunshot so I'll walk down the side street in a westerly direction."

"I'm on my way."

CHAPTER TWENTY

With the sound buffer still in place between the front seats and the cage in the back, Pain was spared Havoc's curses as he guided Bertha to a corner where he found Agony resting on the bench of a bus stop enclosure. He pulled up, leaned over, and pushed the door open as she climbed in gingerly and immediately leaned back to rest her head and closed her eyes.

"That was a whole shitload of work for a whole shitload of nothing."

"So we lost the files and Baran turned. Big deal. I still have Havoc and we're both alive. That counts as a good day in my book."

"We obviously have different definitions of good."

"How bad is Baran hurt?"

"Why? Are you concerned about your girlfriend?"

"Just tell me how bad."

Agony opened her eyes and adjusted her position. "It was an upward angle shot. You were right. She needs to upgrade her body armor. I got her in the armpit—no major arteries, unfortunately—but she will be hurting for a while."

Pain flipped the com to the back on. "Hang on, Esther, we

need to make a side trip."

"Side-trip yourself right to hell, Pain."

He flipped the switch off again. "I guess she's not happy."

"You say that as if I care. Where did you plan to take her and where is this side trip to?"

The detective turned left and thought he could probably put Bertha on cruise control and relax since the minivan should have the route memorized by now.

"Baran's wounded. She needs medical attention and I seriously doubt she will seek it at a hospital. For that matter, Chongrak's hurt too. It seems to me like there is only one place where everything would intersect."

It took Agony only an instant before the penny dropped.

"Baran might still be there. We can multi-task by getting Havoc tended to and check on how the love-triangle between the ghoul, the junkie, and the trollop is progressing." She nodded. "I like it."

The conversation on the drive to Miles and Ignatius Funeral Home consisted of brief recaps of their day's adventures. They were close to their destination when she shook her head.

"I don't know how you lived in that world, Pain. I know someone in blue still has a hit out on me, but that is one betrayal. It's a painful one, but only one. With you spy-guys, it seems like you all should have *Trust no one* tattooed backward on your foreheads so you can be reminded of it every time you look in a mirror."

"It does seem that way, doesn't it? It wasn't always like this, though. There was a time when, despite some petty disagreements, you could trust someone to have your back, but AUNT coming into the picture has ramped the intrigues up. It reminds me of what the outside world would call a hostile corporate takeover."

"Emphasis on the hostile. But in the corporate world, Pain, hostile means jobs, money, and careers being bargained for. In spy-land, it means real hostility and lives endangered. And like I said, you never know where the next danger will come from."

"It does wear on a person—shit!"

Agony saw it too. A metallic-silver muscle car pulled out of the funeral home's driveway and accelerated as it headed in their direction. They were only able to catch a brief glimpse of Baran, who turned and smiled at them as she roared past.

"Double-shit!" Agony couldn't find the words to suitably vent her frustration.

"Should I give chase?"

She sighed. "Bertha's a good girl but there's no way we can catch up to her. Besides, what could we do if we did? She still has fed credentials and we are not licensed to shoot to kill for no apparent reason."

"That's a pity." He sounded as disappointed as she felt.

They watched Baran disappear in their rearview mirrors and with resignation, he pulled into the underworld's favorite mortuary and unlicensed field hospital. He turned the speaker on again.

"We'll be right back, Esther. We have to make arrangements to get your shoulder tended to."

"Fuck you, Pain—and the name is Havoc!"

"Whatever you say, Chongrak."

They exited Bertha and due to Agony's injuries, walked slowly to the front door.

"Do you have to antagonize her like that?" she asked a little irritably.

"Have to? No. Enjoy? Yes. Please don't deny a poor man his simple pleasures."

Agony might have considered him to be acting petty if it weren't for all the trouble the woman had caused both of them.

"Hopefully, with Baran just finished, we can get inside fast enough to not allow Iggy and the floozy enough time to start humping on the drain table again."

Pain opened the door and held it open for her. She was one foot inside the vestibule when she called, "You have company! Make yourselves decent!"

They were both surprised to see Sylvia, wearing proper receptionist attire, step out of Miles' office and frown.

"Oh. You two again. Are you here to see Miles or the doc?"

"Both, eventually." Agony took the initiative. "But Iggy for now."

"He'll be scrubbing up—or down, I'm not sure what it would be called. You know where to find him."

They continued down the hallway and turned right into the surgical room, where Ignatius was drying his hands.

"You just missed your friend. If you had told me you were coming, I would have had her wait."

She tried to put the former medical examiner at ease. "No worries, Iggy. We'll catch up to her another time."

"Well, at least this time, I didn't have to make a house call to take care of her." He donned a fresh lab coat. "She does seem to have an extraordinary talent for placing herself in the path of bullets. Maybe you can suggest she get into another line of work?"

"Or teach her how to duck faster," Pain retorted. "Since you are already all scrubbed up, I will go out and bring in the next candidate in need of your handiwork." He turned to his partner. "Agony, while I go fetch the guest of honor, are you up to visiting Miles' office to see if you can use his computer?"

"And I will need it why?"

"To see if you can find any info on Havoc and her activities. Use your friend Harry T if you have to. Hollund gave us enough information to at least do a rudimentary search. If we can get enough circumstantial evidence, we can hand her over to the cops. Since Chongrak no longer exists, the damage she caused as Havoc will fall directly on her."

"That is if the cops want to put any energy into pursuing it," she countered wearily.

"We need at least a hint of something. We can't simply turn her in and say she's been naughty."

"Why not? Naughty is good enough for Santa."

"Please?" He flashed her his most devastating smile.

"Fine."

"Pouting does not become you."

That response was met with a cocked head and a middle finger. Pain informed Ignatius he would be right back and they walked out, leaving the mortician to wonder if it was too late for him to consider making a career change.

Pain went to fetch Havoc and Agony knocked and entered Miles' office. She was surprised to find him seated behind a very tidy desk. The thin trace of white powder on it was not the kind that came from donuts. In fact, no donuts were visible at all. When he stood to greet her, she could see that his weight had started to drop again.

Sylvia stood in the corner and looked as serious as Agony had ever seen her. "Miles is doing much better now, so don't go fucking with his head, okay?"

"Okay. I'm glad to see you up and about again, Miles."

"Yeah, yeah." He had reverted to his charming self. "Fuck the pleasantries. What are you here for?"

"I need to borrow your computer for a few minutes to look something up. I promise it won't take long but I do need a little privacy."

Miles made sure the lock was in place on the cabinet where he stored his inventory and with his arm linked with Sylvia's, the happy but frowning couple left her to her search. She tried on her own for five minutes, found a couple of crime reports that might have involved the firearms Havoc favored, then gave in and called her reporter-in-the-back-pocket.

"Harry T, don't waste my time."

"It's Agony. I need your help."

"And here I thought you were calling to tell me what I was getting in return for my last favor."

"All in good time, Harry. All in good time."

She gave him a quick breakdown of what she was looking for, including the make and model of the guns. At first, he scribbled frantically—she could hear the scratch of pen on paper—and then pounded some keys. It took him barely three minutes, but she thought it could have taken him only one if he hadn't scanned each report he'd pulled up to see if there was anything he could sink his teeth into.

"I found four police files and three news articles that might be relevant. What's your e-mail?"

She recited it and wished the reporter well.

"If wishes were horses, beggars would ride. No more freebies until I get something in return," he replied bluntly.

"I'm working on it, Harry."

The call ended and she logged into her account. *Damn, that man is good.* She made sure the copier had enough paper and suppressed a slight pang of guilt, put it to use, and made two copies of each document. She only needed one for their immediate purposes, but they might eventually want a hard copy for themselves. Since copy paper and ink weren't free, she ran off the extra set of documents and put all of it on Miles' dime, hence the guilt.

She had heard Pain and their day's acquisition enter while she was still on the phone with the reporter, but once she'd sent everything to the copier's queue, she headed down the hallway to check on whatever progress had been made. When she entered, Ignatius finished the last of a row of stitches as Havoc sat on the table. Pain stood guard on the opposite side of the doctor.

The mood of the current occupants varied. Her partner seemed to be enjoying himself, while Ignatius looked a little on the dour side as he went quietly about the task at hand. As for

Havoc, Agony was glad that her partner was within striking distance if the patient decided to go for a scalpel.

The woman's mood did not lighten when she saw her step in. "Are you here to gloat too?"

"Gloat about what? We wanted the fucking files, not a yesterday's news former spy."

"Oh, are we grumpy because we lost a little fight to a girl?" the bitch snarked.

"No, we are grumpy because no matter how often we take the trash out, more keeps coming to replace it. It's hard enough to keep up with the volume without having to recycle the pieces that haven't yet learned to simply stay where they belong."

Ignatius cut the last stitch and moved himself and his cart out of the way, just in case. He crossed to the sink and washed the blood off for the second time that day.

"Not that any of you people will take my advice seriously, but you will want to keep that in a sling for at least a week." He opened a drawer and pulled one out. "The shot I gave you will wear off in half an hour. You can ask my partner for pain meds on your way out."

Agony wondered what a real mortician would think about a colleague who kept slings as part of their supplies. She had certainly never witnessed anyone being buried while wearing one.

Despite her vocal protests, Havoc held still as he maneuvered the sling into place. His patient all set and ready to go, he was about to try to guide the group to the door but Pain had one more piece of business on his mind.

While Iggy had fussed with the sling, Pain asked Agony quietly how her search had gone.

"Harry T came through for us again. I have twenty pages printing now in duplicate—one for us and one for the authorities."

"Will they be enough?"

"From what little I read, yeah. She's toast."

"Speaking of toast." He turned and addressed Ignatius. "Do you still have Miss Crispy in your custody?"

The man's shoulders drooped. His real workday hadn't even started yet and he already felt exhausted.

"No one's come to claim her yet, so yes. And now I suppose you want to have another look-see?"

"You suppose right."

They followed the doc out and across the hallway. He didn't wait for further orders but opened the door and slid the drawer holding the body out. This duty performed, he tried to look impatient and took a step back. Pain held Havoc's good arm as he stepped close to what was left of the corpse.

"Did you even know her name?" he asked.

The woman shrugged. "She was already dead and donated to the lab. Why bother?"

"Because I think her family has a right to know."

"Then they're shit out of luck as far as help from me goes. I got her from Krayton University's lab, so if you are that concerned, you can check with them to see if they have reported any cadavers missing. I'm sure her family will be thrilled to have a stranger knock on their door to tell them that their daughter is still dead but her body was stolen and then blown up beyond recognition."

Ignatius interjected with his typical concern. "She does have a valid point, Pain."

"Bullshit. Her family has a right to know. The university also needs to be held accountable for their lack of security. She was once a living, breathing, and for all we know, happy person. Dignity should be allowed to remain, even after death."

Agony had an assortment of feelings about her partner, not all of them happy-happy-joy-joy, but she had never been more proud of him than she was at that moment. She would have to remember to tell him that sometime—although maybe she should save it for deflection purposes when he was seriously pissed at her. For now, she stuck to business.

"The files should be done printing now. Should we collect them and get out of here?"

"Please," Ignatius implored.

"Thanks, Doc." Pain led Havoc out.

His partner remained behind for a moment.

"Miles and the bimbo seem to have reconciled. I'm proud of you, Iggy."

"Don't give me too much credit. You guys finally convinced me and I had to tell her that we couldn't keep meeting like we had been and that she either had to make up with Miles or leave. But leaving would have cut her supply chain off, so out of either habit or sincere feelings, she went back to him."

"You all seem the better off for it—except for the no-nookie-for-Iggy part."

He managed to sound both proud and embarrassed. "Miles and I plan to go on double-dates once a week."

"You did say double, not tag-team, right?"

Ignatius nodded, his smile firmly in place. "I did. I am now seeing someone who is only ten years younger than myself as opposed to forty."

Agony didn't have to lie. "Then I am happy." She turned to make her exit but his next comment stopped her dead—no pun intended given the surroundings—in her tracks.

"So is Sylvia's mother."

She turned to stare at him. "Please don't tell me—"

His smile deepened. "Let's say that Sylvia comes from some very good-looking genes."

"And now, if everything works out, your double-dating will end up with a double-marriage, and your business partner will become your son-in-law? Is that the plan?"

"Stepson-in-law but yes, that is a definite possibility."

"Do me a favor, Iggy." Somehow she managed to not gag.

"Anything, if I can. After all, it is thanks to you and Pain having knocked some sense into me that I find myself in my current situation. What is your request?"

"Please don't invite us to the wedding. When it comes to the part where the minister asks if anyone knows any reason why these two—or four, in this case—shall not be joined together in holy matrimony, I might have a hard time keeping silent."

"When did you become such a prude?" His smirk was the last straw.

"See ya around, Doc."

She shook her head, strode to the front, and met up with her partner and Havoc as they left Miles' office. Pain held a stack of printouts in one hand and kept a firm grip on Havoc with the other. The woman walked steadily enough until they reached Bertha, then she balked.

"I don't deserve a cage, Pain."

"Oh, I think a cage is exactly what you deserve, but we're not who will provide it."

As if on cue, sirens could be heard approaching in the distance.

"What the fuck have you done, Pain?" Havoc's anger was now palpable.

"Me? Nothing. My partner might have made a phone call, though."

As she had scrolled through the files Harry T had sent her, she had seen enough to warrant a phone call to their virtually hog-tied chief of police to request a competent homicide detective and a team to meet them in the parking lot. She didn't specify why but he was in no position to argue.

An unmarked sedan and two squad cars rolled in, their sirens now silent.

A man and a woman emerged from the sedan and the woman took the lead as they approached the little group waiting for them next to a minivan.

"I am Detective Scarsdale. Homicide." She flashed her badge. "Are you the ones who called?"

"That would be me." In lieu of a handshake, Agony flashed her PI badge. "We have a live body here that we would like to present to you and a dead body inside who is yet to be identified."

"You mother-fuckers will pay for this, Pain!" Havoc shrieked.

"I assume that means us becoming pen-pals won't happen?" he asked and looked tragically disappointed.

She spat at him but missed and hit Detective Scarsdale on the arm, which didn't help her cause at all.

It took several minutes to explain what they could about the situation and they made sure to mention the matching pins in the wrists and the university lab the burned body had been stolen from. Scarsdale asked the questions as her partner, who had introduced himself as Detective Hernandez, took notes. The more they talked, the more the woman began to resemble a bobble-headed doll.

When they were finished, the detective took their numbers and informed them that she would be in touch. The partners moved to Bertha's doors so the officers could go inside and start trying to make some sense of the situation.

"Yo! Agony!" one of the uniforms shouted. "I had just brought up some paperwork so I was in the squad room on your last day. That was one hell of a punch. The bastard deserved it."

She smiled. At least not all the boys in blue wanted her dead.

"Can we go home now?" Agony desperately hoped for a yes.

"Absolutely. You need a little medical attention too."

"It's all bumps and bruises. Not even enough to warrant your boo-boo-go-bye-bye juice."

"Let me know if you change your mind."

They parked in the lot. It was a Sunday, so George wasn't on duty and they made the short trek to their apartments and managed to almost slip past Kwan's before they were informed that *she* wanted to see them. They assured the doorman that they knew the way, entered, and wound between the late-dinner crowd.

"Do you have any idea what awaits us?" Agony had learned to never get too comfortable when it came to dealing with their landlady.

"I haven't a clue."

The guard outside her office saw them approach and informed Ahjoomenoni of their arrival before he ushered them in. They bowed and waited for an invitation to either sit or expose their necks so that the executioner's blade would have a clean cut.

The Korean woman was in the middle of her dinner and looked as if she was enjoying it. She held her knife and fork in hand as she looked at them.

"No need to sit. Ahjoomenoni just want to say thank you to Agony."

As often happened to her while in their landlady's office, she was at a loss.

"I would say you are welcome, but I am not sure what I did."

Ahjoomenoni sliced off a piece of the meat on her plate and stuck her fork in it.

"You reminded Ahjoomenoni of her roots when you suggested I start including *gae* on the menu." She offered the fork to Agony. "Missy makes for better meal than pet. Taste yourself."

Her hands flew to her mouth in horror. "But I-I...I wasn't serious."

"Should not say things not meant. But it was good advice. Please, have a bite and see how delicious when seasoned just right."

Agony looked at Pain, desperate for him to help her get out of this. He tossed his hands up and took a step back.

"I never cared for *gae*, even when I was in Korea. I haven't developed a taste for it since then either," he told her bluntly.

"Ahjoomenoni. Please. I did not mean for...for, *this*. I don't think I could swallow it."

"Swallow is easy. Just chew, then gulp and is gone."

Pain knew he would have to take the secret to his grave, but he stood deeper into the room than his partner did and could see Miss Missy's bed still snuggled behind Ahjoomenoni's desk. He wondered how long she would let Agony suffer.

Five seconds later, the sound of a dog yapping from the kitchen area caused Agony's stomach to lurch even further. *Do they slaughter them in the kitchen?*

Her horror ended a few seconds later when Miss Missy was returned to Ahjoomenoni's custody and rewarded with a treat as she took to her bed.

"Was time for Miss Missy's walk. Was also time for Miss Goni to learn lesson. Now is time for me to finish dinner in peace."

With two quick bows, the partners left. The old woman dug into her veal with great satisfaction. Her tenants often gave her a reason to laugh at their expense and she didn't have many opportunities for innocent laughter.

Agony led the trudge up the stairs. "That wasn't very nice of her."

Pain was glad he was behind her. It made it easier for him to hide his smile. Instead of offering his opinion of how Ahjoomenoni had cured her of dog-bashing, he informed her that she would be on her own for breakfast the next day.

"I have business to attend to tomorrow morning. I'll call you as soon as I get back."

"Is there anything I should know about in case I have to send out a search party?"

"Nothing of any consequence. I hate to admit it, but I had a cavity start and will be at the dentist from nine until however long it takes."

"Good luck. Don't pass up the nitrous oxide if they offer it."

They reached the top of the stairs and said their *mañanas*. She hurried to the bathroom to start a hot Epsom Salt bath for her beaten body. For her brain, she wandered to the kitchen for a double shot of Jameson's to sip while soaking.

Pain allowed himself one beer from the fridge and sipped it as he inspected his under-armor for any chinks or cracks. He didn't want to take any chances when he went to see his dentist the next day.

Agony spent the next morning feeling slightly cast adrift. She went out for bagels but only bought two and ate them while inside the small bakery-café. Halfway through her first one, she realized how accustomed she had become to starting the day over coffee and bread-stuff with Pain. The realization that she had a friend she could trust brought her a smile.

She toyed with the idea of hitting her training gym but had always preferred to do that at the end of a day when she had extra aggravation to get out of her system, not in the morning on a full stomach.

When she finished her breakfast, she took a leisurely stroll around a few blocks and it dawned on her how much there was about their neighborhood that she didn't know. She took note of a few shops she would visit at another time. Thinking of time, she checked her watch and it informed her that it was just past noon.

Pain had said his appointment was at nine and three hours seemed like a long time to spend in a dentist's chair. She didn't want to seem like she was over-reacting but decided to call him to check in when she returned to her apartment. He saved her from having to do it when he approached her from the direction of the parking lot.

They walked up together and he invited her in. It was never too late for coffee and there was a fair amount for them to talk about regarding the last few days, starting with the fucking dog.

"I've decided to cut back on my derogatory doggy comments," she told him glumly.

"I'm sure that the ASPCA will be happy about that."

They had moved on to more dangerous territory when the sounds of loud banging and cursing came through the door.

Pain took the first sip of his second cup. "Someone on the stairway is not having a good day."

"Someone will have a worse day if this keeps up," she muttered.

"It does sound as if they are having a tough time. Should we go offer to help?"

They hadn't gotten to know any of their neighbors yet other than to nod in passing, but it never hurt to build good relations. Still, it didn't mean she had to be happy about letting her coffee get cold.

Her partner followed a step behind as she rose and crossed the floor. Hoping for a quick resolution to the noise and aggravation, she flung the door open and without hesitating to make sure the coast was clear, stepped into the hallway.

"What the—Pain!"

Halfway down the staircase, two burly men banged the walls and cussed loudly. She spun toward him as he stepped out of his apartment.

"What have you done?"

"Sorry. It's here on a no-return policy. You'll have to learn to live with it."

The muscle on the stairs stopped all their attention-getting noise-making as everyone looked at Agony's reaction to seeing her chair—*her* chair—sitting undamaged in front of her.

"You son of a bitch!"

"You're welcome."

"How—"

"I fibbed about going to the dentist. I hired our friends here and their truck and then paid a visit to a temporarily under-staffed consignment shop. I might have been a little over the top in my negotiating."

"How over the top?"

"Let's simply say no one made a profit from the sale so you don't owe me anything."

"You might have to find a new partner. Once I get this inside, I may never leave my apartment again."

His phone chirped and he saw a number he didn't recognize. It could be business or it could be trouble. More than likely, it was probably a little of both.

"I'll take the call and then, with your permission, may I come over and see how it looks in its new home?"

Agony waved him off and on his way. "Yeah, yeah, sure. Whatever."

Pain headed inside as she encouraged the delivery crew.

"Nice work guys. No damage getting it up the stairs so let's be as careful getting it inside."

"Pain," he answered as he closed his door.

"I'm sorry. I truly am sincerely sorry." He recognized Baran immediately

"You were in the process of drawing down on my partner. It'll take much more than an I'm sorry for me to be able to look past that."

"Come on, Pain, it was the heat of a battle. You know how that can go. Is there any chance of starting over?"

"Over with what and where?" he demanded, his tone scornful

"Over with everything. You and me, somewhere far away from all this fucking agency bullshit."

"First of all, there is nowhere far enough away to be out of their range. Secondly, Oksana, I don't believe I will ever be able to trust you after the stunts you and Chongrak pulled yesterday.

I did not take kindly to her offering to turn me over to Hollund."

"But that was all Esther," she protested. "It's true that I want out and was willing to steal the files. But I would not have aimed to kill Agony and I would never turn you over to the enemy. Now, AUNT will come after me and I will not make it easy for them."

"Good luck," he replied coldly.

"They will be coming for you too," she told him impatiently. "How do the tropics sound? Between the two of us, I'm sure we can manage to disappear and start completely over, or at least pick up where we left off all those years ago."

"The tropics?"

"In the far south-Pacific region. There are dozens of islands to choose from. Eventually, you and me will simply be filed away by AUNT as out of sight-out of mind."

"As I said, good luck. Send me a postcard when you get there."

Pain ended the call, left his phone on his dining table, and headed across the hall. He ran into the two deliverymen coming out of Agony's apartment and about to close the door.

"Leave it open. It will save me from knocking. How much do I owe you?"

"The lady has already paid."

He pulled out two business cards and handed them to the men.

"If you're ever in the mood for some good Korean food, swing in down below, give them a card, and tell them your dinner is on me."

"Appreciate it."

"Thanks, mate."

He watched them hurry down the stairs and rapped lightly on the still-open door.

"Permission to come aboard?" he asked cheerfully.

"Permission granted."

Pain stepped inside and expressed approval of the lack of excess furnishings. "You certainly have the Spartan décor theme down pat."

"Thank..." Now, he saw her. "You." Now, he didn't.

She had the chair placed directly in front of and a few feet away from the window and currently twirled in circles as she rocked.

"Is that where it's staying?"

"I think." Now, he saw her. "Maybe." Now, he didn't. "I'm... trying...to decide...which direction...I should...sit facing."

He was getting dizzy.

"It's a rotating chair." He pointed out the obvious in a slightly rough tone. "It doesn't face in any permanent direction."

She began to spin the opposite way. "Huh, I think...I like the views...coming from...this direction...better."

"Will you stop it?" He was almost pleading.

"No."

"I'm getting vertigo."

"There is...a pail...under the sink...You can use that...as a vomit bucket."

"I don't want a vomit bucket!"

"Fine...but don't...puke on...the floor."

She finally showed some mercy, planted her feet firmly, and stopped facing him.

"There, I stopped. Do you feel better now?"

"Much. Thank you." He sighed with undisguised relief.

"Do you want to try it?"

"Maybe another time when I have an empty stomach."

She shrugged. "Suit yourself."

With her feet still planted, Agony twisted as far as she could toward the right and sang, "Ground control to Major Tom." As a follow-up, she spun counter-clockwise.

Pain headed to the kitchen and returned with the vomit bucket. One of them would need it at this rate.

THE STORY CONTINUES

The story continues with book 5, *Night Moves*, coming soon to Amazon and to Kindle Unlimited.

Claim your copy today!

CREATOR NOTES

JANUARY 25, 2022

Thank you for not only reading this book but these author notes as well!

I'm in Dubai, UAE (United Arab Emirates) – and tired from too much walking.

So, I'm thinking about what to share in this book when I realize that one of my author friends (Marc Stiegler) has been working on a thriller series (and has a couple of books already published by LMBPN. First one is out (Triple Cross (The Dread Nought Book 1)), and the second comes out at the end of March (in a couple of months.)

I figured I could ask HIM if he would mind dropping in to speak about his series and give those of you who like Thrillers another series (and wonderful author) to read and hopefully love as much as I do.

Talk to you in the next book!

From Marc Stiegler:

Hello, everyone. First, let me thank Michael for giving me this opportunity to introduce myself and my new Dread Nought thriller series.

Who am I? Well, I could talk about my time as a Visiting

Scholar for HP Labs or my time as a VP of Engineering for a Fortune 500 company, but more relevant to you are a couple of the more unusual episodes in my life. I spent two years writing computer viruses for various organizations, some of which you have heard of. And I spent one entertaining year writing millions of bad checks for a living.

(*Editor's note: He's not some weird homeless person. He's a world-class computer guru, and he was paid big bucks to do that. Really*)

With that, let me introduce Cassie and Remy, heroines I think you'll like after reading about Pain and Agony.

Who is the predator, and who is the prey?

When the prey are as lethal as Pain and Agony, the hunters and the hunted get stirred like a vat full of fudge swirl ice cream. The underworld is hopelessly unprepared for enemies such as these.

But deeper and darker than the crime families facing Pain and Agony are the black clandestine organizations of the shadow gov and the dark web, so well hidden neither law enforcement nor news media knows of their existence. A favorite new tool of these Forces Who Shall Not Be Named? Conspiracy websites they operate as psychological experiments, selecting the most fully indoctrinated and unleashing them as fire-and-forget weapons in a brutal yet covert battle for domination.

But the game is about to change because Remy, a cheerleader whose inventor parents were taken in a bloody kidnapping, is about to meet Cassie, a cat burglar who should know better.

As they race to escape their enemies across the globe, Cassie and Remy will be fighting, shooting, and sassing their way through all comers.

Together they will fight for survival, and they will fight to protect the crucial secret Remy now carries...but most often, they will fight with each other, combatants handcuffed together by fate, destiny, and Remy's preplanning.

The covert world is hopelessly unprepared for enemies such as these.

If you think Pain and Agony have a troubled relationship as they blow through their enemies, wait until you see Cassie and Remy dance with their would-be kidnappers on their way to a grand, climactic *Triple Cross*.

(Check out Triple Cross here)

In the meantime, I hope you're living your best life!

Marc Stiegler

BOOKS BY MICHAEL ANDERLE

Sign up for the LMBPN email list to be notified of new releases and special deals!

https://lmbpn.com/email/

For a complete list of books by Michael Anderle, please visit:

www.lmbpn.com/ma-books/

CONNECT WITH MICHAEL

Connect with Michael Anderle

Website: http://lmbpn.com

Email List: http://lmbpn.com/email/

https://www.facebook.com/LMBPNPublishing

https://twitter.com/MichaelAnderle

https://www.instagram.com/lmbpn_publishing/

https://www.bookbub.com/authors/michael-anderle

Made in the USA
Coppell, TX
05 February 2022

72979944R00163